HOBSWYKE

C. R. CLARKE

Matador
Unit E2 Airfield Business Park,
Harrison Road, Market Harborough,
Leicestershire. LE16 7UL
Tel: 0116 2792299
Email: books@troubador.co.uk
Web: www.troubador.co.uk/matador
Twitter: @matadorbooks

ISBN 978 1805142 003

British Library Cataloguing in Publication Data.
A catalogue record for this book is available from the British Library.

Printed and bound by CPI Group (UK) Ltd, Croydon, CR0 4YY
Typeset in 10.5pt Adobe Garamond Pro by Troubador Publishing Ltd, Leicester, UK

Matador is an imprint of Troubador Publishing Ltd

In memory of my mother, who always stood by me.

FORWARD BY THE AUTHOR

Firstly, thank you for purchasing my book. Your faith in my abilities is both humbling and much appreciated.
Hobswyke was the first novel I ever wrote and the culmination of decades of work battling dyslexia to a point that I could pen an entire book. Since then, my writing style has changed ever so slightly, and the temptation was to rewrite the entire novel to bring it in line with those changes. But I decided against it, choosing to release it pretty much in its original form to document my own, personal journey.
I've had back and forth discussions with my excellent publisher – Troubador – as to what demographic to aim it at, and that proved almost as difficult as writing the book in the first place! The ages of the main protagonists would suggest targeting it towards the older end of the young adult market. But all who were reading my pages as I penned my efforts were very much adult in their years, and all universally loved the experience of reading it, one 69 year old ex-proofreader from Yorkshire even proclaiming, "It scared me bloody sh!%less!"
I personally have never understood why society's constructs have deemed adults unsuitable for the enjoyment of anything

residing beneath the 'adventure' banner, specially if that adventure is dark, at times frightening, and dips a cheeky toe in the realm of 'horror'. I recall reading what percentage of readers of the Harry Potter series were adults, although what's here is very different to those books.

Life can be cripplingly serious at times, and I believe ultimate escapism is one way to manage those pressures. So here it is, my first ever book, and the third of my efforts to be published. It's a slow burn at the beginning, but soon gets fully in to it and I promise you it's a ride. I hope you enjoy reading as much as I enjoyed writing it… A sequel is already underway…

THE JOURNAL OF LUCY CLAYBOURNE

July 23rd

Who'd have thought that just three weeks ago, the path of my life would have changed so drastically, and so bizarrely. That I would discover so many lies that have encompassed my whole existence leaving me ill prepared to deal with the truth of who and what I am when the time finally came to face it. Perhaps 'lies' is too strong a word? 'Sincerities never presented' is perhaps more accurate and fair. But still, the end result is the same.

Would I have been as guarded if I had found myself in the exact same position? Probably! But still, it doesn't change the fact that everything should have been in place for this to be the most idyllic of summers but, despite that, my world has been turned on its head! I've been forced to grow up so fast this last two weeks, and can feel I've matured, becoming more of a woman than the girl I once was.

If I could have this summer all over again, start it all over again, would I have revisited that damned house? Part of me wants to say no, but just think if I hadn't...

ONE

'COME HOME, DEAR LUCY. COME HOME...'

LUCY CLAYBOURNE reclined on her bed, fingers knitted around the nape of her neck, staring through a ceiling that looked as empty and featureless as the day that lay ahead. After a manic year of revision and exams, she had to come to terms with having nothing of major importance to do. Not something that she could consider a chore, just a lifestyle change that warranted consideration.

It was the laziest of mornings she could ever remember, finding difficulty recalling the last time she felt as relaxed as she did right now. It was the end of June, and the final year of high school was finally over; the exams went well – at least she felt they did; her eighteenth birthday was only one month away, and the mere thought that she'd never again get assigned a quality time-sapping homework assignment induced a level of relaxation that she found near impossible to rise from. For once, in what felt like an eternity to one so young, Lucy found herself free of an agenda.

Physically, she was a girl who'd stepped across the divide

into womanhood. But life had yet to draw back the veil and display to her how wholly cruel and hurtful the real world could truly be to a person ill prepared to face it.

Witnessing her mother's trials and ordeals, she *was* somewhat aware, but until she had to face the full force of life's wrath personally, she was happy feigning blissful ignorance.

'Come on, Claybourne,' she yawned through contorting features, 'shift your arse. You can't be lying here all day.'

She sat up, wiping her hands over her face. She could feel the pressure of her fingers through the back of her eyes as she massages her lids awake.

She stretched her body long, combing her fingers back through what she would describe as *pillowhair*, raking her long, silky blonde tresses into a more presentable arrangement.

She'd been dreaming for most of the night, and not the recurrent nightmare that had been plaguing her sleep for the past eight months: that dream where she was sitting in an exam and turned the page only to find that all of the questions were written in a language she didn't recognise, and certainly couldn't read, before the world around her began to shimmer, then burn, then melt through the floor like a painting in the rain leaving her perched precariously on a jagged pillar of rock, flames licking at her recoiling legs like the fingers of hell trying to seize her and drag her down its fiery depths. No, this dream was different, but equally ominous: she dreamt of 'Hobswyke', the big house, calling to her from atop the hill. Calling her name like a breath on the wind, calling for her to, 'come. Come home,' and she couldn't work out if the calls seemed to be for help, or to tempt her to be curious, and for reasons that seemed far more sinister than anything else.

It had caused her to wake with a jolt, and she'd felt relief that the arrival of daylight had brought with it an end to the torment, giving her reason to rise.

She noticed a blade of light on the wall opposite the window. It looked blindingly bright within the greyscale tones of an unlit room.

The Sun's out, she thought, energised by the prospect. It shone through a parting in the curtains, warming the sandstone walls of the gatehouse to the Hobswyke estate that the Claybournes now called 'Home'.

Lucy swung her slender legs clear of the duvet, and rose unsteadily to her feet. Toes reached and clawed at the butter-softness of the pile of the carpet. She stretched again, and yawned, flicking a cursory glance towards the clock on the bedside table. Her eyes widened at the time, and she hurried from the room.

She made her way with forced urgency along the landing towards the bathroom. 'Ten twenty-seven, you lazy sod of earth!' she muttered to the solitude, a personal rebuke from a confirmed early riser.

The muffled clacks of her mother washing the previous night's dishes resonated from the kitchen, a muted siren hailing the fact that Lucy wasn't alone in the world. It was a sound she found endearing and homely, prompting a call down the spiralling stairwell.

'Morning, Mum,' she shouted, with childlike vibrance warming her voice, aware that such a tone made her mother feel maternal. She draped her slender torso over the landing handrail awaiting a response.

The flick-flack of soft, slippered footsteps approached from the kitchen. A friendly face appeared at the bottom of the staircase looking up. 'Morning, you lazy ape, I was wondering when you might bother to make an appearance?' her mother crowed, sarcastically, but with a smile – her marigold-gloved hand wiping a stray bubble from the side of her nose; the corner of her mouth blowing upwards to clear the itch.

Lucy's mother, Helen Claybourne, her sole parent and arguably her best friend, was an uncommonly attractive woman in her mid-forties, with a tendency to draw attention – desired or otherwise – from pretty much every man she encountered, a curse-or-blessing trait inherited by Lucy. They also shared a sunny disposition, an unquenchable desire to look on the bright side of any situation, an unfaltering drive to help others whenever they may need it, and an innate ability to get along with all classes of humanity, despite possessing what may be considered by many to be a grandiose surname.

'Would you like a cup of tea, love?' her mother asked, in an overtly syrupy voice. Helen Claybourne adored her daughter, and being the sole parent in her life, felt no desire to hide the fact.

'Please, Mum. That would be lovely,' came the response. 'I'll be down in a bit.'

Lucy was fully aware of the love her mother held for her, it having never been anything but freely given. She allowed the corners of her mouth to twitch a smile at the knowledge, painfully aware that many weren't as lucky as she. She felt blessed.

Lucy meandered into the echoing coolness of a porcelain-clad, Victorian bathroom to spend time arranging her reflection, gathering herself together, fortunate enough to possess a face that required very little effort to look good. For sure, she had the freshness of youth on her side – the same as anyone else her age – but it was, in reality, far more than that.

She stared into the turquoise eyes looking back at her from the mirror, hands leaning on the sides of the sink.

'I have nothing to do today,' she informed the face looking back at her, revelling in the fact. 'Did you hear me? Nothing... Ab-so-lute-ly, nothing... Nice huh...?' As usual, her reflection failed to respond, it just stared back at her… 'Hm. Alright then, be like that. See if I care.'

Lucy then caught sight of a looming section of roofline of the large house reflected in the mirror, reaching high above the treetops far in the distance, as though spying on her through the window she had her back to.

An image of Hobswyke materialised through the mists clouding the darker recesses of her mind – just like the dream – the black slab doors slowly opening, stretching long and wide like a gaping mouth, calling to her, calling her name, beckoning. 'Lucyyyyyyyy… Commmmme…' it breathed, but this time, sounding decidedly more taunting than anything that could be mistaken for amiable.

She shook it from her thoughts. 'Stop it! Go away,' she complained, blinking it from her mind.

She spun the taps on…

*

'Tea's ready, love,' shouted a voice from the kitchen. 'I'll put some bread in the toaster for you.'

'Okay, Mum. Coming!' she replied, spitting the tongue-burning mintiness of the toothpaste into the crystal vortex coiling down the plughole.

She twisted off the taps, and dropped the brush back into the glass. It rattled in the beaker like the clapper of a bell, ringing the end to her cleaning routine. The room fell into post-activity silence.

She wiped her hands dry on the towel, and took one last look at herself in the mirror. 'Well, I guess I'll see ya later, if you're still around…' Again, no response. 'Sod ya then.'

*

Lucy sat at the heavy, oak kitchen table and drew the tea and toast in closer. She sniffed the rising steam… Rye bread, her favourite.

Her mother was toying, with rapidly deteriorating patience, with the hot-water tap, trying to stop its recent propensity to drip. 'If you see Peter today, honey, could you ask him to pop over and have a look at these taps for me?' she asked over her shoulder.

'Yeah, sure, no worries,' Lucy replied, happy to oblige, as she scooped another dollop of zesty orange marmalade onto her toast. 'I'll pop over as soon as I've finished this, okay,' she said, lifting her toast into the core of the conversation.

Peter Fletcher lived on the grounds of Hobswyke in an old cottage by the lake. It sat nestled in the forest like it had been there as long as the trees that surrounded it, its yellow sandstone walls streaked black from the autumnal resin that dripped from the dying leaves and branches that had umbrellaed its slates for centuries.

He resided there with his two kids, Hillary – although everyone called her Hilly – and her older brother Sam.

Peter's job description, was 'Everything': maintenance engineer, handyman, groundskeeper, gardener, family friend, gossip giver, gossip receiver, and someone to have an occasional glass of wine with when Helen felt starved of adult company – a chore he often welcomed, his wife having died shortly after Hillary was born.

Owning such a large estate, Helen would've found it impossible to manage without him, often referring to him as 'a gem-of-a-man'. She appreciated him, as much as she could ever appreciate anyone, but there had never been any romance.

Lucy folded the last piece of toast into her mouth, keen to get outside and feel the clement weather against her skin.

Her finger scooped the remaining soup of crumbs, butter and dripped preserves off the plate, and deposited it in her mouth, before thanking her mother with a peck on the cheek, and galloping upstairs to get properly dressed.

*

An hour later, a far more presentable version of Lucy wearing an optimistic yellow summer dress trotted down the handful of steps that swept from the front door of the gatehouse into the midday sun.

She and her mother moved from Hobswyke, the main house, a little over five years ago, as an apparent money-saving exercise, its smaller dimensions being far easier to maintain and, during the winter months, keep heated.

Lucy often felt the slightest twinge at not having the bragging rights that would almost certainly have come from living in a such a house; a building with undeniable pomp and notoriety in the area. But being the gatehouse of such a grand gothic mansion and, as such, the opening gambit of any attempt to impress visitors – it shared many of the style cues of the main building, and much of its intimidating grandeur. A fact that went a long way in helping to take the sting out of the move.

'Hobswyke Hall', the *big* house, had been standing empty ever since. Looming over the world that chose to deny it. Locked up, cold, alone…

Lucy strolled down the footpath that ran parallel to the main drive. A relaxed stroll, not complicated by having any real purpose. Simply walking for the sheer pleasure of walking, although, she did have that message for Peter.

Her slender legs lolloped lazily beneath her. She closed her eyes and hung her head back, presenting her face to an uncluttered sky. She felt her skin prickle as the sun's rays warmed her delicate features.

A cooling breeze from the lake at the base of the hill rolled up the lawned slopes, carrying the smell of freshly cut grass into an eager nose… She drew it in, the sharp, invigorating sensation of fresh air rushing through sun-warmed nostrils heightening her awareness. An awareness of self, of the world around her, and of her own existence within it. She revelled in the feeling of being alive on such a monumentally idyllic day, and the smile on her face sang to the fact.

The path eventually peeled away from the main drive and dropped into woodland… Tall trees lined the narrow walkway beneath their thickening canopies, fans of clustering leaves obstructing the sun, texturing the path with handprints of dappled sunlight. The temporary respite from the heat felt welcome, as was the smell of the flowers, emitting an impressive body of insect-beckoning scents, a floral musk hailing a desperation to be pollinated filling the warm, summer breeze. Lucy inhaled…

The trail led down to a fork, the right-hand path snaking through the trees to the east shore of the lake and Peter's cottage; the left, to the big house.

Lucy hung for a moment in her choices… then turned left…

She made her way across extensive grounds that had a long time ago been contrived to resemble nature, but forced into an orderly queue to create flow and motion.

She made her way along the shingled approach to the old hall that was once her childhood home, and noticed the forest floor increasingly encroaching onto the rapidly narrowing pathway the nearer she got.

Since it was closed up, everything surrounding Hobswyke had been neglected, allowing nature's tendrils to begin the gradual task of reclaiming the building and its surrounding, contrived infrastructure.

The trees and bushes that lined the final stretch of path used to form a neat, arched tunnel, maintained almost purely by regular use alone. But now – forgotten and deserted – the branches clawed in from all sides like obstructing arms undesiring of anyone, or anything passing beneath their tortured limbs.

Lucy had to use her hands to carefully manoeuvre through the final tangle of twigs, weaving her face and favourite yellow dress clear of their cloth-snagging reach.

She swung the last branches open like saloon-doors, and quickly ducked through into the open.

Her eyes scanned her clothing for pulls as she crunched along the gravel towards the big-house – brushing away a couple of leaves that had hitched a ride. The dress still looked pristine, 'You got away with that,' she muttered in her solitude, to her relief.

Her attention swung back to the front… The sight that met her eyes stopped her dead in her tracks.

Lucy hadn't visited the main house for a considerable length of time, what with having to focus all of her energy on her final year exam revision, but maybe, even more than that, to appease a desire to avoid reminders that she no longer lived in such an awe-invoking building.

She was shocked to realise that she probably hadn't visited in at least eighteen months, or possibly even more than two years? But somehow, the house looked different now, almost to the point that she wouldn't recognise it if she happened upon it elsewhere, or saw it in a random selection of photographs of similar buildings.

Lucy drank in the sheer volume of the tenebrous aspect: a slab-flat frontage flanked by turreted wings, topped with a complex, faceted, dormer window peppered roofline. Twisted brick chimney stacks reached far above the trees' canopies, broadcasting the opulence of the building beneath to distant gazes in defiant red-brick, in-your-face Victoriana, before Victoriana was even a thing.

She never realised just how suffocatingly oppressive the architecture was, until now, leaving her feeling compelled to reacquaint herself with her childhood home – the view she was presented with being so at odds with her memories. *Five years,* she thought, *feels like a lifetime.*

Lucy could sense the black, murky windows looking down at her – eleven rows across, three rows high – as if the building looming from atop the bank was reacquainting itself with *her.* She even fancied she saw flickers of movement through the corner of her eye within the deep-set blackness beyond every grime-streaked pane of glass, but she knew she couldn't have done, except in the eyes of her unnerved imagination.

She scanned the vast expanse of the flat, angular aspect filling her view. *All those rooms, so many rooms,* she recalled. And the basement. *That* basement! Deep. Dark. Its creaking wooden staircase that seemed to drop forever into the damp, stale blackness, inhabited by putrid earth, air-hung mould spores and the remnants of negative energy left from the dirty secrets of past occupants.

Who on earth knows what went on down there? God? she wondered to herself. *No, not God,* she decided, recalling the unholy tales she'd been made party to over the past handful of years, now of an age to be told such details. Details regarding the house's long, bloodstained past, so grim in their very essence.

She tried not to think about it, uncomfortable about letting too much dark into the light of her innocence, an innocence she'd taken great pains to maintain for as long as she could. She knew it to be a cruel and nefarious world to live in, and her intention was to push against it.

Her rekindled interest drifted up the gothic facade to the gargoyles spaced evenly along the perimeter of the roofline. Taunting. Hideous. Freakish. Each face contorted with an expression steeped in ill intent.

They all seemed to possess a distant stare, as though placed there to face down anything that dare approach the heavy brick and wrought-iron fenced boundaries of the grounds. Again, Lucy struggled to recall them being so thoroughly grotesque. She swallowed back the bitter taste that had formed in the back of her throat, ingesting her undeniable revulsion.

The house seemed so utterly alien to her now. *Did I really live here?* she thought – the more she looked, the less she seemed to remember…

She receded into her thoughts again, straining to draw out a single, solid memory of actually living in this repugnant building. But any memories she managed to fish from the pond seemed vague at best.

'Luuucyyyyyy…' came a voice, drifting in on the wind, sounding so distant that she failed to hear it, too engrossed in her attempts to remember specific details of her childhood.

The ebbed tide of her attention flowed back into the real world. She lowered her fascination from the house, and found herself gazing at the staircase that ascended to the stone-flagged landing area fanning the main doors… She remembered being told they were a later addition, commissioned by 'Mallette' himself, the previous owner that had single-handedly fuelled two-hundred years of morbid gossip: tales of his necromantic pursuits; of babies going missing from nearby villages, of claims of seeing him floating through the surrounding forests coated in a film of coagulating blood, of overheard chants to unseen demons late into the midnight hours, and of his eventual death, sitting bolt-upright in a high-backed chair, set centre of a Neolithic stone circle located deep in Malory Woods. Charred. Burned. Immolated.

His blackened body had shown no signs of struggle or resistance, so suicide had been suspected, but no one truly knew what had happened to Antoine Mallette.

The staircase he'd commissioned could itself be considered unremarkable, airing towards utilitarian functionality rather than the artistic arrogance one would have expected to see front such a belligerent building. But in stark contrast, the fairly quotidian staircase was flanked by the most overtly ornate, anomalous wrought-iron handrails: wave-form, extravagant, and devoid of a single straight line.

The serpentine top-rails – polished smooth from well over a century of use – snaked up the elongating staircase, rolling in all directions, and Lucy could recall them being impossible to slide down, a detail of her past she *could* remember.

She ambled across to take a closer look, the crunch of the gravel seeming much louder now as it reverberated off the flat, unyielding facade of the building…

She climbed a few steps and squatted to examine the complexity in the design of each panel, rotating her gaze in attempt to ingest every detail.

Wrought-iron braids twisted, rolled and helixed beneath the rails, creating ornate uprights that tied them to the sandstone blocks they climbed.

Lucy squinted, beginning to see symbols that appeared to be hidden within the exuberance. Multidimensional, layered patterns that resolved, then evaporate again as she moved slowly up the steps.

Why have I never noticed that before? she wondered. She considered the possibility that such details may simply have been invisible to the eyes of a disinterested child. But to the retrospective examinations of a seventeen-year-old girl, they were far more apparent.

The sun now sat high on its path through the uncrowded

sky, minimal depth of atmosphere to cool its incandescent radiation. Lucy could sense her shoulders; a sub-dermal warmth pricking at her skin. She crossed her arms in front of her chest and cupped them in her hands, attempting to protect her alabaster skin from turning an undesirable hue of crimson.

Then, she noticed a curious mist rolling up the steps from somewhere beyond the ironwork, hugging the undulations as it drifted towards the stone-flagged landing groveling before the heavy oak doors.

Her brows pinched. She stepped in closer to see from where the fog was emanating…

Oblong pools of water projected out from either side of the staircase, like an incomplete moat that failed to encircle the entirety of the building. They seemed odd to her: meaningless, unnecessary, and somewhat out of place.

Steam swirled over the surface of the water, evaporating to the beat of the sun's rays. 'Haaaaa yes,' she finally remembered, her mother used to warn her to keep clear of them – Lucy never having been the strongest of swimmers. Her memories finally seemed to be rebirthing, little by little. Piece by piece.

Fascinated eyes tracked the rising mist as it vortexed up to the staircase, blanketing the ornate, gothic stonework.

'What the hell?' she whispered, a granite-hard look of confusion galvanising the soft features of her face.

Her lower lids flexed, kissing the coronas of her turquoise irises. She gazed down with unrecognising eyes at intricately carved, balloon-form stonework that she had absolutely no recollection of ever seeing before, projecting out from either side of the staircase, curving outwards, then down into the water from the farthest side of both handrails.

Lucy's eyes couldn't help but broadcast her disbelief at having never before noticed them, but they *must* have been there, mustn't they?

She crouched by the railing, and extended a curious arm through the bars. Her intrigued fingers glided over the bizarre carvings, her eyes following her touch through the spiralling ironwork, face pressed up against the cold, metal rods, darting pupils absorbing the complexity of each and every sculpted detail: venom-spitting snakes, hieroglyphics, encircled pentagrams, stick-form script, swords, knives, naive renditions of naked, frolicking proletariats, and a multitude of peculiar blank areas that seemed intentionally left bereft of detail.

'What are you doing?' barked a voice from right behind her shoulders.

With a stuttered intake of breath, Lucy winced away from the voice, her shuddering arm rattling between the tortured bars as she withdrew it.

Panicked, she scrambled back from the ambushing figure looming over her, pin-prick pupils pleading up at the backlit silhouette, a sense of vulnerability dragging her stomach to her feet!

The black figure leaned further in, eclipsing the blinding sun behind. Lucy's eyes adjusted… '*Sam!*' She exhaled. 'You *shit!*'

TWO

THE PASSING OF A BUTTERFLY

'BLOODY HELL FIRE!' snapped Lucy. 'You sodding idiot!' Reclined on her elbows, legs scattered ungracefully across the steps, she glared her disapproval up at Sam's chuckling, bewildered face. His whole head looked like it was shrouded in a halo, unruly chestnut hair backlit by the sun.

'I'm sorry.' He giggled, mewing the words with forced remorse. 'I didn't mean to scare you.' But there was little truth in *that* statement.

He couldn't help but laugh at the sight of his dishevelled friend. 'Here,' he said, offering an outstretched arm. 'Sorry, Luce,' he reiterated, allowing himself one final smirk.

Begrudgingly, Lucy took his hand, darting a disapproving look his way as he hoisted her to her feet.

She brushed the grit and leaves from the back of her dress. It was no longer pristine.

'What were you doing?' he asked.

'Oh, nothing, really,' she replied, 'I was just...'

'Just what?'

She loosed a sigh. 'Oh, I dunno,' she huffed, turning a

glance down towards the pool. 'I guess it's these steps… I can't remember, or recall, *any* of these symbols?' she said, pointing towards the carvings flanking the pool. She turned a frown to Sam. 'Come here, take a look.'

She walked past the base of the handrail and pointed an accusatory finger towards the unusual carvings. 'I don't remember *any* of this, do you?'

Sam was staring at her face. 'What?' she snapped.

'You've got rust on your cheek,' he explained, circling his finger towards a smudge. He dug out a clean handkerchief from his back pocket, and handed it to her. 'It's all over your arm as well.'

'Damn it!' she whined, rolling her wrist over to see. She turned her back to him and delicately spat into the handkerchief, and started wiping herself as clean as she could without the luxury of a mirror… She refolded the cloth to a clean side, and gave her face a few last wipes.

'How's that?' she asked, turning back to face him. But Sam didn't answer, he'd found something far more interesting to arrest his attention.

He was crouched by the base of the handrail, picking large flakes of rust off the iron bars with his thumbnail. 'These are *really* decayed,' he protested.

'Are you going to look at this for me or not?' she asked for the second time, pointing an impatient finger towards the carvings.

'Oh. Yeah… Sorry,' he said, struggling to his feet and brushing his knees clean.

Lucy handed him back his handkerchief. 'And erm – thanks,' she mewed, her voice tinged with mild embarrassment. 'I'm afraid there's some of my spit…'

He smirked at the rare display of coyness. 'Don't you worry about that,' he said, with an understanding shake of the head, smiling kindly into the crystalline sheen of her turquoise eyes.

It had been a long held belief in Sam's mind that Lucy's eyes had to be as beautiful as eyes could ever be, and he relished any opportunity that presented itself to look deep into their serpentine vibrance.

He carefully folded the handkerchief, and covertly slipped it back into his pocket. He probably *wouldn't* wash it, but he might very well frame it.

Lucy pointed again, this time calmer, and turned her head back towards the stonework. Sam's eyes followed. 'Look! Look at all of that, do you remember *any* of that?'

Sam studied the details of the carved relief with interest. 'Mmm, well yeah. Sort of… But I've never really looked at it properly though.' He stepped in to examine it closer. 'It's weird innit,' he said, rolling his head from side to side, absorbing the peculiarity of what was stretched out before them. He frowned. 'Actually, no. If I'm to be completely honest, I've never really taken that much notice of it. It *is* pretty odd though. What do you think it all means?'

'I've caught a butterfly!' boasted a voice approaching from behind. They both spun round to greet the new arrival… It was Hilly – Sam's twelve-year-old sister.

She walked gingerly towards Lucy, shoulders hunched, hands cupped tightly together. She assumed her brother would probably have little interest in the beauty of an ornate insect, so walked straight past him.

Sam's face complained, looking more than mildly put out, wondering why *he* didn't get a look.

'Let me see,' smiled Lucy, hooking her hair behind her ear and leaning over the young girl's palpable excitement.

Hilly gently uncupped her hands, revealing the butterfly. It was the first one she'd managed to catch since the arrival of summer.

Its wings beat slowly in her palm, proudly displaying its vivid, crimson iridescence within the brilliance of the midday sun.

'I *think* that's a red admiral,' said Lucy, feeling proud of her knowledge, but disguising the pride by forcing a *matter-of-fact* tone into her voice. 'Are you going to let it go?' she asked – as a gentle nudge from an animal lover.

'Um. Yes… okay,' Hilly agreed, smiling up at Lucy.

She looked around for a suitable place to offload her find, then crept towards the steps, carefully extending her arms out towards the handrail.

She rolled her palm over, depositing the butterfly onto the flaking ironwork. The insect settled on its new perch, pulling the flat majesty of its wings up tightly together.

The insect suddenly began to spasm: twisting, contorting, legs curling hard into its body, like the life force was somehow being sucked from it.

Its wings began to struggle, twitching, flinching, beating erratically, then fell limp to one side. It was dead?

A gust of wind blew its paper-light carcass off the rail, and it spun to the ground like a sycamore key.

'What the shitting-hell happened there?' whimpered Lucy. 'I-Is it dead?'

A thermal breeze chased the lifeless carcass over the stone carvings, bouncing it across the relief, and then carried it onto the surface of the evaporating water.

Hilly stepped in and stared despairingly down at the ornate wings wheeling on the charcoal blackness of the pool, visibly distraught. 'Did I just kill it?' she asked.

Sam stepped in and placed a hand flat on the handrail. 'No. It's cold. You didn't kill anything?'

Lucy turned her face to Sam, they both shared a moment of confusion. The corners of Sam's mouth buckled. He shook his head. 'I don't know – I've never seen anything like that before. Have you?' he mouthed – she hadn't.

Hilly edged her stooping body towards the pool, eyes fixed on the dead butterfly carcass spinning on the surface of the stagnating water… She had to squint, struggling to see through the layer of swirling fog.

Her eyes suddenly hardened. She flinched, certain she saw what looked like the end of a stick, or something similar, rising from beneath the water. It seemed to be focused on the insect, chasing it towards the side of the pool.

'I know it's just a butterfly, but that was *really* weird,' Sam whined, while attempting to play down the undeniably freakish nature of what they'd all just witnessed to protect his sister's anguish.

'I know. I know. But insects don't just die like *that*. At least I don't *think* they do?' Lucy responded. 'It's all very weird, everything. Everything about the way this place feels to me is wrong. Can you not feel it?' she asked. 'There's something about this place, something not rig—'

Hilly screamed! A soul-contorting scream. Her scrunched body staggering back from the pool.

Sam turned to front the clamour, and was faced with the sight of his sister driving her fist hard between her teeth, insane eyes fixated on the water.

'What is it?' asked Sam – brotherly instinct rushing to the fore. '*Hilly?*'

Hilly snapped a manic, imploring glare towards him, then back to the pool. She extended a pin-straight finger towards the water.

Sam was shocked by the look he saw in his sister's eyes, barely recognising the face glowering back at him. 'What is it, Hilly, *tell* me!'

'F-F-F-Fingers…!' she stuttered.

'What!?' he exhaled.

'F-F-F-Fingers, came out of the w-water…!'

Sam's sickened face stared coldly back at her words, having never in his life heard her say anything so peculiar, or so sinister. He was briefly repulsed, but not by her, only by the words she spoke.

'Th-They took the b-butterfly,' she stammered.

Sam strode to the side of the pool, leaning in on the railings that encircled it, desperately searching for the iridescence of the wings within the layers of fog. But they weren't there. 'What are you talking about, "fingers",' Sam pleaded.

'Fingers… A h-h-h-hand, came out of the water, and pulled the b-butterfly under.'

Lucy flashed a look across at Sam again, he shrugged.

They both walked over to the tremulous girl and wrapped themselves around her. 'Come oooon.' He laughed. 'It wasn't a hand, it *can't* have been a hand… It was probably, I dunno, a fish or something.' Hilly's head shook frantically – part denial, part shock, part certainty of superior knowledge.

He tightened his arm firmly around her shoulder. He could feel her body quake through his hand.

Lucy looked down at the girl cocooned between them. She stroked Hilly's face with compassion, then turned her attention back to the house…

She broke from the huddle, pulled forwards by the house's morose facade, drawing her up the steps towards it. She sensed it watching them from atop the rise, a building somehow able to project an air of arrogance and superiority.

'Come on. Let's go and have a cup of tea,' chirped Sam – one of his sister's favourite things. She leant her head on him, a blank, doll-eyed stare gazing straight ahead at nothing. Her thumb was firmly in her mouth – something she hadn't done in years. 'Look, it was just a fish, that's all,' Sam reiterated, in an attempt to console.

Lucy stood midway up the steps, watching the house, an ominous feeling infesting her entire body. She felt decidedly nauseous.

The heavy, slab doors that guarded the hall lorded ominously over her from their vantage point at the top of the rise, beckoning, summoning, daring her to be curious…

Sam and Hilly started towards the path, his arm still enveloping his sister's mortification.

He turned to check that Lucy was with them. He saw her standing midway up the staircase, motionless, looking up at Hobswyke. 'Hang on here a sec,' he said to Hilly, 'just wait for me, I won't be a minute.'

He unwrapped himself from his sister, and walked up behind Lucy. She was not moving, searching eyes locked on the monolithic entrance. She seemed in a trance.

'Luce? You okay?' he asked, softly, concerned. She didn't react.

He laid his hand gently on her shoulder. 'Lucy…? *Lucy!*'

She flinched back into their world, turned, and peered at Sam with lost eyes. 'I want to go in,' she proclaimed.

'What…? In where?'

She swung a bone-straight finger up towards the derelict building. '*There*, I want to go in *there*!' she spat, impatiently.

Apart from the multitude of occasions Sam had purposefully made Lucy jump for fun, he had before never actually seen her genuinely come undone. He took a step back from her unquestionable agitation.

The corners of Lucy's mouth buckled with doubt. 'I don't think we moved to save money, I don't think that's why we moved at all!' she said, forcefully. 'I think there's a whooole other reason.'

'Like what?' asked Sam – until now, not knowing that money was supposedly the reason for their move in the first place. 'Why wouldn't it be money?'

Lucy turned a look up at the oppressive morosity of the hard, granite frontage. 'Listen. The other day, I found one of Mum's bank statements open on the kitchen table.' She rolled her head with mild shame. 'And I *know* it was wrong, but I couldn't help but have a look.'

'And?' Sam coaxed.

'Well, of course, I can't – or, or *won't* – tell you just how much, but God-in-heaven, Sam, we've got a lot of money! I never actually realised just how much, until then.'

Sam would sacrificed a limb to know the figure on the bank statement, but he knew Lucy to be honourable enough to never tell, so he'd reciprocate by never asking.

'So, you see, there *has* to be another reason, doesn't there? I mean, for Christ's sake, she's not been up here for over *five fucking years*...! Why...? Why won't she come up here?'

Sam had nothing to say, or add, or any suggestion to make. Lucy had never been this agitated in front of him before. He suddenly felt a strange awareness that Lucy was the boss's daughter, making him feel more akin to an employee than a friend. It was a feeling new to him, and threatened to redefine their relationship. But he *was* her friend, so he pushed through the awkwardness. 'Can't you get the keys?'

'She's *hidden* the keys!' she snapped. 'Somewhere, *Christ* knows where!' Sam took another step back.

Lucy noticed his retreat. 'Oh, Sammy, I'm sorry. I'm so sorry,' she said, caressing her words to take the sharpness from her voice. She walked over and put her arms around him. 'Please forgive me. I'm... I'm just getting freaked out by this *fucking* house.'

Sam closed his eyes. It was moments like this that he realised that he was probably in love with the girl in his arms – to some extent he couldn't yet judge.

The healthy scent of her hair clouded around his entire face within the embrace, he breathed her in.

'Forgive me,' she insisted, the deeper tones of her otherwise angelic voice vibrating through his shoulder, 'I'm just…' She exhaled a resigned sigh. 'I don't know… there's just something very wrong here, Sam, something wrong with this place. With this house.' She turned her eyes distrustfully up to Hobswyke. 'I can't quite put my finger on it, and I know, it's not really based on anything solid. But somehow, I can just sense it.'

She peered up at the stacked rows of murky window panes. 'Thing is, the more I think about it, the more I realise there has to be another reason why we moved from here. A reason *other* than money.'

She release their hold. 'Come on, let's get away from here.'

Sam delivered a smile, and nodded, happy to distance himself from the awkwardness left by their heated exchange.

They turned to leave, making their way across the gravel, collecting Hilly along the way.

Sam's mind was percolating all that had happened, and the things Lucy had said. There were undeniable similarities to feelings that he, himself, had had in the past regarding the house, feelings attuned with Lucy's.

The three of them departed the derelict mansion, Sam turning a parting look back towards the staircase… He knew full well there were no fish in that water.

THREE

A KEY

LUCY STUDIED SAM as she hung back, trailing behind him and his sister, watching as they skirted the lawns that dropped from the front of the big house, happy to follow them along their alternative route that avoided the overgrown pathway, and the potential dress-snagging opportunities that went along with negotiating it.

She hoped her public freak-out hadn't in any way harmed their friendship; that would truly upset her. With the obvious exception of both her mother and her grandmother, she cared about Sam – about his feelings – more than anyone.

She turned her attention to Hilly, who no longer seemed to be needing the comfort of her brother's embrace. *Good*, she thought…

*

Hilly's mind was swirling in a dream-state, rerunning through her mind what she saw, or at least, what she *thought* she saw, rising from the stagnating waters of the pool. As insane as the idea was to her, it *did* look so utterly real, and she couldn't help but wonder if it was, however unlikely the premise, or preposterous the idea.

No, she thought to herself, *don't be so ridiculous. It can't have happened.*

One of the few things Hilly and her brother could truly claim they shared, was a deep and abiding love of all things horror, and it would be a regular occurrence, against their father's wishes, but he would say 'better judgment', to take in a horror movie together, to exercise their fear emotions. So she knew, or at least she *felt* she knew, that she wasn't one to scare easily. *Or do I?* she now had to wonder.

She pondered the possibility that her father's fears about her watching 'those types of film' were justified? Giving consideration to what was effectively a moot point with more of an open mind and less of a defensive stance than she normally would.

Could they be influencing my perceptions, twisting them to see the macabre, before seeing what's real? she considered – with far less ridicule than she ever had before in the light of recent events.

But she shook her head clear of the idea, trying to shrug off any notion that she actually saw a hand rising from the pool. *How could it have possibly been a hand,* she thought, feeling more than a little ridiculous about delivering such an out-of-character outburst…

*

Sam turned to check on his sister… She seemed fine, if a little distracted. 'Thank Christ for that,' he muttered under his breath.

He spun a look behind to Lucy. She quickly snapped her head away, pretending she was looking elsewhere.

Sam dropped a smirk to the ground, heart warmed at receiving any form of attention from one he unquestionably had feelings for.

*

What the fucking hell did you do that for? Lucy thought to herself. *It's perfectly normal to just be looking, now he's going to know I was watching him.* She rolled her head in despair. 'Weirdo!' she muttered, berating herself and her actions.

She flicked a momentary glance back towards him through the corner of her eye, but he was no longer watching, far too gallant to hang back and see if she would look back at him.

That's the one thing she'd always liked about Sam, in many ways, somewhat of an old-fashioned 'gent'.

Although a full year younger than Lucy, because he was so much more knowledgeable about *stuff*, about the *real* world than Lucy was, or likely would ever be, she often found herself looking on him as the eldest of the trio.

Lucy tilted her gaze. She actually thought him really rather handsome, but she tended to try and steer her mind clear of such thoughts, not wishing to risk ruining her most prized friendship.

She watched him strolling down the bank, his frame tall and strong for one so relatively young. He slowly extended an arm up to grasp some low-hanging leaves from one of the trees that encircled the lawns. Lucy's eyes tracked his fingers, the flexing branch attempting to follow his grasp until the leaf stems relented.

She watched his hand drop again from the recoiling limb, clutching the liberated foliage… The sight catapulted her consciousness back up the hill to the side of the pool: to the carvings, the butterfly, the watching windows, to the contorted terror worn tightly across Hilly's face, and the sheer abnormality of the sight she'd claimed she saw.

Lucy recollected a story that Mary Tucker from the newsagents in Deerbourne had regaled with an inappropriate level of effervescent levity only a week before. A tale of how the local priest, a father Dylan, had ridden to Hobswyke to question Mallette about yet another child missing from the local area, strongly suspecting Mallette's involvement.

A land worker witnessed the heated exchange. Hot words were swapped, threats made, and the priest eventually departed in a haze of bad blood, but he never made it back.

His shattered remains were found two days later on the bridleway that ran between Hobswyke and Deerbourne. His body was so broken, and his spine so twisted that his head and shoulders faced fully backwards.

The horse was also dead, something apparently so startling it that it ran into a tree with force enough to break its neck and shatter both front legs.

Lucy pirouetted to walk backwards, staring up at the gothic monstrosity that seemed to be calling to her from the top of the bank... *The keys*, she thought, *where are those keys?*

They all eventually reached the bottom of the slope, and ducked through a break in the hedgerow that cut back onto the path by the fork.

'I'm going to go home for a bit,' Lucy announced. 'I've erm – I've got stuff to sort out, things I need to do. Okay?' She turned to Hilly. 'Are you going to be alright?'

Hilly nodded quietly, forcing an embarrassed smile.

'*She'll* be fine,' said Sam, giving her shoulder a brotherly shake. 'Too much Stephen King, that's all.'

Lucy forced a temperate smile towards the young girl to mask her concerns. 'You'll be okay. And I'll see you both later.'

She smiled her goodbyes, and turned to make her way up the path…

'Oh!' she remembered, spinning on her heels. 'Can you tell your dad our kitchen taps are dripping? Mum asked if he could pop over to take look at them.'

'Okay, Luce,' Sam replied, 'I'll do just that.'

Lucy showed her gratitude with another parting smile, and set off up the path again.

Sam stood watching her leave, tilting a fond-filled gaze, before remembering he wasn't alone.

He snapped from his dreams, and turned to collect his sister. They made their way down the lane towards their cottage…

*

Lucy reached the top of the path. She could see her mother ahead of her up a ladder, pruning the roses that blanketed the outside of the gatehouse. She strode up the bank with conviction to hide her apprehension…

She had questions tumbling through her confused mind about the old house that she begged to have answered. She was unable to shake the notion that there was way more to *everything* than she knew, and her mother – for whatever reason – was keeping it from her.

She sensed that there was something *very* wrong with Hobswyke, call it a hunch, or intuition, together with reconsideration of some of the more unusual events from the past that she'd not thought relevant until now. But five years had passed, she was five years older, five years wiser, and unlike before, *now,* she could *feel* it.

'Hi, love, how are you enjoying your new, school-free existence?' her mother quipped airily over her shoulder.

'Yep, I can't deny it, it's really rather nice,' she replied, trying to ignore the subliminal images of the steps, the house, the pool, the fingers rising from the inky depths flashing sporadically through her thoughts.

'Where did you walk?' her mother asked, amputating a length of Virginia creeper that was growing aggressively through the roses.

'Oh, you know, just around, towards the lake, that sort of thing.'

'Well, it's certainly a beautiful day for a stroll. Some vitamin D on your skin won't do you any harm. You've not been getting much of that of late, cooped-up in a classroom, aye.'

'That's for sure,' she agreed, faking a laugh, trying to find an *in* within the standard banter.

'I um… I also went over to take a look at the big house. I've not been to that side of the grounds for quite a while, so I wandered across to have a look,' she announced, as nonchalantly as she could.

Her mother suddenly ceased pruning, and stood motionless on the ladder… She just stared straight ahead at the wall. '…You went to the house?' she asked. Her voice seemed strange.

'Well? Yeah. I've not seen the place for ages, so I thought – you know – I'd go up and have a look around.'

Her mother said nothing, just stared at the wall. She dropped her head slightly. 'And, did you… '

'Did I what?'

'…Did you, *see* anything?' she asked, twisting her face subtly towards her shoulder. A peculiar tone was infesting her voice, like she was feigning disinterest within her interrogation of Lucy's movements.

'Like what?'

Her mother didn't reply, she just hung static on the ladder… 'Nothing,' she chirped, erupting back to life.

Lucy's mother climbed down from the ladder, then paused at the bottom facing the rungs…

She turned to front Lucy. 'Listen, love. I-I don't want you going over there, to that house – *the* house, I mean.'

'Why?'

'I… I just don't. I don't want you going anywhere near the place. It's dangerous.' She stooped to look into the confusion in Lucy's eyes. 'Until I've managed to raise the money, and we can afford to get it renovated, it's not safe, that's all.' She dropped a smile into Lucy's searching eyes. 'I just don't want you getting hurt, love, okay?'

Lucy gazed back at her, trying in earnest to mask the disbelief burning her cheeks. *How the hell can she lie to me like that*, she thought, knowing that money had absolutely nothing to do with any of it.

But one thing *was* for certain, *now* more than ever: Lucy wanted to find those keys!

A bright but insipid bell rang out. A bicycle approached along the main drive. 'I hear you've got a bit of a drip, and I'm *not* talking about Lucy.'

Peter Fletcher arrived on his heavy, ex-postal service bike, flashing mocking eyes at Lucy.

She returned the favour. 'You can talk. The only drip in these parts, is you,' she crowed, smirking. 'Get the garlic everyone! Run for your lives! It's Count Dripular!' She held out crossed fingers towards him and screamed. He laughed.

Lucy was extremely fond of Mr Fletcher, he was what she would describe as a lovely man.

Having never had an actual father in her life, Lucy – on occasion – would allow him to fulfil that role for her. She was also aware that her mother would sometimes utilise him as a sort of surrogate husband, whenever she felt the pang of single motherhood.

'How are you then, young lady?' he asked, unhooking a bag of tools from his handlebars.

'Yeeeeeah. I'm good thanks, Mr F,' she said, genuinely happy to see him.

He strolled up the path towards her. She walked down to meet him, turning to join him, and linked her arm through his.

They ambled up the path together in rhythm. 'Sam was telling me your exams went well?' he enquired, with genuine interest, you could almost say fatherly.

'Yeah, they did. Well – I *think* they did. I had no problems, so, we'll see. Only time will tell I guess.' She flashed a smile across at him as they sauntered towards her mother.

Over the years, Peter had witnessed Lucy gradually bloom into the caring, beautiful young girl she now was. He had known her, and been there for her, for pretty much the entirety of her life.

They'd always had a very strong bond, but it had changed colour of late as Lucy had become far more adult in her ways, bringing them more on a par as people, becoming more like friends than ever before, with a far more *pally* feel to their interactions, and Peter couldn't feel prouder of having played even the smallest of parts in raising the girl that now linked his arm.

'Hi, Pete,' choired Helen, slipping her gardening gloves off as she crossed the lawn to greet him, leaning in to deposit a friendly kiss on his cheek.

'Hey, Hel. How are you?' He smiled. 'Those roses are looking great. They're really starting to come through.' His elated gaze painted the walls of the cottage, admiring the mass eruption of colour blanketing the brickwork. 'They're erm, they're hanging over a bit. Would you like me to help tie them back while I'm here?'

'Aw would you? That would be great,' she responded. 'But, before you do that, could you *possibly* take a look at the—'

'The taps?' he cut in. 'Of course. I'll sort it out for you right now. It's top of my list.' He beamed at Lucy and gave her arm back. 'It shouldn't take too long, no doubt it'll just need a new washer.'

'Thanks, Pete,' Helen beamed.

He nodded a gracious, parting smile towards the two beautiful women in his life, then made his way round to the front door.

Lucy turned to face her mother, prompted by the rasping of aluminium being dragged against the undulations of sandstone blockwork. Her mother struggled to reposition the unwieldy ladder across to the next floral explosion that needed quelling.

Lucy squinted, the mechanics of her mind in full reciprocation, deciding how far she was willing to push her naturally honest nature out of its comfort zone. She pondered whether a decision to withhold information constituted a lie… Somehow, she managed to convince herself it didn't.

'Mum. Can I borrow your necklace, the silver one I like?'

'Yes, of course, love. You know where it is,' she agreed, happily. 'Oooooo,' she sang in a mocking tone. 'First, your favourite dress, and now jewellery. Who is Lucy out to impress?' she jibed.

'Oh – whatever. No one. We're not *all* desperate for constant male attention you know,' she fired back acrimoniously. Her mother laughed.

Lucy turned to make her way inside 'Thanks, Mum,' she called, glancing back to check she wasn't being followed… She wasn't, her mother was already halfway up the ladder again.

Lucy rounded the corner nonchalantly, then gradually sped up her walk, until she was in a full sprint through the door, across the hall, and up the staircase.

She thundered along the landing and darted into her

mother's bedroom, instantly making for the jewellery box on top of the chest of drawers.

She pulled it towards her, flipped the lid open, and began scanning the tangle of chains, clasps and earrings.

She stirred the chaos with her fingers, scanning for a glimpse of a shape she recognised... She found what she was looking for, and frantically began pinching her fingers towards it before it was lost in the tendrils of the mess again...

'Got it!' she fizzled, triumphantly, drawing out the necklace and carefully folding it into her hand.

Having fulfilled the prerequisite for *why* she was searching in her mother's room, she now retuned her focus to what she was actually there to find. 'The keys,' she said out loud, 'where are those bloody keys?'

With the jewellery box still open, she continued sifting through the detritus left over from a lifetime's worth of dressing-up, but now, harbouring an image of the keys she so desperately wanted to find... But after a minute rearranging the chaos, she realised they weren't there.

'Fuck!' she hissed, closing the box and turning to scan the rest of the room. 'Where would I keep them?' she muttered, attempting to channel her mother.

She strode urgently across to the wardrobe, flinging the doors open.

She scanned the inside of the cabinet, and made for the handbags, opening them all one at a time, scooping her fingers through all of the pockets and compartments, listening for the telltale *jingle* of slithers of metal shackled together by a common fob. But nothing! '*Shhhhit!*' she spat.

She closed the doors again, spun around, and rested her back against them. She rescanned the room... *The drawers!* she thought to herself. *It's got to be the drawers.*

She strode back across to the chest of drawers, and started

pulling them out one at a time, sliding her hands beneath the stacks of neatly folded clothing, feeling for anything not fashioned from cloth. How much tidier they looked compared to the jewellery box.

She heard a noise behind her, she sucked in breath and snapped her head round, half expecting to see her mother, standing in the doorway, wearing a mixture of shock and disappointment across her face. But she wasn't there.

Lucy hung static in the silence, her breaths shallow, listening for any perceivable sounds from the stairwell…

A metallic *clank* rang out from the kitchen and echoed up the staircase. It was Peter.

She exhaled, expelling the coiled panic from her knotted stomach.

She turned back, took a breath, and continued to ransack her mother's belongings…

'Nothing!' she hissed in frustration. 'God damn it!' She was all out of ideas, realising that if the keys weren't hidden somewhere that *she* would expect find them, then they'll likely be stashed in any one of a thousand possible places that it was going to be near impossible to find.

But what she *was* now certain of, was that there *had* to be a very good reason why her mother was hiding the keys, and she wanted desperately to know what that was.

'Lucy. Did you managed to find it?' her mother called, starting up the staircase, every creak of a tread hailing each footstep she was nearer to the bedroom.

Lucy shuddered as panic flooded her whole body with adrenalin. She began to straighten and close every draw before the shadow of her mother appears in the doorway behind her…

She could hear the footsteps getting louder, closer, then become muted. She was on the carpeted landing!

Lucy quickly slid the jewellery box back towards her, while

her other hand roughly straightened the last drawer, before rapidly pushing it closed, and at the same time, slowly sliding the jewellery box back to where it usually lived in an attempt to mask the sound of the drawer.

Her mother stepped through the door just in time to see the box settle, and Lucy turn to face her – she'd timed it perfectly.

Lucy attempted to look nonchalant, but inside, she was quaking.

'Did you find it, love?' her mother asked, as she rounded the end of the bed.

'Yes, I-I did. Here it is.' She opened her sweat-glazed hand to display the trinket.

'Do you want me to help you put it on?'

'No! I mean – I can do it,' she said, not wanting her mother to feel the panic-perspiration coating her neck. 'I need to wash first before I put it on. I-I got quite hot outside before.'

Lucy forced a smile, and pushed past her mother's bemusement, feeling guilt-manifested disappointment in herself for going through her mother's belongings without her knowledge. Something she had never done before, and likely will never do again.

Lucy nudged the bathroom door shut with her hip and locked it.

Her shaking hands stuttered a cold flannel over her face and neck, trying to calm her shredded nerves.

She washed her hands clear of the guilt-sweat and its silver-tarnishing properties, then dropped her chin to her chest, and carefully fastened the ornate trinket around her neck.

She looked at herself in the mirror, inspecting the glinting embellishment to a slender neck. It looked good on her.

Her eyes drifted up to meet her mirrored gaze. 'That, was really *bloody* stupid,' she said, berating her reflection. She sighed. 'What the hell do you think you were doing? Idiot! Stupid bloody idiot.'

She shook a regretful head, disappointed in herself, and her actions. 'Let it go now, okay,' she instructed the solitude, 'there's nothing in this, it's all in your imagination. Just let it go, it's just a bloody house.'

She eventually unlocked the door and made her way downstairs, ambling into the kitchen just as Peter was refitting the handles to the taps.

'All done, young lady. It *was* just a washer.'

'That's brilliant,' she replied, brightly, but with having no real interest in taps. 'Would you like some tea, Mr F?'

'Ahhhh please, I could murder a cuppa,' he replied. 'But Luce, before you do that, could you do me a quick favour?'

'Yeah, of course. What is it?'

'Could you look under the sink for me, and watch for leaks while I run the taps, sweetheart? Your knees are younger than mine.'

'Yeah sure,' she agreed, happy to oblige, wishing to exercise her usual helpful ways in an attempt to appease the gods of 'karma', after her recent foray into mild dishonesty.

She crouched down and pushed her head in amongst the city skyline of cleaning product bottles. The smell of stale detergent, shoe polish and mildew hit her nose. She snorted at the chemical stench. 'Go on then, ready…'

The interior of the unit erupted with the drumming sounds of pressurised water ricocheting off thin-walled stainless steel. She scanned for droplets forming on the bottom of the pipework.

'Anything?' a voice shouted from within the drone.

'Nope, nothing yet,' she confirmed.

Something caught the corner of Lucy's eye, something

beyond the pipework, swinging to the harmonic of the running water.

She repositioned her head a little to better see, and could just make out a loop of old string suspended within the snakes of copper tubing. She manoeuvred to get a better look, and inhaled sharply. 'The keys!'

FOUR

A VISITOR

LUCY THREADED HER ARM through the matrix of cobwebs that time had knitted around the keys. Silently, she wrapped her repulsed fingers around the cluster of cold metal. They felt waxy and damp to the touch.

She snapped her grip firmly downwards, the moisture-rotted string popping with barely any perceivable resistance. 'What was that?' Peter asked, hoping it not be a sprung leak.

'Hm? Oh, it was nothing, I erm, I just banged my head, that's all,' replied Lucy.

'Are you okay?'

'*Yeeah* fine,' she assured him, with a dismissive air, trying to act the way she would if she actually *had* banged her head. Her fingers tightened around the discovered secret.

Lucy rose from the dank stench of the cabinet, her eyes taking a moment to readjust to the relative brightness of the kitchen. 'Nope, nothing. All good, Mr F,' she proclaimed, her fist resting on her hip, enveloping her discovery. 'So, tea,' she barked. 'I'll just pop out and see if Mum wants one, too.'

Lucy trotted out into the hallway towards the front door,

stopping briefly to drop her find furtively into her small, trendy leather rucksack hanging from the coat hooks, making sure they made no sound as they landed, announcing to the world their existence.

She stepped out into the sunlight to receive a grateful, 'Yes please,' from the thirsty pruner – elated at the unexpected offer of an Earl Grey with milk and one sugar…

After gifting mugs to welcoming hands, Lucy checked herself in the hallway mirror, then slipped her slender arms through the straps of her rucksack.

She exited back out into the warmth of the sunshine. 'How's your tea?' she chirped, as she strode energetically past the busy gardener.

'Mmm, lovely thank you, sweetheart,' came the reply, with a twee shrug and a smile. 'Where are *you* off to?'

Lucy turned to walk backwards down the bank. 'Me? I'm just going to see Sam, just to say *hi*.'

'Okaaaay,' her mother replied. Lucy could hear the tone of suspicion in her voice.

'I'll see you later,' she smiled, spinning back to face the front.

Helen watched from her elevated vantage point. 'Remember what I said,' she warned, her voice muted by the flutter of the summer breeze and the increasing distance.

Lucy glanced back up the bank, finding the sight of her mother watching from atop the ladder more than a little disconcerted. 'Don't worry,' she replied, forcing a carefree tone to avert her mother's obvious growing suspicions.

Lucy took the right-hand fork at the bottom of the bank, and continued along the sun-dappled lanes towards the Fletcher's lakeside cottage.

She felt happy in the knowledge that Peter would probably be helping her mother tie back the roses for most of the afternoon, feeling that the fewer adult eyes there were circulating the grounds at that moment in time, the better.

She strode down the lane on the final approach to the cottage, exiting the trees that umbrellaed the pathway. As she emerged from beneath the low-hanging canopy, she saw Sam across the way carrying boxes out to the recycling bin by the garage.

'Sam!' she called. He spun like a top, trying to pinpoint what direction his name drifted in from.

'Sam!' she cried again, laughing. A few pirouettes later, he eventually turned to face the path.

'Hey. Hiya,' he chimed, the vision in yellow considerably brightening his day. A most welcome distraction from his bin filling duties.

Lucy crossed the parking area to join him. He ambled across to meet her.

'How's Hilly doing now?' she asked, as she neared him, darting a look up to the house.

Sam's shoulders lifted. 'Well, she seems okay, I guess.' He flicked a look up to her bedroom window. 'She's upstairs, doing one of her crosswords, you know how she loves words, so she can't be that bad. I think she's finally coming to the realisation she imagined it all.'

Lucy fronted him, peering intensely into his face. 'Did she?' she queried, seeming to question the natural assumption.

Sam's eyes pinched with suspicion at Lucy's real-world baulking suggestion. 'What do you mean, "did she"?'

Lucy popped a shrug in response. 'What if she *did* see a hand?'

Sam laughed. Lucy didn't. He stopped. 'What? You mean, you actually think she saw a hand?'

Lucy shrugged at him again.

'Do you know how mad that sounds? "Fingers rising out of the pool".'

'Maybe,' she replied, with a subtly defensive air. 'Anyway, whatever, I'm going to go back up to the house again, to take a good look around.'

The reaction on Sam's face did nothing to hide the fact that he too, had become increasingly wary of that old building. 'How are you going to get in?' he asked, 'your mum'll go *mental* if you break a window.'

Lucy crimped a mischievous lip between her teeth, flashed her brows, and tugged a few times on her rucksack straps. The keys rattled their existence from within the hollow of the bag.

Sam's whole face brightened to the sound. 'You found them!'

She nodded her excitement. 'Under the sink, looped on an old piece of string. They'd been tied right up behind the pipework. A *reeeally* normal place to keep keys, wouldn't you say?' she mocked – a sarcastic tone woven purposefully into her voice. 'Why?' she asked. 'Why not just put them in a draw like anyone else?'

Sam failed to extricate an answer that wouldn't shore up Lucy's suspicions.

Old memories continued to birth in Lucy's mind. Sam could see her thinking. He tilted his head to align his face with hers, inviting her to share her thoughts.

'I can just about remember, right before we moved,' she said, pensively, 'my mum, and your dad, had just started working on one of the larger rooms. It was the library I think?' She frowned. 'If I'm remembering right, the idea was to redecorate it, or-or restore it, or something along those lines?'

Lucy swung her gaze clear of the distraction of Sam's fascinated face, to aid dragging her memories to the fore.

'Anyway,' she continued, 'it didn't really occur to me at the time, I mean, I must've only been about Hilly's age, or younger even? But one day – for *whatever* reason – we suddenly all just left? Like – *really* quickly, without warning, just like that.'

She turned back to Sam, her palms presented to the sky, inviting an opinion he didn't yet have. 'We suddenly abandoned the place, with absolutely *no* explanation whatsoever as to the reason why, and Mum's never *ever* given me a good explanation?' She loosed a sigh. 'And then, as you know, we both moved into the gatehouse.' She flexed the fingers of her upturned hands and shrugged. 'Why?' she asked. 'For what possible reason…?'

Lucy's words began sparking retrospective memories in Sam's *own* mind, of changes that he'd noticed in his father's mood around the same time. 'Did you want me to come with you?' he offered.

'Noooo! It's okay. I'm not risking getting you into trouble too, not yet anyway,' she joked. 'But later on maybe, another time, I'd be more than happy to drop you *right* in the shit.'

They both laughed, but Sam was having to work hard to hide his growing concerns. 'But hang on?' he interjected. 'Why *would* it get us in trouble? You *did* used to live there.'

'Well,' she said, loosing a dismissive snort, working a *gossipy* tone into her voice, 'that's the other thing.' She leaned forwards into a clandestine huddle. 'I told Mum that I'd been up to see the house, to look around – you know. And when I did, she went *really* weird on me.'

'What do you mean, "really weird"?' he asked, squinting his curiosity.

'Well, I dunno? At first, she kind of went all quiet, and then she asked me if I "saw anything"? "*Saw* anything"? Well, I saw the house? But that's *not* what she meant, I could tell by the way she asked. But it's not exactly what you'd call a normal question now is it?'

'No. I guess not,' Sam responded, trying in vain to think of any other way to interpret such a conversation.

'So… I've found the keys, I've *got* the keys, and I'm going to go over there right now to take a look around. I'll try and find out for *myself,* what it was that forced us to leave that place, and so urgently.'

She started walking backwards away from Sam's contemplations, 'I'll see you later, okay.' She flashed her brows and crimped a smile, then turned to start back up the lane. 'I'll let you know what I find,' she called over her shoulder, as she made her way back up the bank.

'*Lucy!*' Sam barked – unable to disguise the concern from his voice.

'Don't worry,' she fired back in response, 'I can take care of myself… I *am* nearly eighteen you know.'

Sam's hunting gaze tracked Lucy as she snaked her way up the lane. How thoroughly alone she looked, and how utterly vulnerable.

Intermittent flashes of yellow peeked through the thickening woodlands as she receded into the distance… It felt wrong for Sam to not be there to protect her.

Sam had also, at times, sensed something festering within the bricks and mortar of that old manor house, and he now found himself regretting his pretence that he hadn't…

Lucy arrived back at the fork at the top of the rise, slowing to a stealthy creep.

She leaned out from behind the trees and glanced up the bank towards the gatehouse, checking the coast was clear of anything resembling a *parent.* But she couldn't see anyone, so she took her chance, and quickly darted across the clearing…

She made her way with forced resolve towards her old home, focusing her attention on the complexity of the early summer birdsong drifting in from every tree, helping to distract her mind from the fact that her levels of unease seemed to be rising exponentially with every stride she advanced nearer to Hobswyke. She suddenly felt very alone.

She eventually arrived at the end of the path. Once again, having to negotiate her way through the latticework of contorted branches that seemed to be scheming to impede her progress.

'Why the hell didn't you go the other way?' she grumbled, scolding her own lack of foresight.

Eventually, she ducked back out onto the gravelled clearing, but this time, she wasn't checking for snags or rogue leaves, her face was firmly locked on the stones and mortar of the gothic monstrosity attempting to intimidate her arrival.

For the second time in a day, Lucy was confronted with the manor house that the passage of time seemed to be conspiring to alienate from her memories.

She endeavoured to face it down, to be dominant in a staring match between her and the gloom-laden frontage peering down at the tiny figure standing before it.

She was conscious of an overwhelming aura of threat that its morose architecture seemed to emit, taking a deep, shaky breath in attempt to clear the sick-inducing quiver that had manifested in the pit of her stomach.

How she wished Sam was next to her, holding her hand, sharing the fear, doubling the ardour.

She regretted, in wanting to appear strong, that she'd inadvertently given voice to a very real weakness she all too often harboured, namely, an inability to ask for help when she truly needed, or wanted it.

It was something she erroneously felt displayed fragility in her nature. A negative impact that she considered her attempts to practice *feminism* had had on the way she interacted with the world.

Eventually though, she managed to steel herself sufficiently to carry on, and started with rekindled determination – however fake it may have been – towards the heavy, oak doors that guarded whatever secrets lay beyond them.

She locked a blinkered gaze on the entrance, attempting to ignore the pools flanking the stone staircase as she slowly climbed the steps. She feared catching a glimpse of contorted fingers rising from the inky blackness of the stagnating fluid, however alien that concept may have been within the real world she was desperately trying to remain planted.

She reached the top of the steps and exhaled; she'd arrived.

She crossed the stone-flagged landing to the tall, dominating, oak-panelled doors, coated in treacle-thick layers of black, heavily crazed paint.

Two stone columns stood guard majestically either side, drawing Lucy's eyes up to an ornate lunette that crowned the entire entranceway, its concave, vista-like surface painted with depictions of frolicking cherubs lording over all who passed beneath.

As she drank in the details of the vivid artwork, she began to notice each winged child had what looked to be a horned, demonic version of itself peeking from behind each and every one. It was yet another detail that had managed to escape her younger self, and one that sent a slow-dripping shudder sliding down her spine.

She swung her rucksack to the front to retrieve the keys. She started to thumb through the cluster. *So many*, she thought, wondering what secrets each one might unlock. But standing out like a white rose in a bed of nettles, was one key that looked pompous and majestic enough to be charged with the task of unlocking such an imposing door as the one she faced, so she swung it clear of the rest, and carefully slid it into the lock... It fitted.

Lucy had to use both hands and the majority of her strength to rotate the large, ornate key, its sister mechanism having sat idle, unfriended by oil or use for over half a decade.

The tumblers finally broke their bonds, and announced Lucy's presence with a deep, hollow, metallic *clank,* amplified by the entire door.

She pushed, but nothing gave.

She stepped back to scan the heavy oak slab for any other locks, but could see none.

She dropped the keys back into her bag, slipped it on, and leant her whole bodyweight hard against the door again, and with a few determined thrusts, it finally crackled open, the bonds of inactivity relenting to her persistence.

The dry hinges cracked as the door swung open, presenting the interior like parting curtains unveil a stage. But in this particular play, Lucy was a cast member that had yet to read the script.

FIVE

'I'M BACK'

DRY LEAVES AND DEBRIS blew through the liberated entrance, gusting past Lucy's tentative legs. They scattered across the black and white skeined marble flooring of the grand entrance hall, dancing to the tune of the thermal currents that carried them in, until Lucy turned and slammed the door shut behind her, decapitating the wind.

The deep, woody crash rang throughout the entire building, overlapping echoes chasing through the abandoned rooms, hallways and staircases… The multilayered pulse finally dissipated into the stale air, leaving a deathly silence in its wake almost deafening in its nothingness.

Lucy remained static in the quiet. Just listing… her eyes the only things moving within a face searching for the comfort of familiarity. She could feel the thump of her heart pounding in her throat.

She recognised the geography of the space, but each individual detail seemed subtly different to her memories, but she realised they can't have been.

She unrooted her feet and moved further into the chilled

hollow of the vast, open space, the soft tip-tap of her pumps echoing off the walls as she roamed across the flat, marble slab.

It put her in mind of the near deafening gunshot sounds her mother's stiletto heels would make whenever she hurried across this space. Lucy smiled at the memory, and the fact that she'd been successful in recollecting one.

She took time to reacquaint herself with each and every element of the room, rebooting her recognition of a building that the passage of time had pushed to the back of her mind.

Her eyes drifted from one overtly ornate object to the next, soaking up their extravagance, her face luminous with wonder, awe, and a newly discovered ability to appreciate.

She drank in the details of her forgotten past: Chinese vases, too immense to reside in a gatehouse, sitting atop ornate, French side tables with scrolled, serpentine legs recurving down to lions feet, carved from the finest woods, and glazed with the purest of polishes; delicate balloon-back chairs, embellished with red velvet upholstery, set evenly around the perimeter of the room; hung tapestries competing for wall space with portraits of those who had been, and gone; and heavy, painted landscapes chronicling the way the world once looked. All things she had looked upon many times before, but now, only just seen. An eclectic mix of decor that would look ridiculous anywhere else but in a room as ostentatious as this, all sharing a common layer of dust, and a place in the past of a family that had moved on.

She adjusted her focus back to the geography of the room. Directly ahead, opposite the main entrance, were large double-doors that Lucy remembered led into the library. Rising from either side were twin staircases, mirrored in appearance, climbing away from each other before circling back to reunite on a common landing area that overlooked the entirety of the room from above the library entrance.

There were two more doors to her left: the first led into what her mother used to refer to as 'the drawing room'. The other opened into a large dining hall that housed a table so preposterous in its length and proportions, that it made any attempt to eat while sitting at it virtually impossible from laughing so hard.

Lucy dropped her eyes to the floor and chuckled. 'Ridiculous bloody table,' she muttered, the words echoing around the must-scented room.

Her mother never felt that she knew enough people to even consider holding a dinner party in such a huge expanse of room, so in all its time, it remained virtually unused, except as a place for Lucy, Hilly and Sam to play. A reminiscent smile played across Lucy's lips.

Her gaze drifted upwards from the dining room doors… She swelled with awe as gleaming eyes absorbed in wonderment the hundreds of ornate, finial-centred, quad-form plaster mouldings that encrusted the entirety of the huge expanse of ceiling. Its unnecessary opulence bejewelled by an enormous chandelier dropping half the height of the room, thousands of crystal droplets each coated with five-year jackets of dust and delicate veils of cobwebs.

She found herself lost in her gaze, no longer able to focus on the sheer complexity of the patterned ceiling crowning her wonder. Her pupils palpitated, their ability to judge distance confused. *How high is that ceiling?* she thought. *Could be a metre, could be a mile.*

She rocked on her heals, no longer able to judge up from down, and shut her eyes tight to reset her body's scrambled equilibrium.

Lucy felt sure that she has never truly appreciated how beautiful and awe-invoking her old home truly was, until now, seen through retrospective eyes, *older* eyes, now of an age where she was able to appreciate such things.

She came to the realisation that, as a child, she must've rarely ever looked up, probably far more fascinated with life at ground level.

How magnificent and regal she thought the chandelier managed to look, in spite of its time-inherited coating of grime. In fact, the sheer elegance of the entire room still managed to shine through the pungent air of dereliction.

She lowered her gaze from the chandelier to the opposite wall, and popped a smile as she saw the entrance to the games room – much fun was had in there as children.

She remembered how she and Sam would play a version of snooker that used their hands, the cues being deemed out of bounds by her mother as a baize-saving exercise.

The rules were simple, throw any coloured ball towards any other ball, and hope it knocked it into any pocket. And if it did, act as if there was considerable judgment involved, and that the outcome was planned.

She chuckled to herself. 'Stupid kids,' she whispered into the seclusion, pulling herself back from her memories to continue the reunion.

To the left of the games room were a pair of large double doors that led into the old ballroom. She ambled across to take a closer look. The doors to the room had been left ajar. She wandered in…

She felt an inflation of her recollections as memories of the space thrust forwards to the forefront of her mind.

The room still looked every bit as cavernous and majestic as she remembered, mirroring the dining hall on the opposite side, but without the preposterous table to fill the space, it always seemed much larger.

The sensation was not at all what she was expecting, imagining that the room would somehow look smaller to her now that she was older and taller, but if anything, it looked larger, grander, and even more impressive than her rekindled memories would've suggested.

Vivid echoes of the many gatherings held in this impressive expanse of room over the years manifested in her mind. She remembered how her mother would allow her to stay up late whenever she held what she used to refer to as 'a get together', something Lucy recalled with extreme fondness, it allowed her – as a child – to dip a toe into what it might feel like to be an adult.

Her memories seemed to be returning thick and fast now, keying off the visuals of the building, finding immense enjoyment in her reunion.

Lucy's recent apprehension towards Hobswyke seemed to her almost ludicrous now, her prior unease all but melting away with each room she reacquainted herself with.

She turned and made for the staircases, extending an arm and making a grab at the handles of the library door as she trotted past, but they were locked.

Her long legs consumed the treads with ease, two at a time, creaking beneath the first human feet that had graced their boards in more than half a decade.

She reached the top, and turned to take in the bird's-eye view of the hall from the landing. 'Wow!' She exhaled through a face glowing with awe, her voice echoing around the ceiling, unable to contain her pride and excitement at knowing that this incredible building was not only in her family, *part* of her family, but would, one day, in all likelihood, belong to her.

She squealed like an overexcited child, and turned to make her way towards her old bedroom. running along the expansive landings, footsteps padding on the heavily piled carpets, throwing cursory glances into all the other rooms as she rushed past, her excited energy helping to fill the lifeless void left by a five-year absence of human activity.

She spied the door to her old room, and galloped towards it, her excitement rising like a warmed thermometer until she could feel it in her throat.

Reaching out an arm, she grasped the frame, her inertia swinging her in through the door.

She stopped dead, face relaxing out of its smile, overwhelmed by apparitions from her past…

The room was peppered with toys, trinkets and ornaments that would have failed to hold the fascination of a twelve year old girl, but that now – many years on – drew fond memories to the fore in one looking on with a maturer eye. A room filled with inconsequential objects made relevant by nothing more than the simple passage of time.

Lucy wandered into the familiarity of the space, a space that held nothing but happy memories, except perhaps, the day they all hurriedly left – for reasons still unknown.

An ominous image of the library doors pushed forwards from the shadows of her mind. She shut her eyes to shake it away, keen to reacquaint herself with her childhood haven, undesiring of anything negative tainting what she was determined would be a joyous occasion.

She reopened her eyes again, and looked about the room…

Her old bed was sat before her, exactly as she remembered it, still made up with the linen she last slept in the night before they left.

She walked to it, and swiped her hand across the sheets a few times, but there was surprisingly little dust. So, gently, she perched herself on the edge… She recognised the creak-pattern of the springs, she'd heard them a thousand times before. The bed felt soft, welcoming, familiar.

Lucy peered past her left shoulder, watching as her fingers stroked the pure white cotton, her eyes smiling at the multitude of happy memories that were now erupting in her thoughts like fireflies in a midnight sky.

Lifting eyes to the windows, she carefully cleared a tear from beneath her glistening cheek with the side of her finger, trying not to smudge her carefully applied makeup.

She spied her collection of dolls and teddy bears arranged neatly on an old, mahogany toy box. She beamed, and rose to take a closer look…

Stooping, she carefully drew out what used to be her favourite doll from the core of the throng. 'Sandy' she used to call her, because the doll always reminded her of a character from the movie Grease. She crimped her lower lip between her teeth as she spent time rearranging her outfit, stroking her hair into a more current style – the one she was sporting being at least five years out of date. 'There,' she announced with triumph to her old friend and the rest of the toys looking on. 'Much, much better. Very trendy.'

She flinched a regretful smile to mask the inner sadness she felt at having to grow up, and placed the doll carefully back again, this time right at the front – pride of place.

She turned her attention to her right side, and saw the antique, marquetry table that she used to keep her *things* on in the corner: puzzles, music boxes, games, souvenirs, photos, mementos, and a chintzy ceramic pot spilling over with costume jewellery her mother had let her have over the years. She smirked at how small the table now looked, and wondered how on earth she used to sit at it?

She ambled across to it, tilting her gaze at the random collection of memories, brushing her fingers gently over the age-lifted inlay of the undulating table top.

Her fingers rose and fell over the contours of the puckered marquetry. Her mother used to refer to it as 'patina'. 'Like laughter lines worn proudly on a face that's lived a life of happiness,' she used to say. For the first time, Lucy now understood what she meant. She stroked her other hand across the softness of her cheek, comparing the *life-lived* table top to her perfect young skin.

She attempted to imagine what she would look like when she, herself, would be older, then thought of her mother's face, and how elegantly she managed to wear *her* years.

She quickly scanned the rest of the room, grabbing a past-favoured piece of jewellery from the pot as a keepsake, then with her mother still on her mind, left through the door…

She padded back along the corridor a short way, and turned into what was her mother's old room, just two doors down from her own.

She stood in the doorway and closed her eyes, drawing a long, deliberate breath in through her nose… The air in the room was inert, but still charged with the exact same scent as her mother's current bedroom, just markedly less so.

She looked about at all of the beautiful furniture that had been abandoned, then inexplicably replaced by items so similar in appearance that it would be difficult to tell them apart. 'Why didn't she just take these?' she had to ask herself, unable to contrive an answer.

She pondered the detritus left from the move: emptied drawers left pulled out, wardrobe doors ajar, unfavoured clothing and shoes laying piled up on the bed. To Lucy, the room typified one left in a hurry, the condition it was in suggesting a certain level of panic, an undeniable urgency, a desire to '*get out, as quick as we can!*'

Lucy couldn't help but frown at the sight that faced her, wondering what on earth could be so wrong with a building that the occupants just had to leave, and with such immediacy.

With a heavily pensive brow, she amble back out into the

corridor. 'The library,' she said out loud, looking around at all the open doors. 'Why is it the only room that's locked?'

She made her way back along the corridor towards the top of the staircases, determined to find an answer to the question…

As she hit the mezzanine landing, she caught a glimpse through the corner of her eye of the library doors down through the flashing balustrades. A concoction of mixed feelings – nervous, excited, intrigued apprehension, swelled in her knotting stomach.

She creaked down the staircase towards the locked room, taking the keys from her rucksack once more, fumbling to find any visual clues to which one might unlock the answers to her questions. But there were none, so methodically, she began to try them all. One after the other, after the other, after the… *CLACK!* The locks withdrew from their housing.

The pit of her gut lurched and began to quiver. She crunched her stomach muscles and blew through pursed lips to try to clear the feeling. She dropped the keys back into the bag, and slipped it on.

Grabbing both door handles, she tentatively twisted them down, then furtively, pushed them slowly away from her…

The musty smell of antiquated books curled past the doors as they swung open. A spreading fan of light arced across the floor of the windowless room as the doors finally settled into their open position, unveiling a room in utter disarray.

Lucy's fascinated eyes swept the ceiling-high shelving lining the walls of the dingy, semi-lit room. Half of them neatly filled with books, the other half lying empty.

The tomes and volumes that had for so long sat within them had been dislodged from their long-term haunts, and carefully packed in boxes around the perimeter of the floor.

Her pupils finally widened to the relative lightlessness, allowing here to better see the space around her.

To the far right-hand side, in shadow, the carpets that had graced the floor for the better part of two centuries had been unceremoniously ripped up, and piled in a heap against the wall. There was a heavy-set, leather-topped desk pushed to one side that had originally sat in the centre of the room, with the buttoned leather seat married to it stacked on top. Other random objects that had been displaced lay scattered around the perimeter, but it was what lay dead-centre of the floor that arrested Lucy's interest. A sight that fulfilled the least of her expectations.

She gazed in utter disbelief at something that must have always been in this room, hidden away out of sight, out of mind, out of knowledge. Hidden in the house that she had lived in the entirety of her younger years. A secret that must have existed beneath their everyday comings and goings for all that time.

What she saw before her chilled her to the very marrow of her bones, and all she could do was stand, and stare, and wonder if it was real.

Her slender shadow cut across a stack of floorboards that had been lifted and piled up to one side, revealing a large, circular section of floor that dropped down into the centre of the library like the maw of hell.

Lucy walked tentatively past the stacks of planking towards the pit, and could see it dropped down at least half her height, if not more.

As she reached the edge, her freshly acclimatised eyes solidified to the sight they saw. She was presented with what must have been Antoine Mallette's ceremonial circle, hidden for decades beneath their feet, beneath their lives, beneath their ignorance, now uncovered for the world to see.

Emerging ominously from the murk at the base of the pit, stood an elaborate stone altar, draped with illustrated cloths, heavy with mildew, and adorned with black candles; ornate handled knives, and an eclectic mix of paraphernalia that Lucy could see must related in some way to the practice of magic.

She leaned over, rolling her gaze, drinking in the details of the anomaly to ordinary life.

The walls of the pit were entirely covered in writing in all languages, not a single square inch left bereft of script. Writing upon writing, ten layers and many decades deep: complex mathematical calculations, astronomical predictions, life problems – demented solutions, ungodly thoughts, and twisted ideas. Seventy years of the cerebralvomit of a damaged mind, spilling out in written form all over the walls of a rancid secret.

Lucy had listened to stories of Mallette and his skewed existence for as long as she could remember, but to suddenly come face to face with the reality of *him,* was something she was wholly unprepared for.

She crouched at the edge of the well, twisting her squinting eyes to try and decipher some of the scrawled madness...

She could make out English, some French, Latin, something that looked distinctly Arabic, and an ancient stick-form symbology that she knew were called 'runes'. But there was so much of it that within the stark light, it was virtually impossible to make out anything remotely intelligible, and the things that she *could* manage to read made little sense to the interpretations of a sane mind.

'He must have been mad?' she whispered to herself as her eyes drank in the sheer volume of the product of his apparent mental illnesses...

She shifted her gaze to inspect the floor of the pit. A ring of what looked like encrusted salt crystals encircled the entire circumference of the stone-flagged base, fused solid by the damp seeping up through the ground.

A five-pointed star, a pentagram, had been painted within the circle in some sort of deep red, near-black fluid, and in each corner of the triangles created by its intersecting lines, there was more Arabic writing and strange symbology, marked in the same deep-red substance.

Lucy felt a sudden urge to leave the room, to leave the building. The same urge her mother and Peter must have felt when they'd originally discovered it.

Then she heard a sound like slow breathing, and the cracking groan of weight-loaded timbers.

Lucy's breath stuttered, terrified eyes flitting about the space, searching for the source of the sound... She scanned every darkened crevice, sensing something watching, but saw nothing, then her gaze drifted across to the large mirror hanging above the heavy, sandstone fireplace. Reflected in the dust-veiled sheet of glass, barely visible within the blackness of the room, was a crouched figure with knotted limbs, hanging high in the corner of the shelving where the walls met the ceiling, clinging to the timbers like a canker.

She snapped her head away from the reflection to where it was, but it wasn't there? She looked back at the mirror again, and could see it, vividly.

It watched her with eyes as empty and emotionless as those of a corpse, twisting its head as it examined the terrified life cowering before it.

Paralysed with fear, her squat body began to violently shake at the sight of the apparition studying her.

It leaned forwards out of the shadows, pushing its tortured face into the light, its mouth slowly stretching open, extending down, gaping wide beneath its dead-eyed stare.

A lifeless black tongue lowered from its mouth like wet rope, hanging limp, dropping almost the length of its grotesque body.

The tip of its tongue vibrated, tasting the air. The creature exhaled a long, hollow breath. 'Asmodeussssssssss…' it hissed.

Lucy winced from the sound, trying desperately to animate her paralysed limbs, her mouth swinging wide, fear-formed drool dripping from her chattering jaw.

The thing began to draw its tongue slowly back into its mouth again, leaning further from the unlit corner towards her.

Lucy noticed the face and horns of a bull, then the letterbox eyes of a ram emerge from the gloom, writhing violently in the shadows behind the creature's buckled shoulders, their horns cracking together as they wheeled with excitement. Suddenly, she realised, this thing watching her had three heads.

The shock of the vision jarred her into flight mode, and she fought through her paralysis to regain at least partial control of her limbs.

Her stuttering body twisted and fell back onto her hands. She began to scramble urgently towards the door on panicked arms, guided by the illuminated path along the ground.

She flailed frantically along the ribbon of light, manic, unblinking eyes staring dead ahead at her only possible means of escape, expecting to see the apparition cutting her off at any moment.

Two grasping hands lowered down and grabbed her arms, arresting her progress.

Lucy's mouth bit at the air, her arid throat chocking on its inability to cry for help, until finally, she managed a scream, a shrill, manic cry that pierced the very fabric of the house.

The manacle hands gripped her tight, and lifted her off her feet.

Lucy's pin-prick pupils turned to meet those of her captor… It was Sam! Her eyes rolled back into her lolloping head, and everything went black…

SIX

THE BLACKEST OF SECRETS

LUCY'S LIDS fluttered open, allowing the sting of the light to burn through her pancake pupils, shocking her consciousness awake.

She could hear a muted voice calling her name, echoing around the furthest reaches of her scrambled mind, drifting in from the aether… Calling… Calling.

The voice gradually brightened, pulling forward from her distant dreams. 'Lucy…? Luuuucyyyy…?' it called. She spun in her mind, trying to find the voice. 'Lucy,' it called again.

Her eyes ceased rolling beneath her flickering lids, and she groaned awake, reeling in the farthest extremities of her confusion.

The voice suddenly shot forwards to pin-sharp clarity. 'Lucy? Are you okay?' it said. 'Talk to me!'

She felt a hand tapping her cheek. The voice was drenched in concern and familiar tones. 'Speak to me. Are you okay?' it asked – softly spoken, gentle, caring… The voice was Sam's. 'Lucy! Please wake up!'

She drifted her blurred vision towards the question. An

out-of-focus silhouette of Sam was standing by the side of her prostrate body, looking down upon her.

Her drifting eyes finally managed to lock and pull focus, resolving the genuine concern on his face. 'What? Um…? Where the hell am I?' she mumbled, feeling decidedly groggy.

'You're okay, don't worry,' he assured her, 'you're safe now. You're in my room, just relax, okay.'

'*Your* room? What the hell am I doing in *your* room?' She looked around, bewildered. 'W-What? What happened?' she asked – confused by what felt like teleportation.

'Well. I-I *think* you fainted?' he said. 'But I don't really know what that looks like, so I'm not really sure… I've only ever seen it in films. It's actually kind of frightening.'

Lucy had only ever blacked out once before in her life, during a particularly memorable inoculation at school. She'd never been good with needles – the same as her mother. The sensation she felt then as she'd succumbed to her fear of the needle – a sensation of shifting within herself – was very much the same as now.

'I *fainted*?' she slurred, bemused. She struggled to sit upright, and swung her legs off the side of the bed. She stared through the floor for a time, running through her mind anything resembling a recent memory…

Through the swirling collage of images, one alone pushed through, slowly emerging, subtly obvious like an omen. It resolved into an image of the three-headed entity, mouth stretching long, its elongated tongue tasting the air.

Suddenly, she could remember it all. 'Shit, Sam! That – *thing*! What the *fuck* was that *thing*?'

'What do you mean, "thing"?' he asked, startled by her sudden animation.

'In the library, crouched up in the corner of the library!'

Sam looked blankly back at her, not comprehending a word she was saying. Doubt and confusion tugged at his brows.

Lucy couldn't help but react. 'Are you telling me you didn't see that – that *creature*?' she snapped in disbelief. 'You must have done? I don't know what the fuck it was, but you *must* have seen it?'

'No,' he responded, 'I didn't see anything.'

Lucy closed her eyes tight, trying to pull the memory to the fore. 'It said something… A word I've never heard before. Now what the hell was it…?' She cupped her hands over her eyes to lock herself into her thoughts. 'Asmo, Asmo, deus? Or something…? Yes, *that's* it. "Asmodeus"?'

Her words meant nothing to Sam. 'No I didn't see, or hear that. I didn't see or hear anything,' he replied – perplexed. 'All I know is I didn't like you being there alone, so I jumped in Dad's buggy and drove up to join you, and that's when I discovered you on your hands and knees.' His eyes softened. 'You looked so frightened,' he explained, attempting to mimic the expression he'd seen on her face, not having the words to hand to describe it. 'So, what was it you think – I mean, what was it you saw? Think you saw?' he asked, attempting to walk a more diplomatic line, and failing miserably.

'It was a creature, sort of like a man, but *not* a man, if you know what I mean.' She shut her eyes again. 'But it had more than one face, heads I mean? Shit! I don't know what it was, but it was *there* I *swear* it,' she insisted, painfully aware how unbelievable it all must have sounded.

She rolled a humble head, 'I thought you were it. I thought it had got me.' She peered up at him with wet, timid eyes. 'Thank you, Sammy… I'm so glad you came to help.'

Sam flashed the weakest of smiles beneath a brow tight with empathy. She only ever called him 'Sammy' when she was being genuinely compassionate towards him, the sobriquet forming a knot in his stomach, and he sensed his heart beating in his chest, the adoring thump pulsing through to his neck, and behind his eyes. In spite of her aggression, he loved her.

'*I* believe you,' announced another voice. It was Hilly, who'd just walked into the room holding an open book.

'Hilly!' cried Lucy, enthusiastically overjoyed at seeing her.

Hilly carefully closed the book and placed it down on Sam's desk. She trotted over to the bed, wrapping herself around a person who she'd always considered to be – in all but actuality – her older sister.

'Are you okay now?' asked Hilly. 'We were worried.'

'I'm fine, Hill,' she responded into the young girl's dewy gaze, cupping her cheek gently in her delicate hand.

Lucy visibly flinched, shooting a worried look up at Sam. 'Did you tell my mum? You didn't tell Mum did you?'

'Noooo, I didn't tell Helen. She wasn't supposed to know you were there, right?'

Lucy vented a heartfelt sigh of relief. 'Yesss. God. Thank you.'

Sam allowed himself a smile.

Lucy threw another look his way. 'The floor… of the library! What was going on with that floor?' she asked, recalling her ordeal.

'Erm… the floor? What about it?'

'How the hell could you have not noticed the floor!'

'Well, you know, I was a little bit busy trying to carry you out to the buggy, sorry if in trying to help you, I failed to absorb the details of the house!' he replied – more than a little put out by what was beginning to feel a bit like deep ingratitude.

'I'm sorry. I'm sorry,' she mewed, apologetically, ingratitude being the farthest thing from what was in her heart.

'That's okay,' he said with a shrug. 'Anyway, what about the floor?' he asked – his interest spiked.

'I don't know how to describe it. There was a sort of hidden floor that they'd uncovered. Like a big well, a shallow well.'

'They'd?'

'Your dad, and my mum I presume?'

'And…?' he coaxed, keen to know exactly what it was she'd seen. What he'd failed to notice.

Hilly looked on too, her eyes also inviting the details. She flicked a glance towards the book on the desk.

Lucy took a calming breath. 'It was a pit, in the ground, hidden. Like a magic one, for doing witchcraft stuff. I could tell, it was a sort of devil-worship thing.'

'What, in the library?' asked Sam, a *what-the-hell* tone colouring his voice.

'*Yesssssss*! In the library,' she barked, her patience fraying.

Sam dropped his gaze to the floor, gathering his thoughts… 'Wait here, I won't be long,' he instructed, authoritatively. He looked across to his sister. 'Hilly, stay here with Lucy, okay?' Before she could respond, he turned, and rushed from the room.

'Where are you going?' Lucy shouted from the bed, but there was no reply.

They both heard the door of the cottage slam, and the engine of the buggy start and drive away.

Lucy looked across at Hilly, Hilly shrugged…

*

Sam was back at the hall, standing in the library, looking down in awe at Lucy's discovery…

Generations of locals had whispered of such a site, knowing it to exist somewhere within the bones of the old house, but no one had ever actually seen it to confirm its existence. But now,

Sam Fletcher – overwhelmed by a sense of grim foreboding – was looking down into the very place where the notorious Mallette must have performed all of his rituals.

He found the fact that Mallette had gone to such extraordinary lengths to conceal what lay before him more than a little disconcerting, realising that for someone go to *that* much effort to hide something, then it must be a particularly squalid 'something' that's being squirrelled away from the judgment of others.

His eyes scanned the details of the pit, it smelled damp, a centuries old stench of mildew and wet earth burning the back of his throat.

His gaze drifted up to the altar. 'Christ!' he whispered.

He looked about the room for any signs of the entity Lucy described, but he saw nothing. He snorted dismissively and shook his head, attributing her experience to an overwhelmed imagination.

Sam looked down into the well again, fascinated by how macabre it looked in comparison to the studious room it inhabited. He stepped to the edge, dropped to a hand, and hopped into the pit.

He stood upright and was shocked to realises that the walls were nearly his height.

He looked about nervously, but could see no steps apparent in order to climb out again. The ceiling of the library seemed so much further away now. He rocked on his heals at the sense of negative vertigo, feeling unnervingly cornered and decidedly exposed.

He lowered his attention back to the pit, and circled the stone altar, carefully placing his feet to avoid the makings on the ground.

He took up the knife in his hand. The steel had a coating of terracotta rust. He wrapped his fingers around the handle and gripped it tight, and made a few stabbing motions in the air.

He lifted it into the light fanning from the doors, then he realised, the blade was in fact made of a slither of bone, and the deep-red staining, wasn't rust at all.

He ejected the blade from his fingers back onto the altar, wiping the palm of his hand on his jeans, his face twisting with revulsion.

He took a breath, and stepped in again, this time, with a little more reluctance, and began examining the cloths that were draped across the altar. There were three of them, all embroidered with Arabic script and cabalistic symbology, similar to what he'd seen flanking the stone staircase outside.

He decided to take one with him to do some research. He grabbed a corner of the middle one and lifted it revealing the bare stone beneath. But it wasn't the sandy colour he was expecting, it was black.

Sam frowned, and swiped his finger across the top of the altar. The dark substance powdered to his touch. He sniffed at it, but it had no scent.

He rolled the dust between thumb and forefinger, before dabbing it against his tongue. A metallic, almost copper taste erupted across his taste buds. He lifted his hand into the light, the tip of his finger was now stained deep maroon.

Sam gagged, and bent over, spitting his revulsion onto the ground!

He heard a woody creak from the corner of the room, from deep within the shadows high above his head.

His eyes snapped towards the sound, scanning the dimly lit corner from whence the noise came…

He stumbled and pushed his back against the wall, his body stiffened with fear, his erratic breathing almost deafening in such purity of silence.

Sam hovered motionless, continuing to stare into the lightless corner, but he could see nothing.

The groan came again, and it didn't take much of a stretch of his unnerved imagination to think that there could be someone, or something lurking in the unlit crevasses of such an antiquated study.

He finally succumbed to the realisation that there was probably truth in everything Lucy *and* his sister had claimed they saw, despite having seen none of it himself, however bizarre their claims may have seemed.

A crippling sense of solitude began to incinerate his ardour, his only companion being an eerie silence, and the oppressive atmosphere that had been slowly inhabiting the space since his arrival.

He turned, and scrambled desperately at the walls of the well, trying to climb out. His toes slipped on the greasy sandstone, struggling to get purchase, smudging decades of Mallette's notes and scribblings. He finally managed to rise up onto his hands, hooking a knee on the edge, and heaved himself to his feet.

He started to back out of the room, nearly taking a toss over the stacks of floorboards.

He regained his footing, and stumbled out into the entrance hall, erratically grabbing at the handles of the library doors and slamming them shut behind him.

Sam sprinted, magnetised to the slither of *outside* that he could see across the hallway.

He thought he heard the doors of the library opening behind him, but he didn't dare turn to look, hoping it was just the birth-child of his unnerved imagination, and not something far more real.

He darted through the gap into the sunlight, and turned to heave the heavy doors closed with everything he had within him.

They *crashed* shut, the sound echoing through the trees surrounding the house. Then he realised he didn't know where the keys were.

'Shit!' he spat, shying from the monolithic entrance towering above him, wondering if he really did hear someone, or something following…?

He froze, and stared, expecting the doors to creep open… But after the longest minute of his life just watching and waiting for movement that never came, he released his held breath, and dropped to his knees – exhausted by his not inconsiderable apprehension.

He finally managed to gather himself together again, clearing his mind of what he assumed must have been some kind of fear-induced paranoia.

But he was less able to reason his mind free of the things the two girls had claimed witness to.

He turned his back on the house, his eyes gravitating towards the steps. He could see sunlight glinting off the pools through the twists of the elaborate railings.

His intrigue in his sister's claim, and the utterly terrified look he'd seen in her face – a look that he felt sure would be seared into his memory forever – drew him slowly down the steps until he was resting his weight against the rusted handrail.

He watched the water, and noticed the swirling mists had cleared. He turned his curious gaze skyward. The sun had begun dropping towards the horizon, and along with it, the temperature.

Wisps of cloud were beginning to form from the moisture the baking, midday heat had lifted from the soil.

Sam peered down into the tar-blackness of the water again, and saw the assembling clouds reflected off the stillness with the clarity of a scrying mirror.

Sam leaned towards the inverted sky, mesmerised by the sheer perfection of the veneer to all that existed beneath the surface.

He scanned for an imperfection: a ripple, a bubble, the iridescence of drifting butterfly wings, or God forbid, fingers rising from beneath the inert glassiness, breaking through the film into the world above. *His* world. But all he could see were the clouds.

He leaned further in, magnetised by the image. The handrail digging into the tops of his thighs, but he failed to feel any pain – far too mesmerised by the serenity of the onyx-sheen...

He heard a sharp, metallic *snap!* Then suddenly jerked forwards and out of his trance.

The rusted handrail sheared! The tendrils of decayed ironwork snaking beneath bending to the force of Sam's body weight, lowering his panic-stricken body towards the inky water.

He shuddered as he went weightless, flailing his arms back, blindly grabbing for anything substantial enough to halt his descent.

He managed to grasp a section of the railing still fixed solid, and heaved to pull himself back from the stagnant water.

His other hand pushed frantically against the disintegrating section, and with a loud *tink,* the entire panel broke away, and dropped into the pool.

'Oh *sssssshit*!' he cried, finally regaining his balance. He took a moment to steady himself, then looked around to see if there were any disapproving eyes looking on. There weren't, he was alone.

Anxiety twisted his stomach into a fist as he considered just how much trouble he could be in. It *was* an accident, but the reality was, that although he lived on the grounds, this *wasn't* his house. But worse than that, as close as the families were, this building belonged to the boss. His *father's* boss!

He pondered his situation. *But for what good reason would I be here? Leaning over this pool?* he asked himself. *What good reason could I give, that wouldn't get Lucy in trouble?* Questions he was not sure he could answer with any level of validity – given that the house lay unlocked, and he had no reason to be there, at least none that related to his usual daily habits or chores.

Damaging the property of what was in reality, his father's employer – however friendly the two families may have been in their everyday interactions – wasn't sitting well.

He suddenly felt nauseous, uncertain of the reaction he'd receive should 'the parents' learn of what had been going on. Potentially, he was very much in trouble.

He carefully leaned to look down at the pool… He could just see the corner of the panel protruding from the water.

Sam strained to lean out further, trying to better see it. One of the wrought-iron twists had bent back into a loop, and was hooked onto some of the carved details on the stonework buttress.

He desperately tried to evaluate his options in the midst of his panic, and decided the only one open to him, was to try to retrieve the section, and temporarily wire it back in place in the hope that no one would notice. Then, on a day when the grounds were free of parental eyes, he could return, and attempt to repair it well enough that no one would ever know it had been broken.

His father had recently taught him how to MIG weld, a skill he'd always wanted to learn, but he wasn't expecting a chance to practice to come along quite so soon.

He scanned the area one last time to check he was still alone, then carefully, started to edge himself across the stonework towards the pool.

He looked down at his feet, and noticed the archaic details in the weathered sandstone were crumbling under his shoes. 'Oh, crap!' he barked, quickly manoeuvring his feet to areas without detail, keen not to do any more damage than he already had.

He squatted, and strained his fingers out towards the ironwork panel, but he was unable to reach it.

He noticed other areas with no detail, and stepped across to one of them, and reached out again... He was a matter of inches from being able to grab one of the bars.

Frustration started to percolate in his gut, but he had to try to quell it, the panel potentially just one clumsy fumble away from being lost in the pool forever, and not knowing how deep it was.

He noticed a couple more of the blank areas on the stonework, closer to the submerged railing, and stepped across to them, and tried one more time...

He squatted down, straining his arm out, the ends of his fingers just about kissing the metal, carefully making micro lunges, trying desperately to wrap his fingers around one of the bars...

'H-H-How are you d-doing that?!' implored a voice from somewhere behind him.

Sam's heart leapt into his throat, and he turned his head towards the question. Lucy and his sister stood static on the gravel, just staring at him, both wearing as shocked an expression as any face had ever worn.

Lucy had her hands clapped tightly across her mouth, hiding a lip curling with fright. Her widened eyes shook at a sight beyond comprehension.

'What's wrong?' asked Sam, confused.

'H-How, are you d-doing that!' begged Hilly.

'Doing what?' he fired back.

Lucy dropped her hands from her mouth. 'L-Look. Look at yourself,' she whimpered, a tear curling from the corner of her eye and meandering down her cheek.

Sam carefully unwrapped his fingers from around the bar, and stood. But he didn't rise higher, weirdly, he extended *out* from the side of the pool?

He turned his attention selfward, and it suddenly dawned on him that Lucy and Hilly lay horizontal across his vision, but he was standing up? 'What the…?!' he said, looking around cluelessly. He bent his eyes down to his feet, and stammered a breath laced with utter disbelief. He appeared to be standing, but on the *side* of the stonework that flanked the staircase!

His head was level with the rest of his body, hanging parallel to the surface of the water… He could reach out a hand, and dip it into the pool.

Sam had been so engrossed in retrieving the panel, he hadn't noticed that he'd been walking around the curvature of the carvings, arcing towards the pool. And now – somehow – he defied gravity.

He started to quake at the impossibility of what he was apparently doing, but he tried not to panic.

Lucy and Hilly were still staring at him, terrified by the surreality of what was unfolding before them – so at odds with the known laws of physics and the real world.

Hilly began to weep uncontrollably, struggling to handle what was beginning to feel like a nightmare, a nightmare that she was unable to wake from.

Lucy was so frozen in her own universe, that she didn't even noticed Hilly's distress.

Sam was totally paralysed, trying to come to terms with gravity that seemed to be pulling sideways.

He turned his head to face forwards, looking down at his

reflection in the onyx sheen, backdropped by the sky of newly formed clouds above, *and* behind him.

His mind fought to form anything close to a cogent thought. He took a deep breath, and tried to exhale the heaviness from his stomach, and reason away his fears enough to be able to motivate his limbs.

He looked to his feet again, and noticed the blank areas he was standing on had rings of complex symbology surrounding each one. Looking on retrospectively, they seemed designed, almost purposeful, *meant to be*, left blank for a reason, and the more he examined them, the more he realised they looked more akin to stepping stones than anything else.

He compiled a theory, and felt ready to test it… He lifted one of his feet, allowing a moment for his balance to settle, then tried placing it down on an area heavy with detail…

Sam suddenly felt a force wrapping its fingers around his internal organs, and start to drag him towards the water! He quickly lift his foot again, and placed it back where it was before. The force suddenly swung back through his feet, and with a jolt, sucked him onto wall again. The severity shocked him.

He steadied himself, and turned to look at the girls.

'I think it's the blank areas,' he cried, 'they're holding me here. I don't know how, why, or what the fucking hell it is that's happening – but they are. They're holding me.'

He glanced at the other blank patches, then back to Lucy. 'They're kind of like, like stepping stones, or something? But I'm not sure,' he explained. 'Come here. Don't be afraid. Come and look!'

But all Lucy could do, was stare, shaking uncontrollably.

'Come over and see,' he insisted. '*Please*, Lucy, it's okay.'

She had to fight hard to unstick herself, but somehow, she managed to summon enough ardour to unglue her feet from the gravel. Cautiously, she walked across to the pool, her legs close to buckling at the site she was being forced to behold, barely able to carry herself towards something she was fundamentally ill-equipped to comprehend.

They both stood in eerie silence, ninety degrees apart, witnessing the impossible.

Lucy shuffled past the base of the handrail to the side of the pool and tilted her head, inspecting the intricate symbology surrounding Sam's feet. 'There are some more of those blank areas I think you're talking about,' she said, 'there's like – a whole row of them.' She rotated her gaze. 'They seem to keep going, down to the water.'

She panned her eye across to meet his. 'Try another step,' she suggested, 'go on, try…'

Sam's whole face *gasped* at her suggestion, a suggestion far easier to make from the side of the pool, than to actually contemplate while hanging above it. But he also knew it was the natural thing to attempt next, so was unable to turn his exasperation into an argument against the idea.

He steeled himself and, with determined eyes locked on the next featureless step, strode with conviction to it…

It landed, and he was still dry. He took another deep breath, and stepped across to the next one in line… Again, it worked!

His nose was now just inches from the surface of the pool, and Lucy *gasped* at a sight that was so completely alien to everything she'd ever known. Her gasp transformed into manic laughter, laughter that infected Sam, and he couldn't help but join in.

He turned his face down and peered into the ink, and saw his elation reflected back at him. The flawless sheen, mesmerising in its perfection, quelled his hysteria, and his face relaxed out of its joy.

He drew a hand tentatively to his shoulder, then slowly,

and deliberately, started lowering his arm towards the pool.

Lucy stopped laughing, and watched with breath held...

Sam's fingers touched, then broke the surface of the fluid. His brows flickered – expecting it feel much colder, and more like water than it did. What the hell was it?

A meniscus of the inky liquid sucked up each finger as they were lowered into its mesmerising sheen, his hand dropping deep below the surface, until his whole arm was completely submerged before him.

He stirred it in the fluid, but to his surprise, felt no resistance, no discernible drag – not at all what he was expecting.

The sensation unnerved him, and then he remembered the fingers Hilly said she saw rising from the pool.

He quickly snatched his arm from the water, startling Lucy. 'What is it?' she snapped. Sam didn't answer. 'Sam. What is it? What's happened? What's wrong?'

Sam stared at his arm, his expression blank, cloaking his confusion.

He placed his other hand flat against his arm, dabbing it several times over... 'It's dry! It's completely dry,' he whispered, turning to Lucy. 'It's not wet at all, not a single drop!'

His words did nothing to alleviate Lucy's confusion, and she couldn't bring herself to say *anything*. She felt like she was inside a bubble, just watching events unfolding in a world that she didn't herself inhabit.

Sam turned his attention back to the carvings in front of his feet again. He could see a couple more of the steps – the ones Lucy was talking about – dropping to the surface of the water, the last of them half submerged.

Counter intuitively, his actions fuelled purely by uncontrollable curiosity, he strode to the next blank footprint... it landed, he breathed... He took, and held a full breath, then stepped again, his face pushing through the surface tension of the ebony film.

Lucy gagged on a failed attempt to shout '*stop!*' But for whatever reason – maybe a selfish desire to know what was there – she didn't try twice.

She released a yelp as she watched Sam step down the wall, and drop beneath the surface. Tides of viscous-black fluid washed across his back, colliding along his spine, engulfing him, and he was gone… Hilly sprinted to the pool's edge, joining in Lucy's shock and disbelief, and screamed her brother's name towards the last of the ripples as they dissipated.

Lucy had no idea how to react, or what to do. They both just stood, watching the place where they last saw him…

Seconds past, feeling more like minutes. Maybe they *were* minutes, neither of them could tell anymore, their inner monologues unable to judge anything with a level of certainty anymore. Years of tuning 'what we know to be true', completely undone by a series of events so bizarre as to cause a crash in the very logic of their existence.

Hilly flinched and grabbed Lucy's arm. Lucy looked at her, then followed her needled gaze down to the pool. There was a bulge forming on the surface, pushing up from beneath – then it split, and Sam emerged through the fluid, striding from beneath the midnight-sheen, like a newly forming volcanic island rising from a prehistoric ocean floor.

They watched him walking up the wall, his pin-sharp concentration focused on accurate foot placement…

He arced over the curvature of the buttress like a windscreen wiper blade, until he finally stood upright again, and stepped through the gap in the fractured handrail onto the stairs.

Lucy and Hilly burned him with looks of disbelief in their eyes. The curtains of water that Lucy would have expected to see cascading off the hems of his clothing didn't exist. He looked completely dry! But how?

She started to sob, she didn't know what was happening anymore.

'Where did you go?' asked Hilly. 'Why aren't you wet?' Questions the young were far better equipped to ask than anything resembling an adult, far less inhibited by knowledge or logic.

Lucy watched Sam as he slumped down onto the steps, waiting for a response to Hilly's questions.

Sam stared at his feet, visibly close to succumbing to the effects of shock, but they could both see him actively fighting it.

'What happened…? What is it, what did you see?' asked Lucy softly, seeing how understandably shaken he was.

Sam lifted his gaze to meet hers. He peered deep into her tear-glazed eyes, his face paper-white and ashen. 'It was…' He took a deep breath. 'It was this house,' he said, with a quick glance behind him, his voice soft, as though barely able to convince itself of what it was saying.

'What…? What do you mean?'

'Down there… Below us… There's, there's another *here*, another Hobswyke Hall.'

Lucy pulled Hilly into her side – more for her *own* comfort than anything else. 'What does that mean, "another here"?'

'There's another place, Lucy. Through there. A complete other, what's the word? *Realm*? Yes, realm.'

He shook his head at what he heard himself saying. It sounded ridiculous, and he knew it, but he'd seen it. 'It's another place, with another house, another grounds, a whole other world, a different world, but it looks every bit the same as this one.'

He flicked a look at the pool and nodded, 'Through there, through the water.'

Lucy's face contorted. 'I can't believe it. Are you being serious?'

'*Yes*! Yes I *am*...!' he barked. 'It seemed to be a world that looks exactly like ours.' He reconsidered his words. 'No,' he said, 'not exactly, somehow, it felt different, it felt – wrong?'

He looked down at the pool again, then turned to face the girls.

'Lucy, I could sense this place I was in was evil, it was bad... It was *putrid!*'

SEVEN

THE CONSULTING OF AN ORACLE

SAM LAY IN HIS BED, the idea of sleep an alien concept in light of the day that had been. The atmosphere of everyday life had attained an unreal quality after the events of the day.

Neither he, nor Hilly had said anything to their father of what had happened, it seemed such a natural thing for the young to have secrets from those much older than themselves. But secrets of this magnitude have power-enough to eat their keeper's away to nothing – unless their burden is lessened by the act of sharing.

But he couldn't, to do so would betray a trust, and besides, who would believe him?

He pulled his pillow up around his face – trying to block out the world. It was still woven with the scent of Lucy; he could smell her hair, and her skin, and the fragrance she wore, the exact same scent that clouded his face whenever she held him. It was comforting, and reminded him why it was he needed to harbour everything he saw that day.

He sat up in bed, frustrated at being unable to sleep.

He turned to his bedside table, switched on the lamp, and grabbed a book that Hilly had handed to him after they got back to the cottage.

She'd marked a page with a torn-off slip of paper, apparently prompted by something she'd overheard Lucy say after she'd come to.

The book was extremely old: well-worn, weighty, and heavily laden with centuries of ingrained dust. All makings had been worn off the outer cover, but it seemed to be a book about witchcraft, the occult and demonology and, for whatever reason, their father had it in his bookcase.

It had that odour old tomes attain with age: musty, earthy, a subtle oakiness wafting into the air when the pages were turned.

As a lover of books, Sam found the smell comforting in its woody familiarity, he would even say *homely,* if it wasn't for the disquieting nature of the subject matter.

He wormed a finger between the pages next to Hilly's bookmark. It fell open in the middle of a section that appeared to chronicle all of the known demons of the world.

He was faced with a crude, block-print image of one in particular – 'Asmodeus', an apparent prince of the underworld. A Judaeo-Islamic demon of lust and wrath.

Sam found the image grotesque, depicting a crowned entity with three heads: one decidedly impish in appearance and the easiest to relate to, one of a bull and one of a ram, sprouting from its hunched, almost skeletal shoulders.

In the diagram, the demon was shown riding aback a dragon-like creature, and the more he studied it, the more he realised this had to be what Lucy said she saw in the library.

But it seemed too incredible to believe, but was it truly anymore incredible than what *he*, himself, had seen that day?

He grabbed his mobile from the side table and photographed the page, then took another, zoomed in on the block-print picture.

He opened the images, clicked on Lucy's name, and hit [SEND], tagging the post:

Is this what you saw?

He studied the page again as he waited for a reply, trying to imagine how it would feel to come face to face with something so surreal and terrifying…

A deep hum emitted from his phone, and he tapped Lucy's thumbnail:

Yes. That's definitely it. Hilly showed it to me earlier after you'd left the cottage. That is exactly what I saw.

The phone vibrated again:

Me and Mum are going to see Grandma tomorrow, I've got a feeling she must know things, things about the house. Don't ask me why I know, I just have a feeling. There's things she's said to me in the past that meant nothing then, but that now make perfect sense. Almost like she was trying to warn me.

She's lived in Hobswyke Hall her whole life, so she has to have seen something!

I'm going to try and talk to her, but only if I can get her alone.

Please keep away from the house while I'm away, for me!

Try to sleep. Luce X

Sam shut the book and slipped it under the bed. He opened his phone again:

> *Don't worry, I'll stay away. Goodnight, Luce. Sam X*
> *PS Let me know if you find out anything.*

He placed the phone on the bed, rolled onto his side, and wrapped his face in Lucy's scent again… After an hour, exhausted by the events of the day, he finally managed to drift off…

*

The morning sky hung bright and inviting, the air alive with the smells of summer.

Lucy and her mother made their way along the Gloucestershire roads to Furnhurst Gardens Retirement Home for their weekly visit to Lucy's grandmother.

Furnhurst Gardens was a care home for the extremely elderly and decidedly wealthy. Her grandmother moved there some nine years ago, a decision she'd made herself. After having led a life of 'doing', she now yearned for the relative simplicity of care-home life.

The approach to the grounds was predominantly made through twisting country lanes, single-track roads lined with trees and ancient blackthorn hedgerows that occasionally broke, revealing intermittent vistas of undulating landscape. Flashes of a vibrant sea of green, peppered with islands of yellow rapeseed swaying in the summer breeze, receded into the haze of a sun-warmed horizon.

Lucy peered through the window into the blur of the passing landscape. She had no idea *how* she was going to broach the subject of Hobswyke with her grandmother, or even how she was even to wrangle getting time alone with her away from her mother?

How was she even to start such a conversation? 'Hi, Nan, how are you? Did that problem with your leg clear up? Oh good. Here, I've got you some chocolates, your favourites. Oh yeah! Isn't the big house bizarre, what's going on with that then? By the way, Sam walked down the illustrated wall into and through the water and found what seems to be another realm of existence. Weird or what!'

'You're quiet today, love, everything okay?' her mother asked, sounding concerned that Lucy wasn't her usual chatterbox self.

'Hm? Oh, yeah. I'm fine. Just thinking.'

'A penny for them…'

'Oh, nothing really, just stuff,' she replied, smiling wide to waylay her mother's concerns.

Lucy spied a row of shops ahead that they'd planned to stop off at along the way to get some bits and pieces for their visit.

She turned a furtive eye to look to her mother. She seemed lost in her thoughts and distracted, and drove straight past.

Lucy said nothing, allowing them to miss the stop. She was now in possession of a plan to get the time she needed alone with the old lady.

*

'Here we are,' her mother chirped, turning through the gates of the retirement home.

Lucy smiled. The grounds at Furnhurst were picturesque, colourful and well-tended, and she always enjoyed their visits, even this one, despite the task she'd set herself…

'Hellooo, Helen. Hi, Lucy,' sang the woman behind reception, 'lovely day.'

'Isn't it,' Helen replied. 'Might take Mum for a bit of a stroll, if she feels up to it? How's she been, do you know?'

'Oh, you know – cheeky, a bit saucy, with patches of naughtiness blowing in from the south, giving way in the late afternoons to spells of forgetfulness and mildly daft… And that's the forecast for the weather in Violet Claybourne today.'

Lucy and Helen laughed as they made their way down the corridor. 'She's way too funny to be a receptionist,' whispered Helen.

'I know what you mean.' Lucy smirked. 'What a waste, having to deal with all these crumblies… I suppose I'm just glad she's able to laugh about it.'

'*Crumblies!*' Helen sniggered. 'You'll be a *crumbly* yourself someone day… Blimey, "Crumblies", the respect of the modern juvenile.'

Lucy giggled. She thought it funny to dip her toe into the realm of *disrespect* on occasion – but of course, with no actual intention behind it…

They both turned through the door of suite No. 14 – it was already open.

'Hi, Granny,' warbled Lucy, trotting across and bowing to deposit a kiss on her grandmother's cheek. The old lady's skin had that deep, doughy softness that only comes with ninety-five years of living.

She was sitting in a high-backed chair, observing the passage of time through the window. Lucy squatted to bring their eyes level, her grandmother turning a smile to Lucy's happy face.

'Hello, Lucy, my love. It's lovely to see you both,' she said in a voice as brittle as fine bone china, stroking her hand against Lucy's cheek.

Lucy could feel the crinkle of her parchment skin against her face. 'You get more beautiful with every passing day. Doesn't she, Helen?'

Helen placed a kiss on top of her mother's head, and gave her arm an affectionate rub… 'Hi, Mum… Yes, she does.'

Lucy stood and manoeuvred a couple of chairs into a crescent circling the main attraction. They both took a seat.

'So, tell me how you've been? I see they've finish that work on the east wing,' said Helen – more as a social pleasantry than anything, considering they talked on the phone most days.

'I *think* they have. The builders weren't here on Friday. Anyway, I'm fine, thank you. Actually, I'm very well. But I don't want to talk about me, I want to find out what my Lucy's been up to. I hear you've finished school? And that you think you did well in your exams?'

'Yep, finished last week. So I've decided, I'm going to shamelessly lord it up as some sort of lady of leisure for a bit. Live a carefree existence, until I get bored, then I'll work out what I'm going to do next. You get the general idea.'

Violet smiled. 'Tell me what you did yesterday? That *was* your first day off, right? It was such a lovely day. Very clement.'

'Oh, I didn't do much. I just walked around the grounds mainly, that's all, nothing too earth-shatteringly exciting. Oh, I saw Sam and Hilly, they send their love by the way.'

'Aah, that's nice. They're such lovely kids,' she said, fondly reminiscent.

Lucy turned her eyes slightly towards her mother. 'I, erm, I also went up to take a look at the Hall, you know, because I've not seen Hobswyke for a while, what with being so busy.'

Her mother flinched, and turned a look to Lucy. Violet couldn't help but notice the disquiet passing between them.

'And how is the old place?' the lady asked, watching for a reaction.

'I told her, she needs to keep away from the house, Mum,' Helen interjected. 'I explained to her why, and that it's dangerous.'

Violet's face turned to amazement. She looked shocked. 'You *told* her?' she said, her voice ringing with disbelief. 'You mean, you told Lucy *everything*?'

'*No*! I mean. No... I-I explained to her that it needs renovating, and that until the work's been done, it's not safe to go up there.' Helen flashed steely eyes towards her mother. 'She just needs to keep away. I don't want her going up there. *Okay?*' Helen looked sternly into her mother again. 'Can we just change the subject please?'

Lucy's mouth hung open, *They do know something*, she thought to herself, *both of them do.*

Lucy turned to her grandmother, and was shocked to find her already looking back at her with a most peculiar look in her eyes.

The old lady's lower lids flexed, as though trying to work out what Lucy may, or may not know. Time to put her plan into effect.

'Oh bloody hell, Mum! The shop. We forgot to go to the shop.' Lucy whined, unleashing her best attempt at acting surprised.

'Oh crap! I totally forgot,' Helen said. She sagged theatrically, and peered down at her watch. 'I'll go now. There's no traffic.'

'Oh you don't need to bother,' Violet said.

Lucy snapped stern eyes towards her grandmother, giving a subtle shake of her head.

The old lady's lids pinched. 'Oh – well, actually, if you could, love. I *am* running a bit low on things,' she said, changing her tune. 'I do hate to be any trouble though.'

The old lady glanced towards Lucy, and winked.

Helen took up her purse and car keys from her bag. 'It's no trouble, Mum. You stay here with your nan, I'll be back in a short while, okay?'

'Okay, Mum. See you soon,' Lucy replied, watching as she hurried from the room.

She kept her eyes locked on the door as she listened to her mother's footsteps recede into the distance, listening until she could no longer hear them.

'So, what is you want to know, young lady?' asked Violet – the question jarring Lucy back into the room. '*Is* it the house? It is, isn't it?' she said, fishing for information. She rolled in her seat knowingly. 'It *is* the house, I can tell.' The old woman breathed a disgruntled sigh. 'That damned place, is it misbehaving again?' she asked.

Her grandmother's words shocked Lucy. Not only could this old woman read that something was troubling her, but also decipher what it was. Lucy realised her grandmother was not the prisoner to her age people often assumed she was.

'Yes. It's the house,' Lucy replied, in a semi-whispered voice. 'What is it I don't know, Nan…? What is wrong with that place? There's something isn't there?'

Violet loosed a sigh, then nodded reluctantly. 'Yes, there *is* something,' she replied, wishing her answer could be different.

Her grandmother turned to look out of the window, her stare – distant. 'I'm ninety-five years old now, Lucy, and I sometimes think, if I died without telling you everything, chances are, no one else ever would… So maybe, this is the time? Maybe you're ready?'

Lucy watched intently as her grandmother gazed far away at nothing, sunlight fluorescing the faded colours of her irises, the whites of her eyes stained yellow with age.

Violet turned her attention back to her granddaughter,

seeing how hungry she was for information.

She adjusted herself in the seat to get comfortable, ready to tell her tale…

'During the war – the second one that is – many of the larger houses like Hobswyke, ones that lay predominantly in the countryside, away from the bomb-attracting lights of the cities, were converted into homes for refugee children, children that lived in cities that were in danger of being bombed, to live in relative safety until the war was over… And Hobswyke Hall was one of them.'

Violet motioned to Lucy to close the door, preferring to keep her words private.

Lucy walked across and shut it, and took to her seat again. She leaned in on her elbows.

'Now where was I? Oh yes. So, Hobswyke Hall had children come from *aaaall* over the country to live in it. The dining room was converted into a sort of dormitory. Filled with dozens of makeshift beds, for dozens of makeshift upbringings.' She smiled. 'I was a child myself then of course, so you can imagine all of the new friends I made, all the children I had to play with. They were fun times, in many ways.'

Lucy stood, and moved to the small kitchen area to make tea. 'Carry on, Nan, I'm listening.'

'Well of course, in time, the war ended, and the children were free to go back to their proper homes.' She looked up at Lucy. 'But not all of the children could leave.'

'Why?' asked Lucy.

A sadness moistened the old lady's eyes. 'You see, some of the children weren't so lucky, their parents didn't survive the fight, or the scream of the nightly bombings. Many of the children had no other family, no other place to go, so they remained at Hobswyke Hall. Lost, homeless, and without families to love them, or raise them.'

'That's awful,' whimpered Lucy – sadness swelling her heart.

'Yes,' Violet whispered, looking towards the floor. She smirked, dismissively. 'The glories of war…' she mocked.

Lucy handed her grandmother a cup of tea, sat, and wrapped herself around her mug.

'Anyway,' Violet continued, 'after the war, Hobswyke Hall became, or maybe it would be more accurate to say *remained*, an orphanage. And it stayed an orphanage for the next thirty years.'

Lucy looked on, utterly engrossed, wondering why she'd never been told any of this before.

Her grandmother continued. 'Of course, the years rolled past; I grew older, and the house was passed to me by your great-grandparents when they eventually both died… So, I continued to run the children's home that I'd inherited the way it had always been.'

The old woman fell silent, receding into her memories, visibly toying with how open to be. 'Lucy… Do you know, or, did your mother ever tell you, that *she* was adopted?'

Lucy's eyes widened. 'No… No I didn't. *She* didn't,' she responded – shocked that she was only now just finding out.

'Oh… Well. I wasn't sure if she had or not.' She took a regretful sip of her tea. 'Well… Now you know, I can't take that back,' she said, flashing a weak smile towards Lucy. 'Your mother arrived at Hobswyke as an unwanted child… Her own mother – from what we understood – used to drink, and take drugs, and apparently had little interest in raising a child, so…'

Violet looked across at Lucy and smirked. 'I'm surprised you hadn't guessed, what with you two possessing those incredible *cerulean* eyes, and mine all muddy-brown. Not to mention you being two of the most beautiful girls to have ever graced this earth, and me with this battered old excuse for a face.'

Lucy allowed herself a laugh. 'You're beautiful, Nan. Stop it.'

Violet laughed back. 'Well, that's very kind of you, dear. You may have the most gorgeous eyes, but they obviously don't work very well.' They both share a giggle, helping break the tension.

Violet took a moment to finish her tea… 'How long will your mother be?'

'A while yet, Nan, the shops are quite far away.'

'Okay. That's good.'

Lucy took their mugs, and walked to the sink to wash them. 'Carry on, Nan, I'm still listening.'

'Well – your mother – she was the most beautiful little girl you've ever laid your eyes on, like you were. It seemed incredible to us to think that anybody could fail to care for such a lovely little child.' She shook her head at the outrage… 'Anyway, she soon befriended a little boy called Thomas, another orphan.' She laughed to herself. 'Now, these two were inseparable – Gemini – and you would always see them around, holding hands, wandering here, wandering there – you'd have thought they were glued to each other.' Violet let go a sigh laced with sadness… 'Then one day, they both went missing. They just vanished. Disappeared without a trace.'

'Missing?' said Lucy. 'What do you mean, "missing"?'

'They'd just gone, both of them.' The old woman flashed her brows. 'Of course, the police were called in, searches instigated, rivers and canals dragged, but nothing. No one ever found anything. They had simply vanished.'

Lucy's mouth hung agape. 'So, what happened?'

Violet turned away, sitting in her own, sad silence for well over a minute. Then eventually turned back to face Lucy, a tear in her eye. 'I don't know, and I wish I did, but I still have no idea where those kids went.'

'But – my mum, she's here now?' Lucy said, confused.

'Yes, she is. Thank the Lord.'

'So… How?'

Violet stared down into her lap, unsure of how to go about describing to Lucy a series of events that to this day, she herself still didn't understand. She'd rehearsed this conversation a thousand times, but it wasn't making anything any easier.

'*Please,* Nan… Please try,' implored Lucy.

The old lady exhaled a resigned sigh, and gathered her thoughts. 'The children were never found, nor any clues as to where they'd gone. And of course, no one was under suspicion of foul play – as they call it now – but no orphanage can survive an event like that, *kids going missing,* creates as much scandal as it does gossip. So of course, Hobswyke, "the orphanage", had to close down.' She looked towards the window. 'The remaining kids were homed, or moved to different orphanages, and Hobswyke Hall – after all those years – became a house again.'

Lucy ached to hear the details of how her mother came to return, but she didn't want to push her grandmother too hard. But she couldn't help but push a little. 'And my mum?' she asked. 'How, did—'

'How did she return? Well, that is still a mystery. Ten years past, the whole ordeal by then just a bad memory, like a forgotten nightmare. Until…'

'Until what?'

'Well… *We* – your granddad and me, who I'd married shortly after the closure – we had both decided to renovate the dining room, it having been left as a dormitory for all that time, and we wanted to restore it to the way it used to be, put it back to the way it was before the war. Anyway, we'd taken a large mirror down from above the fireplace, and laid it flat in the centre of the floor to try and keep it safe while we worked on the wooden panelling around the perimeter.'

The old lady leaned a clandestine gate towards her granddaughter. 'Then one night, we both heard an almighty crash from downstairs? We thought it must be burglars or something. But that's not what it was at all.'

Lucy listened expectantly. '…Well? What was it?'

'We scouted around the whole house, trying to find what had made such a God-almighty noise. And when we finally looked in the dining hall, there, sitting in the middle of the mirror, among a thousand shards of glass, was a young girl.'

'A young girl? How young?'

'About your age.'

'…And who was she?'

'I didn't know. She looked so lost, so frightened. She had cuts to her hands and legs. And when I went to help her, she looked up at me…'

'And…?'

'And, I found myself looking into the most lost, confused, beautiful turquoise eyes I'd ever seen, and instantly, I recognised her. It was Helen – your mother, the girl who'd been missing for over a decade.'

Lucy looked on in shock, listening to a story so fantastic she wouldn't have believed it — if it wasn't for the knowledge she already possessed.

Her grandmother continued, 'And do you want to know the weirdest part?'

'Yes,' Lucy whispered.

'The young girl – your mother – was with child. She was pregnant… Pregnant with *you*.'

Lucy rocked back on her seat, then stood to pace the room. Sitting still, hearing such incredible revelations about her own life had grown far too intense for her to cope.

'But that's not all,' her grandmother added, 'when we were clearing up the broken glass, we found shards of mirror with bevelled edges. But the mirror that lay on the floor had been fitted with plain glass? And to this day, I have no idea where those other shards came from?'

Lucy paced the room, trying to calm herself, then sat opposite her grandmother again.

'Anyway, we still had your mother's papers on file at the hall, and with surprisingly little trouble, we managed to adopt her. Thing is, your grandfather and I were unable to have children ourselves. So we almost saw it as a kind of blessing, you might even say a miracle.'

'But, where did Mum say she had—'

'Had been? She didn't, she couldn't remember a thing. None of it. She has a huge chunk of her life with no memory. Even to this day, she remembers nothing... If *you* ever ask her a question about her younger years, she makes up the answer.'

'And Thomas?'

'No – nothing. Thomas is just another forgotten child to add to the list – a statistic. Your mother only has fleeting memories of him now as a little boy.'

Lucy rose again and paced the room, trying to digest all she'd been told.

She turned with resolve back to her grandmother. 'Nan... Yesterday, me and Sam discovered something up at the house, something really kind of frightening. And I'm not even sure how to describe it.'

The old lady twisted in her seat to face her. 'Try Lucy. What is it you found, tell me?' she insisted, face racked with concern.

'We found – well, *Sam* found, something in one of the pools. The pools by the stone staircase. It was a—'

'I'm back!' warbled Helen, bursting through the door with armfuls of shopping, the silence shattered by the crashing door, and the crisp rustle of carrier bags colliding with eager knees.

'Sorry I was gone so long, they've set up road works along the main road since we arrived, can you believe it, we've only been here a short time? Anyway, I've got you some nice things, Mum, some bits for you to nibble on.'

Lucy and her grandmother smiled up at Helen, feigning a look of *pleased to see you back*.

They both glanced towards each other and exchanged a knowing nod, a non-verbal agreement to keep all that had passed between them a secret – at least for now…

EIGHT

A SIMILAR WORLD, UNLIKE ANY OTHER

SAM'S PHONE BUZZED. It was a message from Lucy:

We're back. Can you meet me at the fork? L. X

Yes, I'll be there in 10, is that OK? X

Perfect. Please don't bring Hilly, there are things I have to tell you that I don't want her knowing. At least, not yet anyway. X

K...

Dusk was beginning to soften the evening light, the cooling air lifting moisture from the forest floor infusing the surrounding woodland with the fresh scent of the pine trees.

Sam paced the path at the fork. He figured that if anything resembling a parent should hove into view, then he could just keep walking in whatever direction he was traveling, as though he had a purpose other than to keep a clandestine assignation with Lucy... A far easier lie to present.

Eventually, he saw Lucy coming down the bank, her long legs striding towards him with a discernible sense of urgency, occasionally bursting into a light jog.

She turned to look behind her – checking she wasn't being followed. 'Hi,' she whispered through a face shining with excitement, keen to relay the stories she had to tell. She gestured to Sam to start up the path, away from the houses.

'So…?' Sam asked, under his breath, cocking an ear towards her, inviting her to tell all.

'Well,' she said, allowing her voice to elevate to soft-spoken – having created sufficient distance between themselves and any unwanted ears. 'I managed to speak to my nan…'

She proceeded to unload every minute detail of what her grandmother had relayed to her earlier in the day. Then ran through all of the odd and confusing events that had ever happened to her over the years that for some reason, stuck in her mind. Things she saw, or overheard, that at the time made little sense, but that now fitted within the narrative of the secrets that her grandmother had finally made her party to.

They ambled the grounds for well over an hour, Sam listening quietly, absorbing every detail spilling from Lucy lips, furnishing himself with all the facts he may need to formulate an opinion, should Lucy ask for one…

They ended up sitting on a bench overlooking the lake. The sun had dropped below the horizon, underlighting stacks of striated clouds stretching over the silhouette of the tree-lined hills in the distance. The air grew cold.

Sam removed his hoody and wrapped it around Lucy. She thanked him with a smile and rested her head on his shoulder.

'I don't know what to do, Sammy? Do I talk to Mum? *Nooo*, that wouldn't be good.' She sighed, answering her own question before Sam could even open his mouth. But he was already shaking his head in agreement.

'God, I wish I hadn't found those damn keys.'

'But you did,' said Sam, 'so there's no use wishing for something you can't change, and besides, is it such a bad thing?'

Lucy couldn't make her mind up if it was, or if it wasn't... 'What did it feel like?' she asked. 'What did you see, Sammy, when you went through? I didn't like to ask yesterday, you looked – well – too shaken up.'

Sam rolled his eyes to the sky, trying to put words to his experience. 'It was like– like dipping beneath water, but coming out of water all at the same time,' he explained. His brows furrowed. 'I pushed my face under the water, or whatever it is, but it felt weirdly dry. So I opened my eyes, and I was rising from the other pool, the one on the other side.'

Lucy peered onto the still surface of the lake, trying to clear her mind of extraneous thoughts so she could attempt to imagine what Sam was describing. 'So what does it look like? The other place?'

'Thing is. When I came out on the other side, I was rising from the pool on the *opposite* side of the steps. And also, after I'd looked around for a while, it occurred to me that everything was the wrong way round to the way it is here.'

'The wrong way round? What do you mean the wrong way round?'

'Everything was – what's that way of saying it? "Mirrored". Yes. Everything was mirrored. You know – right is left, left is right, everything flipped the other way. But other than that, it all looked pretty much exactly the same as it does here.'

Lucy sighed, still no closer to knowing what to do next. But there was one feeling that she was unable to shake – despite having been trying for the past twenty four hours.

She rose from the seat and walked to the edge of the water, toying the toe of her trainer among the pebbles. she turned back to Sam who was watching from the bench.

'Tomorrow. Please, Sam, if you would… I want us both to go through to look around.'

'*No*,' snapped Sam.

Lucy shook a defiant head towards his sharp refusal. 'I'll go anyway, with or without you, I have to. But I'd much rather you were there with me.' She tilted her head. 'Please, I need to go through. I need answers, answers I don't have, and I think the only place I can get them is through that pool.'

Her pleading gaze pawed at him – beseeching. 'Where did my mum disappear to, Sam, for all those years? And how did she get pregnant with *me*!' Lucy peered deep into Sam's eyes. 'And how is it, she ended up sitting among shards of glass in the middle of a mirror ten years later? But more than any of that, how the *fucking hell* is it at all possible that there's a fucking doorway to another world sitting outside of my old house?'

Sharply delivered swear words emitting from such an angelic face shocked Sam, and he could see she was never going to be swayed. He'd seen the exact same look of determination in Lucy's face before, and knew it to be unshakable. He sagged… 'Tomorrow?' he asked, reluctantly.

'Yes. Please. Sometime in the morning?'

Sam sat silently for a while, toying with the notion… 'Okay, tomorrow morning it is, you and me. We'll go through and see what's there.'

Lucy strode to him and flung her arms around him. 'Thank you, Sammy. I can't do this without you. I-I need you…'

Sam escorted Lucy back to the gatehouse, hardly a word passing between them the whole way there, both of them uncertain of what they might find on the other side of the water.

'Well, goodnight then,' said Lucy, 'I'll see you tomorrow morning. Oh, and thanks for everything,' she added.

'That's okay,' he replied, 'that's what I'm here for. See you tomorrow.'

*

Lucy wandered into the kitchen having hardly slept, beckoned downstairs by the sounds of breakfast being prepared.

She'd already dressed, but today sported an old pair of jeans and a T-shirt. She'd also had the foresight to dig out a bag of waterproof makeup she once purchased for a holiday to Florida, just in case.

Her mother was standing at the stove turning bacon. Lucy walked up behind her, and pecked a kiss on her cheek. 'Good morning, Mumster, is any of that for me?' she asked, with a cheeky grin.

'Of course, sweetheart. I was actually using the smell to lure you out of that bloomin' bed,' she joked, with a smirk and a jaunty nudge of the shoulder. 'Sleep well?'

'Um – nah, not really. Couldn't shut my mind off, kept thinking about stuff, you know how you do.'

'What kind of things?' her mother asked, with mild concern.

'Oh, nothing important really, don't worry about it. Just stuff.'

'Why don't you go and get back in bed for a bit?'

'Nahhh, I'll be fine. A cup of tea'll wake me up. Want one?'

'Mmm, please,' Helen replied, leaning a big smile over her shoulder.

Lucy filled the kettle and slapped it on.

She looked across at her mother cracking eggs into the pan, then down at the tea cups, trying to work out how quickly she could get away.

Stealthily, she took up her phone and sent a text to Sam, to see if he could meet in about an hour, before quickly swiping her phone onto 'silent'.

A reply flashed up on the screen:

No problem, Luce. I'll meet on the path near Hobswyke. X

*

An hour later, Lucy – heavily laden with breakfast – strode along the path towards her old home, an expectant fizz in her belly.

She'd not felt this apprehensive or excited about anything for a very long time, probably since childhood, when everything seemed to be an adventure.

She could see the occasional glimpse of Sam through the trees as she traipsed up the path, his face looking anything but excited.

'Hi, Sam,' she warbled.

He watched her on the approach, forcing the most unconvincing smile Lucy had ever seen.

'Oh, Sam, please don't fret,' she said, caressing her words.

'I'm not bothered about me. It's you.' He shook his head a couple of times as she finally arrived, leaning a kiss onto his cheek. 'If anything ever happened to you. I couldn't—'

'Oi!' she snapped. 'I can look after myself you know. I am – after all – a *woman*.' She punched him hard on the shoulder and giggled.

'Owah!' he complained, rubbing his arm and grimacing. 'Well alright then, if you're sure. On your head be it.'

'*Yes*, I *am* sure. I've thought of nothing else all night. So let's do this – okay?'

'Okay.'

They both crossed the gravel towards the break in the handrail.

The fizz in Lucy's stomach intensifying. She wished she hadn't had such a large breakfast.

Sam turned to address her. 'I'll go first and check it wasn't all just some weird hallucination or something, and then you can follow.'

Lucy gulped back her nerves. 'Okay.'

Sam positioned himself in the break, then checked to see there was no one else around.

He breathed deep to calm himself. 'So you have to keep your feet inside the blank areas, they seem to be what stops you from falling.'

'Okay. I understand.' She nodded.

He started making his way across the stonework, making sure to land each tread accurately.

He had to work to keep balance as his body, once again, began arcing over the curvature of the carved, stone buttress, and down towards the pool. *So it wasn't a dream!* he thought to himself. *It was real.*

Lucy watched, feeling every bit as amazed as she did the first time she saw it.

'Here,' said Sam, 'take this.' He stooped, lifting the broken section of railing from the water, and passed it up to Lucy.

She crouched down and took it from him, taking care not to upset his balance, and heaved it up the wall. She laid it flat on the ground and stepped into the break.

Sam walked down the wall a few paces, then whirled his hand towards Lucy, instructing her to follow. 'Come on, just step carefully. Do exactly what I'm doing,' he said, 'and don't worry, you'll be just fine.'

Lucy manoeuvred to the top of the curvature, and began to mimic Sam's actions, treading carefully, fighting to keep balance, until she too, began to arc over the stonework and down towards the uninviting membrane to another place.

She started to laugh – half joy, half mania.

'Shhhhh! Concentrate,' Sam barked.

Lucy attempted to rein it in, but she just wanted to laugh uncontrollably at how amazing what was happening felt.

Sam's face fronted the surface of the liquid for the second time in two days. He took a full breath as before, and stepped through.

Lucy watched the viscous ink engulfing him beneath her elated gaze. She gasped!

A hand rose elegantly from the water like an Arthurian legend. She could see by the watch that it belonged to Sam.

He flexed his fingers a few times, inviting her to take hold...

She took a moment to fortify her nerves, then gently, wrapped her fingers around his, and he guided her slowly down the wall to the surface of the pool...

She paused for a beat, steeled herself, then closed her eyes tight, and took her leap of faith through the midnight sheen...

Lucy could feel her face and hands passing into the fluid, a tide of pressure swiping over her face, past her ears and the back of her head to her ponytail, as she sank further under.

She swung her hands and body through until she felt certain she was completely submerged, and fought to not panic, amazed at her own actions given her inability to swim.

'Open your eyes, Lucy. Go on, open your mouth. It's okay, breathe,' instructed Sam's detached voice.

She was aware – as Sam had predicted – that she didn't feel at all wet, or any of the pressure of being submerged in a liquid as she should.

'*Trust* me, Lucy,' he urged, 'just open your eyes...'

Lucy relaxed her squint, allowing her eyelids to part a little.

Slithers of blurred light cut through her lashes, resolving as she opened her eyes into an image of Sam's excited face looking down at her. She un-pursed her lips and took a breath…

'Come on,' Sam enthused, guiding her up the wall, 'let's go.'

They both walked up and over the mirrored buttress until they were standing against a handrail, a handrail that looked every bit the same as the ones at Hobswyke.

Lucy then realised – as Sam had described – that they'd risen from the pool on the opposite side of the steps, rising from the pool on the right, when they dropped through the one on the left?

Sam clambered over the railing, then leant across to assist Lucy.

Safely on the steps, she could at last drink in awe the sight she beheld… It was a view wholly familiar to her, but in a place she'd never been before.

She broke from Sam's side to walk slowly up the staircase towards a gothic manor house, overgrowing with thorn-laden brambles, each barb an inch long, twisting through the architecture of the building. But still, she was able to make out – through the tortured snakes of spiked foliage – a building that looked identical to Hobswyke Hall! 'What *is* happening?' she muttered.

She pivoted around at the top of the steps, and looked out from the front of the house.

It all looked the same as home, except, the pathway from the hall peeled away from the opposite side of the clearing, the lake was to the right, instead of the left, and there was a greyness to all she saw, as though the colour and joy had been drained from all her eyes could see.

Everything was overgrown and crumbling. In an advanced state of decay, rotting, rusting, untouched by caring hands.

'Hands!' Lucy shouted.

'Hands?' Sam replied.

'Yes... Who lives here...? Someone must. Hilly saw a hand?'

She turned her focus back towards the house and noticed the main doors hanging slightly open. She walked cautiously across the flagged landing and presented her eye to the gap, and was amazed to find that everything she could see inside also looked the same as home.

She spun her excitement back to Sam. 'I think Hilly *did* see a hand. Someone must be here to have opened this!' She began to push the door. 'Let's see if we can find who it belongs to.'

NINE

THE OTHERS

LUCY HAD TO SHOVE hard to get the door to open, dislodging what looked to be many years of dirt and rotting foliage that had settled around the base of the entrance. Sam ran up to help, and after a couple of coordinated heaves, they both managed to squeeze through inside.

The initial excitement of entering a new world was slowly subsiding, giving way to deeper feelings of unease, what Lucy would describe as *dread.*

There was an undeniable atmosphere of foreboding that seemed to permeate everything: woven through the brickwork, staining the tattered drapes, hanging insidiously in the musty air, soaking slowly into their hair and their clothes. Lucy could now understand Sam's choice of the word 'putrid'.

The desire to investigate the newly discovered world was just about managing to overpower Lucy's impulse to *run.* She looked back to check Sam was still with her, then took hold of his hand.

They wandered across the hall, the flecks of the marble only just visible through heavy layers of dirt.

'Is this real?' Lucy asked out loud.

'Yes,' Sam whispered. 'I'm seeing it too.'

Elongated strands of cobweb bunting criss-crossed the ceiling, a gossamer net spanning the droplets of the chandelier, wafting strangely with a languid grace in the moving air as the two visitors passed beneath.

Sam halted... Lucy turned to look at him, prompted by the tug on her hand. He was staring dead ahead, his grip tightening, squeezing Lucy's fingers hard together.

'What is it?' she asked, concerned, turning her face to follow the direction of his gaze...

He seemed to be staring at the library doors – they were open.

Lucy levered her fingers free of his vice-like grip, and wandered tentatively towards the room.

Light spilled from the opening, a slow morphing flicker of tangerine reflecting off the panelled door. She edged around the frame, and stepped into the room.

A cold shudder stroked its icy fingers along her spine. She was confronted with a room entirely lined with black candles, many hundreds in number, sitting atop decades-deep tides of wax.

Hanging strands of nero candle grease dropped from every row of shelving like pinguid stalactites, thousands of rods imprisoning the books that lay behind them, each pillar of wax stretching long, dripping into stygian puddles that coated the floor.

She turned her attention from the shelving, and saw in horror – sitting defiantly in full view in the centre of the room – another stone altar, streaked deep red with ribbons of dried blood.

Sam joined Lucy in the doorway. 'Oh Jesus,' he said, drinking in the image of the bloodstained stone, tinted red by the dancing flames of a thousand candles.

'It's the same as the one that's at Hobswyke,' Lucy said.

'I know, I saw it,' he explained, placing a comforting hand on her shoulder, 'but no one's made an attempt to hide this one.'

'I know, but why is it here?'

Sam stepped cautiously further inside the room, drawn forwards by the insatiability of his morbid fascination. Lucy followed…

A loud, hollow, mechanical *clank* rang out, causing them both to stiffen like granite! '*What was that?*' Lucy hissed, stepping closer to Sam.

'I-I don't know,' he replied, spinning like a top, 'but it *seemed* to come from in here.'

They froze to statues, and listened, but nothing. The corners of Sam's mouth buckled, shaking his head at Lucy. 'God knows.'

Lucy released Sam's arm, and crept towards the altar, drawn there by fascination, her whole map galvanised with a look of disgust… She could see what looked to be coagulated blood coating a bone-handled knife lying upon the slab, still fresh enough to be crimson.

She backed away from the horror of the find, hand clutched across her stomach…

Her foot caught something that rang out, she looked down to see what it was.

Piles of animal collars scattered the base of the stone, some with tags, some without. Lucy stirred them with her toe. Many of the tags seemed to have names: Bonzo, Pippa, Mittens, Petra. Most of the tags were spattered with deep crimson specks…

Lucy shied from the altar, biting at the side of her hand in horror. 'What the *fuck* is this place, Sam?!' she cried, flexing her throat in an attempt to quell a sudden impulse to vomit. 'How can any of this be?'

Sam had no answers. 'I don't know.'

She scanned the rest of the room for some other muse to distract her mind.

Her face slowly uncrumpled, her gaze locking with astonishment towards the opposite end of the library.

She was focused on a cluster of candles sitting atop one of the shelves ahead of her… She squinted, peering at the flames… '*Sam?*' she whispered, but he didn't respond.

She leaned her spiked interest further in, studying each lick of flame lifting from every candle. They all seemed to be curling gradually in slow motion, creeping gracefully towards the ceiling – the gentle tumble of each flame mesmerising in its lethargic elegance.

Clank! The metallic sound rang out again, jerking Lucy from her trance.

She spun towards the sound, and could see Sam on the opposite side of the library, staring into the innards of an imposing long-cased clock that presided over the room.

He was staring into the cabinet, something arresting his attention. Lucy wandered across to see what so fascinated him.

'What is it?' she asked.

'Look. Just watch,' he whispered, nodding towards the pendulum.

She watched, but saw nothing, the clock didn't seem to be working. She looked towards him and shook her head.

'No, look again,' he snapped, 'just keep watching. There…'

She looked again, hanging utterly still – then she saw it. The pendulum was swinging slowly behind the dust-coated glass panel, creeping through its arc in a motion only just perceptible to a studying eye.

They both stood, watching, mystified, as it slowed towards the end of its swing…

Clank! – rang out from the clock again, their hearts missing yet another beat. 'Shit!' Lucy stabbed, darting a furious glare towards the clock's internals.

The pendulum arm halted, hovering motionless, then gradually, started a creeping arc back in the opposite direction.

Sam turned his eyes up at the clock face, then down at his watch. He extended his hand towards Lucy. 'Look,' he whispered, 'the second hand.'

She grabbed his wrist, holding it still if front of her face… She watched as the second hand crept past each number, once again, almost too slowly to be perceptible.

'Time seems to be running slower here, but – I don't understand how?' he explained, confused by what he was seeing.

Lucy pointed to a nearby candle flame. Sam stepped in closer and studied the creeping flicker…

He looked about the library, then leaned forwards to grab a book from the shelf. He stepped back and held it out in front of him, then let it go…

It hung motionless in the air, as if to test their trust in their own observations. Then slowly, it started to drift towards the ground. The pair of them watched, in utter astonishment, the tome slowly sink to the floor…

Sam began wafting his arm around rapidly in front of his face. 'Time apparently, runs slower here, I think?' he explained. 'But it doesn't seem to affect the way we can move *within* it? I don't understand how that can be? It doesn't really make sense… But, we're doing it?'

He looked to Lucy. 'Am I getting older at the moment? Or – or not?'

She shook her head, and shrugged. 'I-I don't know.'

Soft pads of fast running footsteps rushed past the doorway behind them. Lucy flinched. 'What was that!?' she hissed, shying from the sound.

Sam grasped her hand. 'I-I-I don't know,' he stuttered.

They edged towards the opening, leaning their faces out in the direction the sound passed…

Lucy faltered, inhaling a sharp lungful of air. She could see two faces peering at them through the balustrades at the base of the staircase.

'Look!' Lucy whispered, nodding towards the stairs.

Sam finally saw them. 'They're children.'

He took a cautious step forwards. 'Hello,' he called, in the friendliest voice he could muster.

One of the children rose quickly from behind the railings, it was a girl. She shuffled towards them, stooping, shaking her head frantically at the sound of his voice. 'Shhhhhh… !' she hissed, through teeth clenched hard together, face tight with what looked to be blind panic.

She darted her eyes about the room, then beckoned them to follow.

The other child was still cowering behind the rungs, Lucy could see it was a young boy – he looked terrified.

Both children had long, matted hair that looked never to have been touched by scissors, soap nor brush, their clothes stained deep-grey with filth. They shared eyes of a pale orange hue, fixed with a look of utmost concern. To Lucy, their features and age look so similar, that she divined that they may possibly be twins.

The young girl was still edging forwards, inviting them to follow.

Lucy looked across at Sam. He shrugged, then nodded.

They walk out into the marbled hall towards the girl. She turned to collect the boy, taking his hand. She guided the group towards the farthest side of the room, continually ushering Sam and Lucy to stick close by…

Sam could see a panel that had been removed beneath one of the side tables, revealing what looked to be a tunnel behind the wall. He nudged Lucy and lifted his chin towards it. 'Look,' he said.

The girl continued darting frantic eyes about the space, until they neared the table. 'What's she looking for?' whispered Lucy.

'I don't know, but whatever it is, they seem afraid of it.'

The girl kept a keen lookout as the boy disappeared through the hole into the wall space, before she too followed suit.

She reappeared, face peering out from the hole like a frightened rabbit, wafting her hand toward the puzzled visitors, urging them to follow. They complied.

Sam followed Lucy through and past the ushering child. The girl reached out, lifting the wooden panel across the opening, and with a tug, wedged it in place.

Sam smiled at their huddled faces, under-lit by a single, slow-dancing candle that the girl held in her willowy hands. '…Erm? So, what are your—'

'Shhhhh!' the young girl gestured with her finger, shaking her head again with frantic energy, cutting off his question.

The children pushed past, peering up with suspicion into puzzled faces as they crossed, then scurried off down a passage.

Lucy and Sam exchanged shrugs, then followed…

They had to scramble to keep up with their new discovery, the adeptness the children displayed at traversing the tunnels making it obvious they'd done so many times before. There was such an air of *second nature* to the way they both clambered through, and over every obstacle, it became painfully apparent – this was 'home'.

The passageways snaked for what felt like forever. Narrow, cramped; changing from brickwork, to wood, to timber laths oozing with crumbling plaster, criss-crossed with rungs of exposed pipework regularly cutting across their path, making them have to work to keep up.

The copper tubes felt damp to the touch, heavily oxidised, staining their clothes and fingers green as they manoeuvred though them.

Sam could see Lucy struggling ahead of him, her slender physique not cut out for this particular form of athletics.

He gently pushed past so he could help lead the way, and assist her over the more challenging obstacles. She happily allowed him.

Sam studied the children as he worked to keep up. They were both wearing what looked to be old fashioned nightgowns, hand-me-downs from a long-gone era.

He also noticed, as he observed the children climb and dart throughout the tunnels and passageways, their gowns floating ethereally behind them, flowing gracefully in the wake of their every movement, giving them all the appearance of being underwater.

Sam remembered the creeping clock mechanism, the slow lick of the flames, the grace of the falling book – it all seemed so utterly dreamlike.

He found himself wishing it *was* a dream, at least he could wake from that. It put him in mind of a saying his father often used: 'Be careful of the things you wish for, nightmares are dreams too.'

They continued the chase, climbing a long series of crooked rungs and water pipes lined up inside the cavity like a ladder.

Lucy felt thankful she'd had the foresight to wear jeans, and not her usual choice of a cute, summer dress.

They passed by many junctions, different tunnels branching off that seemed to lead to other parts of the house. Sam wondered if similar tunnels existed in Hobswyke, assuming they must.

Eventually, they stepped through a hole into a small room. The children were huddled together in a corner.

The girl held out her arms, caging the boy behind an iron-clad stare of mistrust.

The visitors scanned the space, the whole floor blanketed with scavenged objects: bedclothes, silverware, books, cushions, trinkets. Random junk gathered over time to feed an interest in a world they shared with something yet unseen…

The ceiling of the room was heavily lofted and porous, providing little insulation from the strange world outside. It felt cold.

Sam ran through his mind the directions they'd traversed, and the turns they'd made, making considerations for the 'mirrored' aspect of *this* world…

'We must beeee…? In the ceiling space of the east wing I think?' he concluded. 'Somewhere above the servants quarters?'

'Yes, I think you're right,' Lucy agreed.

She stooped a little to try and make her height less intimidating, and started to approach the children. They both responded with a mistrusting glare.

'Please, don't be afraid, we're not to going to hurt you,' Lucy said softly, smiling her kindest smile. 'What are your names?'

The children looked at each other – they seemed confused.

'Your names?' she asked again. 'Do you have names?'

The children just looked blankly back at her.

'I'm not sure they can talk?' Sam interjected.

'Mm, we can talk,' the young girl said, quietly, startling Lucy who was now squatting down before her.

'Oh, okay. Well, *my* name, is *Lucy*, and this, is *Sam*,' she explained, gesturing behind her. 'So, do you have names? You must be called something.'

The girl eventually nodded. 'Um… My name, is "Girl", and he's called "Boy".'

Lucy frowned, unable to help huffing a solitary laugh. 'You can't be called *Boy*, or *Girl*... Don't you have proper names?'

The young girl just looked blankly again, and shook her head.

'Oh. Well, I tell you what. Why don't we call *youuuu?* Jack, and Jill. How's that?'

The young girl allowed herself an insipid smile. 'Jill. That's a pretty name.'

'A pretty name, for a very pretty girl,' Lucy added, 'and you, you look just like a "Jack" to me. Doesn't he, Sam?'

Sam watch as Lucy interacted with the strange children, he could see how easily she'd take to parenting one day. 'Yes. You look *just* like a "Jack",' he agreed.

Lucy watched them silently for a time, gathering all of the questions that came to her mind. 'Do you live in here?' she asked, her face addressing the tiny space.

They both nodded in unison.

'And, Jill, who is it you keep looking around for? Is there someone else here, someone you're afraid of? Are you scared of something? Or someone?'

Jill nodded.

'Who?' Sam coaxed. 'Who is it you're afraid of?'

Jill turned a glance back at Jack, then edged nervously towards Lucy, looking about the room... She leaned cautiously towards her. Lucy presented an ear. 'We're afraid, of *Him*,' she whispered, her voice trembling with fear.

She looked about the room again, and leaned back into Lucy's ear. 'N– The-The Master. We're afraid of The Maste,.' she whispered, barely audible even in the stillness of the loft space.

'What does "*he*" do?' Lucy mewed, her face racked with genuine concern. The girl just shook her head, lips pressed tightly together.

'Why don't you leave?' Sam asked, slightly naively. 'Why don't you both just get away from here, go somewhere else?'

Jill's brows furrowed at the question, turning to look at Jack… Nothing discernible seemed to pass between them, just the telepathy of knowing each other so wholly.

Jack nodded to Jill in response to her apparent silence, and they both made for another hole in the opposite corner of the room.

Jill beckoned them to follow again. They complied, curious to discover more of their world.

The new passage was much shorter, they all climbed down more rungs of timber and pipework, eventually exiting out through a hole into a coal store off the side of the house.

Jill was leaning out, splaying her hand back towards the group. Sam presumed to check the coast was clear of 'Him'.

Her fingers snapped shut. 'Come on!' she ordered, running across the gravel towards a bank of overgrown hedgerows. They all followed…

Jill turned worried eyes up towards the windows of the house as she crossed. Sam looked too, but could see nothing.

They all darted into undergrowth, and made their way along well-trodden paths that meandered beneath tunnels of contorted branches, hanging heavy with thick, brown foliage.

Eventually, they emerged out into a clearing. The sky looked darker than it did before. Overgrown grass lay flat to the ground, collapsed under the weight of its own unchecked growth, they continued following the children as they trotted on ahead.

The going under foot was spongy, feeling like they're walking on cushions. 'Where is she taking us?' asked Sam.

'I have no idea,' said Lucy, looking towards the heavens as they traversed the wide-open clearing.

A deep, grey vista, heavily set with swirls of low, brooding cloud hung ominously above their upturned gazes. A slowly rotating vortex of oppression and foreboding blanketing the skies crowning this peculiar world.

They finally neared the boundary of the grounds. Jill seemed to be heading them towards the metal railings that surrounded the estate, but unlike Hobswyke, these were overgrown with rambling hedgerows.

Lucy pirouetted around, trying to get her bearings, finding the mirrored world confusing to navigate – spatial awareness never being one of her strong suits.

They all finally reached the boundary. Lucy and Sam peered with astonishment above their heads. The swirling sky was bowed, looking flat and two-dimensional, curving down to meet the ornate tops of the tall, iron fencing buried deep behind the overgrowth. A spiralling dome of mist and fog capping the children's world, almost like the angry sky had been folded over them, trapping them there. They could almost reach up and touch its billowing surface, and if they had a ladder, they could.

Jill extended her arms into the twigs and started to part the branches, clearing a passage to the railings.

The flexed limbs seemed to remain where they'd been forced, like they were devoid of spring. But gradually, they began creeping back towards their original position.

Jill pointed through the opening she'd made. 'Look,' she said, lifting a finger towards the perimeter fencing, urging the visitors to pass through to investigate.

Lucy and Sam carefully threaded themselves towards the ironwork, Jill continuing to flex the slow returning branches clear of their efforts.

They arrived at the railings, and presented their faces to the bars to see what was there…

Sinking mist fell like dry ice from the edge of the concave sky above their heads, occasionally clearing long enough to allow them to see what lay beyond the bars.

Sam found himself peering out into something he had on many occasions tried in vain to imagine. 'Nothing'. Pure and unmistakable 'nothing'. Not a vacuum, nor the emptiness of space – *nothing*, a total and complete absence of anything.

In the past, as one who took more than a passing interest in the sciences – touching on the theories of quantum physics – he had stood in places devoid of the pollution of man-made light, and peered long and hard into the eternity of space crowning his wonderment, trying in vain to comprehend a finite state that would in effect be *an absence of all matter and energy.*

But to clear a mind so completely of all things, to allow oneself to comprehend, or even imagine 'nothing' is a feat of impossibility for any, and all creatures.

Yet now, at this very moment, he stood staring out into the unimaginable – a *no*-thing, beyond just sheer blackness. Gazing out at a complete absence of all matter, concepts, ideas or time. Watching something that *didn't* exist to *be* watched.

Tentatively, he extended an arm through the bars out into the void… He couldn't feel his hand, nothing there existing to stimulate his skin. No warmth, no cold, no touch, or breath of wind. Nothing!

'Oh Jesus!' Lucy whimpered, tears bursting off the edges of her lids, rolling down an expressionless face overwhelmed by feelings of emptiness that witnessing the absence of all things had left her with.

'Come away!' said Sam, pulling her back from the bars. 'Come on.'

He escorted her back to the clearing. They stood for a time in their own spaces, attempting to deal with a feeling of ultimate sadness that filled their souls, trying to reason with yet another experience too impossible to truly comprehend. 'Come along. Come on, let's walk,' Sam insisted, Lucy agreed, allowing herself to be led away.

Jack watched the visitors set off, bewildered by their reactions, never having had an opportunity to learn enough of life to know any better.

A view out into *nothing* would have had little meaning to one who'd never been given chance to see much of anything.

Jill took hold of his hand and they followed – having to break into a trot to catch up.

Lucy stopped suddenly, and turned to Jill. 'Where are your parents?' she asked with a frown. Jill shrugged at the question.

'Where's your mother?' asked Sam. 'Or-Or your father? Don't you know where your father is?' He quickly turned to Lucy, who had never known her own father, his identity remaining, to this day, a mystery. 'Sorry!' he mouthed for the insensitivity of his question.

She blinked a smile towards him. 'Don't worry,' she responded in hushed tones, 'it's okay.'

She'd spent years making peace with the fact. The existence of Sam's own father in her life making it a much easier battle to have won.

'What's a "mother"?' asked Jack.

It's the first time they've heard him speak. Hearing how gentle and timid his voice was, softened Lucy like butter.

She walked across to him, and dropped to her knees. 'Erm… A mother, is… is someone who looks after you. Someone who raised you. Someone who cares for you, and cares *about* you. Keeps you safe, gives you love when you need it, and teaches you about life.'

Jack looked into her face, with no flicker of recognition behind his eyes at anything she'd described.

Jack knew nothing of what it was to have a 'mother', but by Lucy's words alone, he could imagine that he would've liked to.

Sam could see by their reactions that they were both parentless. 'Lucy,' he called, quietly shaking his head when she looked over. She nodded in agreement.

'I'm sorry,' she whispered to Jack, wrapping her arms around him... He stiffened in the embrace, shocked at receiving an act of tenderness from a total stranger. The only care he'd ever received in his life before, was from Jill. He had to fight for it to not overwhelm him.

'Where did you come from?' asked Jill, from somewhere outside of their embrace.

Lucy leaned back, and looked to Sam to share in the responsibility of producing an answer.

Sam made his best attempt. 'Erm. Well. We come from another place. A place on the *other* side from here.' He jostled his thoughts. 'Above here – no, below?' he stuttered. 'It's just another place, a different place.'

'But how did you get here?' Jill added, darting a glance towards 'The Nothing' beyond the boundary.

Lucy rolled widened eyes at Sam. Sam shrugged. They'd both done a lifetimes worth of shrugging in the past two days, answers and knowledge becoming somewhat of a luxury in such strange times.

Lucy made *her* attempt. 'Hm – Well... You see, we came up through the pool, the one by the side of the steps, the steps at the front of the house,' Lucy explained, baulking at how insane it must sound.

'Oh... Okay,' Jill responded.

Sam pulled a face towards the girl, realising just how warped the children's lives must be to not react to such a bizarre explanation. He couldn't even begin to imagine the things they must have seen in their limited little lives.

'What do you eat? What is food around here?' asked Lucy.

Jack looked at Jill. She nodded, and he turned, and ran off to a different part of the grounds.

He reappeared a minute later proudly brandishing an apple. 'These hang from the trees, and there are other things, different things, hanging off different plants.'

Sam looked around the grounds, surprised that anything could grow in such a dank, miserable world.

He took the apple from Jack who was offering it to him enthusiastically, examining it with suspicion, then took a reluctant bite... Instantly, he spat it out again, to the confusion of the children looking on.

'What's it like?' asked Lucy. 'What's wrong with it?'

'It's horrible,' he complained, rubbing the taste off his tongue on his T-shirt, 'really bitter. Disgusting.'

He offered it to Lucy to try. She screwed her face up. 'Erm. No thanks,' she said, pushing his hand away.

Jack crept forwards, and snatched the apple back. He ran away and began tucking into it with all the apparent relish of someone eating a slice of the finest cake. Sam watched him, bemused.

Lucy became distracted by something in the distance. She stood to her feet, and walked away from the group, towards whatever it was that had arrested her attention.

Lucy, once again, was feeling the same sensation of being in a bubble, seemingly observing a world detached from her own.

The sensation felt akin to a description a school friend once gave her of a phenomenon called 'astral projection', an event where a person's inner self leaves their terrestrial being, and wanders free of the constraints of its physical host. She imagined it must feel very much the same as this.

Peering out from within her veil of isolation, she looked on at the gatehouse, her home, looming ahead of her. It was a perfect, mirror image of the one on the other side, and in all but just a few details, it looked exactly the same.

She could see tortured brambles growing where roses should be. Darkness beyond the glass instead of the light of a home, lived in and loved.

The domed swirls of the rapidly darkening, oppressive sky kissed the tops of chimney stacks that rose majestically from a roof, thickly blanketed with lichen and moss.

Seeing her home, empty, cold and neglected, saddened her heart. Sat crumbling as a result of an alternative history, a history where it never became the nucleus of a loving family's everyday comings and goings. A place where people ate, slept and shared tales of their lives.

She circled the perimeter, examining the paradoxical replica, exact in every detail except the ones that truly mattered.

The others walk up to join her. 'Try the door,' Sam suggested.

She nodded in agreement, climbing the steps and wiping the handles clear of a coating of dirt. She tried the handle, but it was locked.

She turned her attention to the children. 'In the other place – where me and Sam are from – *this,* is the house where I live,' she explained, their faces alive with genuine interest. 'You see, this world, and our world, are both kind of the same, well – at least they *look* the same, but they're also very different.'

'Different, how?' asked Jack.

She tried hard to think of the most diplomatic answer she could present. 'I guess, they're different in the way they feel, and the way they *make* you feel. Our world feels, I don't know, kinder? Happier? If you understand?'

'I think so,' Jill responded – but not really knowing enough of happiness to truly comprehend her words.

Lucy frowned, then drew her hand from the pocket of her jeans. She opened her fingers, revealing her house keys.

She looked across at Sam, turning her hand to show him… His face brightened and he nodded encouragement.

She stepped up to the door and slid the key into the rusted lock, and tried to turn it, but it didn't move. Her shoulders sagged.

'Lucy,' Sam called, 'the other way.' He whirled his finger towards her. 'You have to turn the key the other way. Everything's opposed, remember?'

She tried turning the key in the other direction, it baulked, then broke free its bonds of inactivity, and began to turn… There was a sharp *clack*, and Lucy swung the door open…

TEN

HOME FROM HOME

LUCY SWUNG THE DOOR into the unlit lobby, unveiling a house that felt as if it had never been lived in.

Apart from the colours – drained by whatever negative force in this world saps their vibrancy, plus everything being mirrored to the way she was familiar – all that Lucy's eye fell upon looked recognisably the same.

She placed a tentative foot inside the door, then turned to face the others. 'Come in,' she sang, inviting them to follow, briefly forgetting this wasn't *actually* where she lived.

They all slowly wandered in through the door and looked around. The house seemed to be furnished, but somehow, it felt more like a show home than anything lived in, a sense that the chairs had never been sat on, the tables ungraced by an elbow or knee. The floors having never, until that moment, been laden with so much as a single footstep.

'Sam,' Lucy called, 'this furniture. I recognise this furniture?'

'So do I,' he replied, trying to place at what point in his past the memory lay.

Lucy's face suddenly lit up. '*This* is the furniture that was in the gatehouse when we first moved in,' she recalled, 'it had been in there for decades. Remember?' She strained to resolve her faded memories. 'We ended up moving it all out, and storing it in the stables. Do you remember?'

'That's right,' he agreed, 'me and Dad helped.'

He walked across the living room to the window. 'Hang on. This sofa, I remember this sofa. It was broken.' He inspected it. 'Do you remember? Dad ended up smashing it into firewood.' He leaned a leg against it, and gave it a healthy shove. 'There, look, this one's coming apart in the exact same place.' He showed her, it jerked her memory.

'Yeeeees, you're right. I *do* remember.' She turned and looked Sam hard in the face. 'What *is* going on here? What the fuck is this place? How can it exist like this?'

Sam ambled about the room, working his mind. He lifted a heavily tarnished candlestick off a side table and turned it over. The base was stamped, but all the letters were back to front. But he could make out one of the words – 'Silver'.

He looked across to Lucy. 'I think, at some point in the past, someone, somehow, managed to create a sort of parallel world, an exact copy of our one.' He knitted his thoughts some more. 'Or maybe, they just created a passage to a parallel world that already existed?' He shrugged. 'I'm not sure, I don't really have an answer, but I'm almost certain it has to be *something* like that.'

He peered about the room. 'Look. Look at all this furniture, it's all really old. I reckon it *is* the furniture that remained in the gatehouse when your family took over Hobswyke, it must've been left over from when that guy owned it before. That French guy. The weirdo who did witchcraft.'

'Mallette,' Lucy murmured, turning her face to the wall.

'Yes, *Mallette*, him.' Sam paced the room some more... 'I think Mallette must have created this place, for whatever reason.

But whatever the reason, it's not going to be for anything good, we know *that* much.'

Lucy was wiping a thick layer of dust from a mirror on the wall above the fireplace, revealing her face looking back at her. She smiled into the reflection.

Sam looked through one of the heavily streaked windows, out over the decay and neglect outside. It seemed to be getting darker by the minute.

He turned his attention back into the room. 'But this *isn't* an entire parallel universe, it's just a small piece, a fragment that exists alone, but why?'

Lucy was still staring at herself, playing her fingers through her hair, then wiping a hand across the contours of her face. 'Do you think I'm beautiful?' she asked in a faraway voice.

Sam had to take a moment to consider the question, being at such a disconnect from the current conversation. 'What?!' he murmured.

'Am I beautiful?' she repeated, gazing deep into the mirror. 'I am, aren't I? You think so, you think I'm beautiful.'

'What the fuck has that got to do with anything?' he barked. But she didn't hear him, too engrossed in her own visage. 'Hey! Are you listening to me? You bloody moron! Are you going to answer me or what?!' he spat.

Lucy heard nothing, just rolled her face, eyes fixated on herself.

'Will you get your face out of that damn mirror!' he shouted, gnashing his jaw. 'I'm talking to you, you fucking idiot! Get your face out of that bastard mirror before I-I…!' He stopped himself, staggering back out of a billowing cloud of rage, straining to rein himself in… But he had to fight to subdue an anger that was building up inside him.

He'd never spoken to anyone that way before, especially

Lucy. He could feel himself changing inside, morphing into someone he wasn't.

He sensed his inner rage closer to the fore than he had ever felt it, bubbling just beneath the surface, ready to erupt. 'We have to get out of here,' he said, 'Lucy, we need to leave, this place is changing me.'

'Hmmm?' Lucy responded, distant eyes still admiring her reflection.

Sam strode to the mirror. He could feel the anger trying to break free again. He fought to push it back. 'Lucy, *please*,' he insisted, taking her arm and turning her from the wall. 'We have to leave. *Now*!'

He suddenly shied away from her, startled. Lucy's eyes had changed.

She smiled an empty smile, peering through his shocked expression with distant eyes glowing vibrant orange. 'Okaaay…' she agreed, in a voice rapidly detaching from reality, slowly rolling her face back towards the mirror.

Sam grasped her by the arm, and dragged her toward the door.

He called to Jill and Jack. They appeared at the top of the staircase. 'Come on, we have to go,' he insisted. They looked at each other, then trotted down the stairs.

Sam strode with conviction towards the big house, towing Lucy by her arm. The children had to run to keep up.

He was aware of the rage brewing, he could feel it swelling inside him, inflating, unsure how long he could contain it.

'Do I look young, Sam?' Lucy asked. 'People say I do. Do you have a mirror I can use? I need to see.' Lucy was acting as if she was unaware of anything else that was happening around her.

They reached the clearing that led to the steps. Sam knelt before Jill and Jack. They looked confused at the changes they were seeing in their new friends' emotions. 'Listen, we can't just leave you here, we're going to take you across with us to our world.'

Sam had to strain briefly to force back the anger swelling in his gut. He took a breath… 'We can't stay here any longer, we have to go now, but you're coming with us.' He looked up at the house. 'I don't know what, or-or who it is you're afraid of, but I'm going to get you away from here, okay?'

The children agreed.

'Come on,' instructed Sam.

They all ran across the gravel towards the steps, Jack and Jill darting concerned eyes up to all of the windows overlooking the clearing.

They reached the staircase. Sam straddled the railing, helping Lucy over to the side of the pool. 'Lucy, go. I'll deal with the kids. Just go, and be careful.'

She started across the stone carvings, carefully placing her feet as before. She began to swing over towards the midnight sheen of the waiting pool.

'Come on,' urged Sam, taking hold of Jack who'd been watching Lucy's path down the wall with astonishment.

Sam tried lifting him over the handrail, but he struggled. He adjusted his grip and tried again, but it was as if someone was holding him back.

He looked to see if Jack's clothes were caught on the ironwork, but there was nothing obvious snagging him. He tried lifting him again, but it felt like an invisible hand was holding him fast, some force unseen.

Jill suddenly screamed, sinking to the ground, her eyes fixed towards the house.

A tall, dark figure loomed behind one of the top-floor windows, its drawn, emaciated face pressed up against the glass, watching them.

It raised skeletal arms and placed its bony hands flat against the pane… It screeched a piercing scream spiked with more rage than Sam has ever witnessed in his life.

The thing turned from the window and vanished into the murk.

They could hear it crashing through the house, thundering along the corridors and down the staircases.

The air filled with echoes of smashing wood and shattering glass. Livid shrieks of unbridled anger erupting from the walls.

'*Quick, come on!*' cried Sam, trying to pull Jack over the handrail, his shaking grip tugging in vain, but he was unable to overcome whatever force was holding the child back.

'Go. Just go!' shrieked Jill. 'We'll go to that place, the one we just came from, *Him* won't find us there. But please, just go, you have to go *now*!'

They both sprinted towards the trees, darting petrified looks back towards the hall.

The large double doors crashed open. The tall, dark figure stood looking at Sam, seething… The *Thing* was long and gangly like an insect, with thin, taught muscles stretched tight across its bones like cables, knotting at the sight of the intruder to its world.

It began striding towards him, its ferocity boiling, and gradually broke into a sprint, its twisted limbs cascading towards the pool.

Sam turned to run down the wall, but Lucy was still there – hanging above the surface – gazing at her reflection. 'Lucy! Go! We have to leave *now!*' he yelled. He shook her frantically to snap her out of her trance. '*Goooo…*! For fuck's sake, go!' he screeched at the back of her head. She finally heard him and dropped away into the fluid.

The twisted figure's spidery legs clattered down the staircase, a deep hollow wail gusting from its gaping mouth.

Sam could hear its breath above him. He sensed an arm reaching down to catch him!

He stumbled down the wall, stepped to the surface, and dropped his head beneath the onyx sheen, black tides lapping across his back, and with a final determined stride, he was through!

ELEVEN

TO PEEK BEHIND A CURTAIN

SAM OPENED HIS PETRIFIED EYES and was instantly blinded by the stinging brightness of their world. He held a hand out in front of his face to block the sun, still instinctively leaning his body away from the grasp of the twisted figure that had come for him.

His blazed retinas managed to calm enough for him to continue his path up the stones, rising from the wake of his rebirth back to safety.

He finally swung over the top, and into the waiting arms of Lucy.

'Sam!' she cried, pulling him in tight... He allowed the comfort of the hold to hang for a moment, his arms cocooning Lucy from the trauma of their recent ordeal, but he eventually succumb to his worries and wrestled himself free of her embrace to pull her back from the edge of the pool, making sure to remain close enough to watch for anything attempting to come through.

'Are you okay?' he asked, eyes burning the surface of the water for movement.

'Yes, I'm fine,' she replied. 'I-I'm sorry.'

'Sorry...? Sorry for what?'

'I don't know what was happening to me through there? I was changing, I could *feel* myself changing.' Her head bowed to the weight of her shame. 'I really started to feel, kind of, self-absorbed? Is that the word?'

'Yes, I know what you mean,' Sam confirmed.

'I felt – I don't know – engrossed in *myself*, I could feel I was starting to not care, or think about anyone else but *me*!' She looked to Sam for understanding. 'But it was strange, the *real* me, the *proper* me, was still inside, and I was screaming at myself to stop. It was horrible.'

Sam finally allowed his attention to relax from the pool, calmed by a passage of time, and the absence of anything rising to disturb the perfect sheen of the inky fluid.

He stooped a little to inspect Lucy's eyes – they were now transitioning to a bright shade of emerald, shrinking flecks of yellow being engulfed by striations of peppermint green, their vibrancy fading as he watched, fascinated.

Lucy flinched away from his studying gaze. 'What's going on with your eyes?' she shrieked.

'Why? What do you mean?' he asked.

'They've changed,' she told him. 'They've turned red! My God, you look frightening, what's happened to them?' she asked, her face squirming.

He rolled his eyes down towards his cheeks, foolishly attempting to look at himself. 'So mine changed as well?' he said.

'As well?' she responded, unaware that the phenomenon was happening to them both.

'Yes, through there, your irises turned orange, a *really* bright orange, but now,' he stooped again to check, 'they're changing to a sort of pale green. They seem to be slowly returning to your natural colour?'

Lucy rubbed her eyes and turned her back on the house, she'd seen enough of its morbid facade for one day thank you.

She suddenly made a leaping flinch backwards, screaming towards the leafy-tunnel that snaked away from the clearing. Sam turned to look…

There was a face watching from within the clawing branches reaching across the path. 'It's okay, Lucy, it's just Hilly.' He called to his sister.

Tentatively, Hilly slowly unfurled herself from behind the tortured arms of the thicket, and stood at the edge of the gravel watching them with a subtle air of mistrust.

'What's wrong, Hill…? Come over here,' Sam mewed. She padded on the spot indecisively, then shook her head.

'What's the matter with her?' Lucy murmured.

'I don't know.'

Hilly took a tentative half-step towards them. 'Sam…?' she called, nervously. 'Is-Is that you?'

Sam pulled a face. 'Of course it's me?'

Hilly cocked a wary eye. 'Well – okay, tell me something that only you and I would know,' she said, taking a cautious step back towards the thicket, looking every bit as though she was readying herself to run.

'It's me, Hilly. It's Sam, your brother?' He turned a frown towards Lucy's equally bewildered face. She shrugged… 'Okay, okay…? Well, let's see…' he said. 'Your name is Hillary, but you kind of hate it because you think it sounds old-fashioned… Yoooou love Scrabble, and crosswords, and you've *always* been better at both of them that I *ever* have.' He squinted towards her, collecting his thoughts. 'What else? Oh yeah, you like to draw, and paint, but you're not really very good at either, but you enjoy it anyway, so…' He pressed a quizzical finger against his bottom lip, turning his eyes to the sky. 'You think too much makeup on a girl makes her look trashy, and you don't really do fashion, you just wear what you like. Oh, and last year you tried to cut your own fringe, but you mucked it up, and ended up looking like Jim Carey did in *Dumb and Dumber.*'

A big smile extended across Hilly's face, her stance softening, and she sprinted across the gravel to the welcoming arms of what she was now sure was her brother.

She enveloped him in her relief. 'Wasn't sure that was you I saw coming out of the pool,' she said, glancing at them both. 'You seemed – different, not the way you normally are.' Her face puckered with disgust. 'And your eyes! Your eyes looked horrid. They still do a bit?'

'You saw us?' asked Sam. 'You were here, watching us come back through?'

Hilly nodded. 'I didn't know where you went. I heard you sneaking off early this morning, so I thought you might have gone into the water again. So I ran up to see. I got here just as you were both coming back. It was frightening seeing Lucy coming through the pool.' She turned to Lucy. 'For some reason, it-it didn't really look like you. You looked like an imposter.'

They all held each other for a time, needing a few moments of closeness to settle their shredded nerves.

'So, tell me where you went?' Hilly asked, leaning out of the huddle.

'Come on,' her brother said, throwing a final cautionary glance to the pool, 'let's have a walk down by the lake, and we'll tell you everything we saw.'

'Okay,' she agreed – glad to be leaving the place. 'And I'm *not* rubbish at drawing!'

They paced the grounds, regaling Hilly with an account of everything they saw, things they'd both divined, and truths that had been shared by those who'd long guarded the secrets connected to the house. For more than an hour, they languished fantastic details upon ears that have to work hard to trust the honesty in the bizarre things they were hearing.

'How old are these children?' Hilly asked.

'I don't know?' replied Sam with a shrug. 'About your age – possibly? No, I think maybe even younger? But, I'm *really* not sure.'

He glanced down at his watch, it seemed to be running normally again. 'What time do you make it, Hilly?'

'Erm? Hang on,' she said, twisting her wrist over to see. 'It's just gone twelve thirty.'

Sam rotated the face of his watch towards Lucy. 'We went through there just after nine.'

Lucy peered at the watch. 'Ten twenty-seven?' she read out loud.

'And we came back just over an hour ago,' he explained. 'A little after eleven.'

'But we were down there for what? An hour and a half…? Two hours?' Lucy reckoned.

'*Yes*. About two hours,' Sam said. 'We probably came back through just after eleven. Nine, ten, eleven – two hours. But by my calculations, my watch must only have moved on about five or eight minutes.'

He paced the lawn, circling the girls. 'I've been trying to work this out… I think something, or *someone* – maybe Mallette – has created a sort of parallel world, a world where the *perception* of time is the same as here, but that somehow, all matter *within* that world is tied to a different path, a path that advances at a far slower pace.' He flicked a look towards two very confused faces. 'I know, I know, it doesn't seem to make sense.'

He began circling the other way. 'We were moving *within* that world as we normally would, but – candles burned, objects fell, water splashed, clocks ticked, everything did everything much, much slower than it does here.' He stopped and turned to face them. 'And maybe: plants grew, wood rotted, matter decayed, and *we* aged much, much slower too? That's what I think was happening.'

'Oh hell, Sam,' Lucy despaired, 'I just wish I could speak to Mum about all of this. She must remember *something* about all that time she was missing. What she did? Where she was? There has to be some answers there somewhere.'

Lucy's shoulders sagged. 'I mean, to not remember *anything* at all of nine or ten years of your life, seems incredible to me, far-fetched, even. I can't believe she doesn't at least remember some details, however small.'

Hilly looked deep in thought. 'I once saw a program,' she said, 'it was a documentary, about this boy who went missing. He was only missing for a few days, or was it a week? Anyway. He was eventually found wandering around the town where he came from. People knew who he was because he'd been reported lost, and everyone had been looking for him. But apparently, something had happened to him that had made him forget absolutely everything about his life. He had that thing? I can't remember the word? He was suffering frommm...?'

'Amnesia?' suggested Lucy.

'Yes! That's it. He was suffering from amnesia. He didn't recognise his mum, or his dad, or remember anything at all about his previous life. He'd forgotten everything!'

'And? What happened?' Lucy asked.

'Well, one day, quite a bit after, he was crossing a road and a speeding car had to brake hard and swerve to miss him. He was okay and all that, but seeing the front of the car jogged something in his memory. He suddenly remembered that he'd been hit by a motorist, and they must have driven away. It had knocked him into a ditch, or was it a hedge? It was something like that. Thing is, as soon as he remembered *that* part, he started remembering loads of other stuff, and by the end – if I've got it right – he ended up remembering everything about his life that he'd forgotten.'

'So, what are you saying?' her brother asked.

'Well – maybe there's something you could do that might jog Helen's memory?'

'Like what?' asked Lucy.

'Well, I don't know. You could maybe, put something somewhere? Or-Or make her think? Or do… Oh I don't know, it was just an idea.'

Sam sniggered. 'Maybe we should drive into her with a car,' he joked, 'knock her into a ditch and leave her there for a few days.' He laughed affectionately. 'If I had a pound for every time I'd had to listen to one of your mad ideas… I'd have about three pounds.'

But Lucy wasn't sure the idea was so mad. On the contrary, she thought there was something there that may be worth trying.

*

The evening sky had attained the flatness of light that comes only from a sun drifting low to the horizon, diffused by an ever-deepening layer of haze-filled atmosphere. Lucy and her mother were just finishing eating dinner.

Lucy rolled the last mouthful of pasta, cheese and arrabiata ragu onto her fork with her thumb, and wrapped her whole face around it. Her taste buds fizzled to the fiery heat of the sauce.

'That was lovely, Mum,' she said gratefully, collecting the bowls and carrying them across to the sink. 'I'll wash up.'

She slipped on a pair of yellow rubber gloves, and whipped on the taps…

Her mind worked overtime to formulate an effective plan to try to jog her mother's memories. She had one idea floating about in her mind that she wasn't particularly happy with, but in the absence of anything better, she found herself willing to run with it.

'There. All done,' she announced, blowing into the cuffs of the gloves and teasing them off her fingers, 'and while I'm in a cleaning mood,' she added, 'there's some tidying I've been meaning to do up in my room. So I'll do that now.'

'Blimey! Well, don't let *me* stop you,' her mother responded, airily.

Lucy jogged up to her bedroom and shut the door.

She scanned the room, and began formulating a scenario that fitted her ideas...

Helen heard a crash from Lucy's bedroom, and lifted her attention from the newspaper she was reading towards the sound, trying to work out if it was sufficiently out of place enough to react to...

She sprung to her feet and rushed from the kitchen, sprinting up the staircase. 'Lucy, are you okay?'

'I think so, Mum,' came the muted response from inside the room.

Helen rushed forwards and swung the door open. She froze...

'I don't know what happened,' Lucy whined, 'one minute I was cleaning my mirror, and then it just slipped off the chest of drawers, knocking my stuff everywhere.' She peered across at her mother. 'Mum, are you okay?'

Helen stared down at a floor strewn with keepsakes and ornaments. And lying face up – dead centre of the chaos – was Lucy's antique mirror, glass shattered into a hundred jagged pieces, a sight that sent a shudder dripping down Helen's spine like ice-cold molasses, for, lying prostrate among the shards of reflected ceiling, was a porcelain doll that Lucy's grandmother had bought her for her thirteenth birthday.

Lucy watched on at Helen quaking at the sight of the diorama she'd contrived in an attempt to jog a displaced memory, and could see the image she'd created was far from alien to her mother's recollections.

'Mum?' she asked softly. 'What's wrong, Mum?'

Her mother remained silent, frozen to the spot, shaking visibly.

'Mum?' she called again, but still nothing – eyes glued to the doll. 'Mum?' Lucy prodded, 'Mum, please…' Lucy took a breath, and steeled herself. '…Thomas!?' she blurted.

Helen erupted from her trance. '*What* did you say?' she slurred, her words laced with a subtle air of threat.

'I-I said – "Thomas".'

Her mother staggered back from the name, a sickened look saturating her contorting features. 'Why did you say that?' she asked, trying to decipher from Lucy's expression how much she may, or may not know of the name she'd had the audacity to introduce into a conversation they weren't even having.

'Because, Mum, I know… I know about Thomas… and I also know about *you*.'

'*W-What…!*' she stammered. 'But who told you?' she demanded. Then her face widened to the realisation. 'Mother!'

'Yes. It was Grandma,' admitted Lucy, 'but don't blame her, *I* asked.'

'You asked?' she said, looking at Lucy with a face wilting with disgust at the rashness of her daughters actions. 'So – what else do you know?'

'A lot, well – I think *all* of it,' she replied.

Her mother staggered to a chair, grasping at the back to

steady herself… She lowered her shaking frame gently onto the seat… 'And what else did she tell you?'

Lucy swallowed back her reluctance to say more. 'Well, I know why me and you have blonde hair and blue eyes, and Grandma and Grandpa don't.'

For a briefest of moments, Helen had to pause to decipher Lucy's words, then lifted a shocked hand across her mouth. 'She told you *that*!' she hissed, through splayed fingers. Lucy nodded. 'But *why…?*'

'Because I wanted to know. I wanted to know what it is that you're so scared of… Why you seemed to be so afraid, of… of Hobswyke.'

Helen began shaking her head frantically, rejecting the reality of her daughter knowing her secrets.

Lucy steeled herself again, forcing her resolve. 'I've been to the house. I've been *in* the house. I've seen the library. I've seen it all, Mum.'

Helen reeled back, clapping her hands across her eyes, head shaking in denial. All the years carefully keeping Lucy protected from a dark secret crashing down around her.

Lucy stepped in and knelt before her. Tears streamed from her mother's eyes. 'It's okay, Mum, *please*, you can talk to me about it now.' Her mother shook her head again. '*Yes!*' Lucy insisted. 'We *can*… and we're going to.'

Helen sat rocking in denial, breathing hard, trying to bring herself to terms with the fact that her attempts to shield her daughter from a truth she found repugnant had failed.

Eventually though, she managed to fight through her reluctance to speak, took the deepest of breaths, and slowly emerged from behind her splayed fingers…

'Okay… Okay,' she agreed. 'But I need a drink first.'

*

Lucy turned from the kettle holding two mugs of tea. She handed one to her mother who was sitting at the kitchen table, still visibly shaking.

'Here you go, Earl Grey with one sugar,' she said, trying to pacify her mother with a warm smile.

Helen stared into the mug, wishing it was full of something a little stronger than tea, absinthe maybe. But as the smell of the bergamot filled the air, she actually found herself glad of the slight misunderstanding.

They sat, and sipped in silence for a couple of minutes, Lucy thinking it better to let her mother take the lead.

Helen eventually lowered her mug… 'What did you want to know?' she asked, sounding reluctant.

Lucy shrugged at the awkwardness, trying to find an effective opener for such a conversation. But she felt very much the holder of the upper hand, so she made a start. 'Do you remember anything at all from the time you were missing?'

After an uncomfortable pause, Helen shook her head unconvincingly.

'*Mum!* If we're going to do this… *Please*, is there anything?'

Helen's whole demeanour sagged, then she lifted her eyes. 'I have dreams, but they're just dreams.'

'Dreams?' Lucy asked. 'What are they, these dreams?'

Her mother looked dispirited. She shrugged… 'There's one in particular, one I have a lot – all the time in fact,' she said, her brows flashing lightly.

'Tell me.'

Helen loosed a resigned sigh… 'Well, in this dream, I'm sitting on the floor of the dining hall at Hobswyke. But it's strange, it doesn't *feel* like Hobswyke?' She frowned down into the mug. 'It certainly *looks* like Hobswyke, but in the dream, I can somehow tell that it isn't. It feels, strange. It feels, wrong. This place is run down, dirty and has an odd atmosphere.'

Lucy had to fight hard not to show recognition of her mother's description. '…And? Go on,' she said.

Helen took another thoughtful sip of her tea… 'I'm holding a hand mirror. An ornate, silver-backed hand mirror – a bit like that one your grandma Violet has.' Lucy nodded her understanding. 'So I'm holding this mirror and I'm watching myself in the reflection. Sort of like – like I'm *admiring* myself, like I'm *proud* of how beautiful I look, or-or, how beautiful I *think* I look, which believe it or not, really isn't me at all.' She winced an embarrassed smile towards Lucy.

'But you are beautiful, Mum.'

Helen rolled her eyes. 'I guess. But anyway, that's beside the point. In the dream, I briefly place the mirror down on the floor next to me, so I can brush my hair, to make it nice, you know how you do. And when I've finished brushing, I look down, and…'

'…You look down, and?'

Helen looked pained to be forced to relive something that's plagued her nights for decades.

'Please, Mum… The mirror's on the floor, and you've been brushing your hair, and you look down.'

'…And when I look down to take up the mirror again, I can see the ceiling reflected in it. But the thing is, in the reflection, everything looks perfect: clean, polished, free of the dust, dirt and cobwebs that hang from the ceiling above me. The whole room – *in* the reflection – looks immaculate, and feels somehow different. Brighter. Warmer. Safer.'

Lucy leaned in and placed a comforting hand on her mother's arm. 'Go on, what happens then?'

'Well, when I take the mirror up off the floor, the image of the ceiling suddenly changes, it shows the room dirty, dark and rotting again. So I place it back down, and once again, the reflection of the room looks perfect.'

Her mother supped the last of her tea. 'Another one?' Lucy asked. Helen nodded timidly, and smiled her appreciation.

Lucy carried the mugs to the kettle, and turned to keep listening. 'So, what happens then?'

'So, after that – in the dream – I stand and struggle to take down a large mirror from the wall, and lie it flat on the floor, in the exact same position as I placed the hand mirror, and suddenly, I can see the whole room looking immaculate – clean, pristine, well tended to. The mirror somehow makes it all look like a far nicer place, a place you'd much rather be, and then I notice something strange and out of place.'

'And what is that?'

'There's an edge encroaching on the reflection, cutting across what I'm able to see. It looks kind of like, like there's a hole beneath the surface of the mirror, that isn't quite lining up with the frame, if you know what I'm saying. So I manoeuvre the mirror around to try and square it with the hole, so I can see as much of the beautiful version of the room as possible.'

'And does that work?'

'Yes, it works. I can now see the whole thing in all its glory. So I kneel down in the centre of the glass, and gaze down into the reflection of the room looking majestic and inviting.'

Helen shuffled to get comfortable. 'The thing is, and this is what's *really* odd, is that for some reason, I'm not able to see my own reflection, even though I'm kneeling right in the centre of the glass. I seem to be invisible, casting no image, like a vampire.'

Lucy placed a fresh mug down in front of her mother, and took to her seat again. 'And – is that it?' she asked.

'No – no, unfortunately not... So I'm peering at the reflection, pushing my face against the glass, turning my eyes this way and that, to see as much of the perfect version of the room as I can, when suddenly, the mirror starts to crack beneath me. Splinters start growing away from my hands and knees like spiders webs.' She shut her eyes tight. 'I can feel the popping of the glass through the palms of my hands and my knees. Then, it gives way, and I drop through the floor into total darkness.'

Lucy gave her mother's hand a comforting squeeze. 'That sounds horrible.'

'It is. It's a horrific dream, and I have no idea what any of it means. I just keep having it, again, and again, and again.'

Lucy leant in further and gave her mother's shoulder an affectionate rub.

Helen's eyes flicked briefly towards the sink. 'How did you get in the house?' she asked.

'It doesn't matter, Mum,' Lucy insisted, with a shake of the head. 'I found a way in, it really wasn't that difficult... I saw what you and Peter had discovered in the library, I can certainly see why you decided we all needed to leave,' she said, laughing lightly.

'It was a horrible thing to find,' her mother recounted. 'Sometimes, I think I should have burned the place to the ground. Maybe I should,' she added.

'Nooo. Don't worry, okay, we'll just keep away from the place, let it crumble.'

Her mother snickered. 'Okay.'

Lucy hated lying to anyone, especially her mother. But on this occasion she felt justified, even if just to save her mother unnecessary anguish.

Helen stared into her mug. 'You know, I often think of Thomas, and wonder what happened to him.' She started to weep.

Lucy rose, and rounded the table, wrapping herself around her mother's pain.

'Promise me you'll stay away from the house,' her mother pleaded.

Lucy smiled softly. 'Of course,' she agreed, from within the embrace – her fingers crossed tightly behind her mother's back.

Lucy decided to push the subject no further, already in possession what she wanted – an answer.

TWELVE

A FACE THAT FITS?

A DEW BEGAN FORMING on the lawns as darkness descended on the grounds, Lucy could feel it soaking through her inappropriate choice of footwear as she trotted down the bank towards the old stables.

She'd arranged to meet Sam at ten o'clock, having had to carefully sneak past her mother's newly spiked awareness of her actions, a major downside of confronting her for answers.

Lucy hadn't snuck from the house since she was a child, and the excitement of reliving her past set a fizz in her belly.

She could see one of the stable doors hanging open as she neared the block, Sam must already be there. 'Sam, is that you?' she whispered.

'Yep. I'm in here,' he confirmed.

She rounded the open door and found him rifling through a stack of old furniture, the exact same furniture they'd seen at the gatehouse in the other realm.

'Hi,' he said, with an excited smile, introducing Lucy to the furniture with an extended arm. 'There, we were right, it *is* the same stuff. *Exactly* the same.' He started tearing tape from the lid of a battered cardboard box. 'I'm sure my theories are right, it *is* a parallel world.' He straightened to consider his words. 'No, not parallel – it's an *opposite* world…'

He bent down again, and continued to ransack the mound of forgotten belongings. 'Ah!' he cried, triumphantly, lifting a heavily tarnished candlestick from the mildew-speckled box, scooping a couple of dead spider carcasses from the hollow of the base. The stamp inside read 'Silver'. 'You see, I'm right on this. It's like – like, there's a world beneath our world – an *under*-world.'

Lucy watched on as Sam conferred with himself, she *would* find it amusing, if it wasn't for the fact that everything he was saying made perfect sense.

'I spoke to Mum, about her disappearance,' she announced.

Sam ceased rummaging. 'You *spoke* to her. But how did—?'

She smirked. 'Now don't laugh, I used Hilly's idea. I set something up to jog her memory and, amazingly, it worked.'

'Shit! So how did you do that?'

They both sat on the forgotten furniture, illuminated by a single low wattage lightbulb dangling from a pendant above them. Sam listened open-mouthed as Lucy described the ruse she'd used…

'…and *she* thinks it's a dream she's having,' Lucy explained, 'but *I* reckon, it's actually a memory.' She extended a finger in the direction of the big house. 'That place through there, I think it might be where my mum was trapped for all those years.'

Sam nodded slowly in agreement. 'I think you're probably right, I've had similar thoughts myself.' They sat in silence, deep in shared reflexion. 'That's incredible, if it's true,' Sam muttered. 'Accidentally aligning those mirrors, and creating another way *in*. Well – another way *out* to be more precise.'

Lucy popped an incongruous smirk. 'Crazy isn't it?'

Sam burst from his thoughts, taking his phone from his pocket. 'Look at this,' he said, excited, 'I went back up to Hobswyke, to take a proper look around those steps. I took some photos. Here. Look.'

He sat down next to Lucy and opened his picture files. 'Remember those symbols carved on the stones, and the ones you noticed hidden within the design of the handrails? Well, I did some investigating.'

'Let me see,' she fizzled – her curiosity pricked.

He sidled close, his phone illuminating the fascination in their faces. He pointed his pinkie at the screen. 'See that symbol there, the one that looks like two linked crosses with a trident at one end.' Lucy nodded. 'It's carved in the stones as well. Well, I found a version of it in that book of Dad's.' He swiped to a photo of a page from the book. 'See it there, it's a talismanic symbol called "The Seal of Exu". Apparently Exu is a sort of entity, a guardian of the doorways and passages to and from this world, passages that lead to other realms – well it was something like that anyway. Thing is, I found this seal carved *all* over those stones.'

Lucy looked and listened, fascinated, and more than a little unnerved. She never really gave much credence to magic, spirits or superstitions before, but she found herself having to re-evaluate her whole perception of the way the world *was*, and the way it worked. 'Do you think that's what chased us?' she asked. 'This "Exu" thing?'

Sam huffed a shrug. 'Maybe?'

He swiped a few more times to a different photo. 'Now this one, this is just *one* of the designs hidden in the railings.' Lucy took the phone from him to look closer. Sam leaned in. 'You can just make it out if you line it up right...' He circled the end of his little finger around an area of the screen. 'See there, that detail there, it *seems* to be an image of a serpent spitting what looks to be a wall of venom in front of that shape you can see.' He lifted his face from the light. 'I looked it up. That shape is an Egyptian hieroglyphic symbol called an "ankh". It's supposed to represent the human soul.' He turned to Lucy. 'I found other symbols with similar themes hidden in there too. I *think* all this stuff in the railings is some kind of barrier, a-a talismanic force field that blocks passage to the other realm. And *I* accidentally broke through it!'

'So, do you think that's why we're able to pass through?'

'Yes, I do. And I also think the fact that the handrails on the other side are still whole, is what created a force that stopped me from bringing anything from *that* world, through into *ours*.'

Lucy sat, absorbing it all… 'What do we do now?'

Sam shrugged again, clueless. 'I don't know.'

'Well, we can't just leave those children in that awful place!' she insisted.

'I know that, and I don't think either of us was planning to. I mean, there is the problem of what the hell we would do with them if we *did* manage to bring them through.'

'Maybe they came from here in the first place?' Lucy suggested. 'Maybe they've been missing for years?'

'I never thought of that,' Sam said, 'but they seem so oblivious to this side?'

'But whatever, we can deal with that problem when we come to it, *if* we come to it,' Lucy said.

Sam gazed through the open stable doors, the chimney-lined silhouette of Hobswyke just visible in front of the evening sky, looming over the trees far in the distance. 'We *will* try. Christ knows how we'll do it, but we'll certainly try.' He turned his attention back to Lucy. 'But we need a plan.'

'Yes,' she agreed. 'Sam… what *was* that thing watching us from the window? Do you think it was that "Exu" entity?'

He shook his head. He'd been trying hard to forget about it. 'God alone knows. Maybe it was, or it may have been Antoine Mallette.'

Her brows furrow. 'But didn't he die? Burned wasn't he?'

'Apparently. But maybe he just died in *our* world? Maybe he sacrificed his physical self so he could exist through *there*?' he suggested, extending his chin out towards the looming silhouette. He sat in contemplation for a time… 'Or maybe it *wasn't* him they found. Have you ever considered that? Maybe they just assumed it was him?'

'What does that mean?' Lucy asked.

'I don't know,' he shrugged. 'Maybe the body they found *wasn't* Mallette. How could they know, they didn't exactly have dental records to refer to then did they. They might have just *assumed* it was him, just because he wasn't around anymore.'

Lucy tried, but failed to pick a hole in his logic.

'Think about it…' he said. 'What if it was just some random guy Mallette sacrificed to please a god, or a demon, or something like that – not that I know how any of that stuff works.' He sat quietly, honing his theories… 'Maybe it was a sacrifice made as an offering to create a passage to that bloody awful place. Or maybe it could have been something to do with actually *creating* that place?'

He rose to his feet and walked to the door. He leaned against the frame and gazed out across the grounds…

'But why?' Lucy asked. 'What would be the point?'

Sam tortured his thoughts, trying to concoct a scenario that might fit… 'If *I* was him, why would *I* do that…?' he muttered into the night in an attempt to channel Mallette.

He spun to face Lucy. 'Okay. Imagine you were him, right. You've grown really old, but you're not yet ready to let go of life, what do you do?'

Lucy shrugged.

'What if he, what's the word? *Conjured*! What if conjured into existence another realm where he can slow time down. A place to exist within, where your physical body hardly ages.'

Again, Lucy failed to find a hole in his reasoning, however insane it sounded in light of all that had happened, and on the contrary, she found herself giving increasing credence to the possibility of its truth.

'Didn't you have some records somewhere, Luce, that would show when those steps where added to the Hall?'

'Yes, we did, somewhere?'

'Can you find them?'

'I could look, why?'

'Because, if they were built not long before he died, or vanished – whatever the hell it was that happened to him, then that would confirm at least the *possibility* of what it is I'm saying.'

'Okay, I'll have a look around,' she agreed.

Lucy peered out at the pitch black sky. 'It's getting late, I have to go. I'll let you know what I find tomorrow, alright?'

'Alright,' he said. 'Come on, I'll see you back home.'

'Okay,' she smiled. After all the talk of witchcraft, demons and sacrifice, Lucy found herself glad of the company...

*

The morning sun lifted into yet another cloudless sky, charging the air with its warmth. The rays streamed through the east-side window of the gatehouse, warming Lucy's shoulder.

She sat cross-legged in front of the large bookcase in the living room, searching out the documents Sam had mentioned.

She could hear the turbine whine of the vacuum cleaner upstairs, so knew her mother's interests were elsewhere.

Frantically, she leafed through the file of old paperwork

her mother kept on the bottom shelf, flicking through every document, searching for anything resembling a set of plans.

The vacuum fell silent. Lucy froze, barely drawing breath… She could hear muffled knocks of her mother banging around in one of the bedrooms, then a door close, then open again…

The vacuum cleaner fired up, and Lucy exhaled. 'Crap-in-hell,' she murmured, clapping a hand to her lurching stomach…

She carried on leafing through the documents: deeds, wills, insurances, something called Premium Bonds? Then came across neatly folded, heavily aged documents, yellowing at the edges, and carefully opened them… 'Got it!' she cried, holding up a set of drawings detailing the stone staircases of the old Hall. She refolded them, and carefully placed them to one side. They had a smell of ancient books, and the aroma took her back to the library at Hobswyke. The arid face of the demon flashed through her thoughts. She shuddered.

Carefully, she straightened the folder and slipped it back onto the shelf, and ensconced her find quietly into her rucksack…

*

Lucy arrived at the stables again, dead on ten thirty as they'd arranged. Again, an excited Sam had beaten her to it.

'So, you found them?' he asked, holding up his phone that displayed her last message. Lucy nodded, and withdrew the discovery from her bag.

Sam carefully flattened the delicate plans out on a table he'd cleared. Lucy looked on. 'So, what do you think?' she asked.

Sam scanned the drawings. 'Yes, this is them,' he said, studying the details of the stone staircase that rose to the plateaux ahead of the main doors. He pointed to the plans. 'See, there are the pools.'

There were other drawings folded in with the main plans, detailing the carved designs for the stone masons to follow, including rough sketches of the desired symbology for the railings, hand drawn, and also folded in with the main plans. There was a faint signature just visible in the corner of the sketch – they were penned by Mallette.

Sam spied a faded date – 13/4/1862.

'It fits,' he bubbled, 'it bloody fits.' He squinted his curiosity towards Lucy. 'Your family took over the house in the late eighteen hundreds, right?'

'That's right,' Lucy confirmed.

'Well, Mallette commissioned the staircase in eighteen sixty two…! So it fits. He *planned* it, he *planned* it all, and when they were finally finished, he suddenly disappeared.'

Lucy could see it all slotting into place, however, none of it explained the existence of the children. But she couldn't bring herself to care too much about such an extraneous detail, all she could think about was getting the kids away from the horrific entity they'd encountered inhabiting that oppressive world. 'So what do we do?' she asked.

'I have a few ideas, but whatever we do, we would have to do it quickly. Remember, we were only over the other side for roughly two hours *our* time before it started changing us. So, it figures, we'd only have a two hour window to find the kids, take them to the stairs, cut the railings and get them out.'

'It's possible,' Lucy proclaimed.

Sam shrugged a *maybe* in response. 'It *is* possible, but it's tight!'

Lucy paced the stable. 'What do you think was happening to us through there?' she asked. 'When we were changing.'

'I've been thinking about that. Everything else seemed

to be flipped over on that side – in opposition to *our* world – so I guess, it figures, that maybe our personalities would too?'

Lucy frowned.

'Think about it. What is one of *your* major personality traits?' he asked. She shrugged. 'It's that of someone who *always* thinks about others before themselves. You're caring, considerate, kind. Really, you're one of the most selfless and lovely people I've ever known.'

For Lucy to hear the way Sam perceived her felt odd, but heartwarming. She felt an urge to hold him, an urge she'd felt many times before. She wondered whether the tendency was bound in any way to a feeling of love? But this wasn't the time to ponder such distractions.

'...So, I ask, what's the opposite of *you*?' Sam continued. 'Someone narcissistic, uncaring, self-absorbed, and that's *exactly* what I was seeing in you the other day.'

Lucy had to agree, she couldn't find fault in anything Sam had reasoned up to that point. 'So when do you think we should do this?'

'I'm not sure?' he said, sitting again to rest his excitement. He had a troubled look.

'What's the matter?'

He rocked on the seat. 'I'm just not sure we know enough of what we're getting ourselves into. I think I'm right about the handrails, well, actually, I'm *certain* I am. But it wouldn't hurt to see them first. And we need to find the kids and let them know what it is we plan to do.'

Lucy could see his point.

'We need to go through and set this up properly,' he continued, his expression turning resolute. '...Lucy, we have one chance at this, and it has to go right.'

'I agree.'

Sam stood. 'So let's go through tomorrow. I'll get some things we might need together. We'll find the kids, and explain what they need to do.'

Lucy nodded. 'Tomorrow it is then, let's make it midday. Mum's away all day.' Sam agreed.

They left. Sam made for his father's workshop to collect what they'd be needing. Lucy headed for home…

*

The day that had been, seemed to have passed in the blink of an eye, and hour as a minute.

Lucy lay in her bed, gazing through the ceiling, unable to turn her back on her thoughts.

She could hear the stuttering whistle of a tawny owl drifting in from the woods through the still night air. She rolled onto her back so she could better hear it, trying to use its haunted song to distract her from her worries.

A delicate breeze passed through the open window, tickling the hem of the curtains. Lucy watched them float gently on the breath of the midnight wind…

A blinking light caught her eye within the darkness over by the door to her room. She adjusted her gaze towards it…

It came again, the briefest of flashes, something shiny catching the light up in the corner of the room.

She lifted her head clear of the pillow and pushed her face towards the glinting. She peered into the darkness, straining to see…

A black spot materialised in the shadow, then started to expand like an ink blot, elongating towards the floor…

She heard a breath, and a chatter, then a salt-white face pushed out into the moonlight, staring directly into Lucy's terrified face.

A dry, black tongue lowered out of a mouth hanging long beneath a lifeless gaze, a hollow groan drifting from a protracting face, filling Lucy's paralysis with panic.

She tried to scream, but her desiccated throat remained silent.

The demon dropped slowly from the shadows, crawling down the wall. A woody clatter of horn shocked the silence as the heads of the bull and the ram begin fighting behind shoulders pulled taught with ill-intent.

The end of its tongue lowered towards Lucy's horrified face, ashen white and drooling with terror.

The tip of the tongue started to oscillate in front of her mouth, tasting the fear-drenched breath from Lucy's muted screams. It drew the tongue back in, bringing its face down to Lucy's ear. She shook beneath its arid stare…

Its thin-lipped mouth stretched further open, and it leaned in, exhaling its cold, rotting breath – 'Assssssmodeussssss…'

Lucy jerked awake! Beaded sweat soaking her pillow. 'Holy shit!' she muttered, sitting up on her elbow.

She looked up to the corner of the room, but there was nothing there. She exhaled, attempting to abandon the moment with a dismissive laugh, but failed. She leaned out and flicked on her bedside lamp, far too afraid to contemplate more sleep. She decided to read instead – far less frightening a proposition.

Sliding her bedside drawer open, she spied her copy of *The Handmaids Tale* and reached for it…

A bony hand thrust from inside the open drawer, and wrapped its spidery fingers around her wrist. She screamed!

A long, emaciated leg extended from the opening, folded at the knee, and lowered its foot onto the carpet.

The drawer slid further out, revealing a gaunt, skeletal face grinning up at her.

Wiry arms began unfurling from either side of its grimacing features, unfolding like a birthing insect, and reached out towards her…!

Lucy flinched awake again. 'Jesus fucking Christ!' she cried…

THIRTEEN

A PLAN

SAM PACED THE GRAVEL at the base of the staircases that rose to Hobswyke, flinching the occasional nervous look up to the windows.

If it wasn't for the existence of the children, he would arrange to concrete over the pools, and dump as many tons of gravel on top as was available. Then he'd probably make a start destroying all of the mirrors.

Lucy hoved into view, walking up the lawn towards him, her arrival a most welcome sight given his current slavery to his nerves.

'Did you find everything you wanted?' Lucy asked, as she crunched across the gravelled clearing.

Sam nodded, shaking a full leather tool bag towards her as proof. 'I've brought everything I think we'll need, plus some other stuff, just in case.' He opened the bag to show her. Lucy peered in: there was a cordless grinder and cutting discs, a hacksaw and spare blades, knives, wire, wire cutters, zip ties, pliers, torches, and a sink plunger.

'What's that for?' she asked with a mocking frown, nodding a furrowed brow towards the plunger.

'I-I don't know. I bought it just in case… Well you never know, do you?' he replied.

Lucy smirked…

Sam frowned, taking the plunger from the bag and placing it on the ground. 'It was just a thought,' he said.

Lucy chuckled fondly at the vermilion hue flushing his cheeks. 'You *do* think of everything,' she said affectionately into his embarrassment. 'Come on then. Let's do this.'

They walked to the handrail, and were faced with the bleak reality of having to descend into that frightening world again, but this time, fully aware of the livid entity residing on the other side.

Lucy blew hard though pursed lips, clutching a hand to her stomach.

'Are you going to be okay?' asked Sam. 'Do you think you can do this?'

Lucy nodded. 'I'll be fine, once I'm through, I just had a pretty rough night, that's all.' She winced a less than convincing smile in his direction, he reciprocated the gesture.

If it wasn't for the children, Sam would end this now. But the reality was, discovering the existence of Jill and Jack had seeded in them both a knowledge they'd simply be unable to live with, unless acted upon.

'So what do we do?' Lucy asked, leaving the planning to Sam – having never once beaten him at a game of Risk.

'What I think is this… I go through first and check the coast is clear, and if it is, we both cross over.' He shook the leather holdall in his hand. 'I stow the bag of tools in the undergrowth, somewhere close by the staircase, then we'll go and search for the kids. I think we should check the gatehouse first of course, you know, because it's the least dangerous option.'

'And if they're not there?'

'Then I guess we'll have to check the hall.'

Lucy agreed. 'Sounds good. Well, actually, sounds terrifying. But let's do it anyway.'

Sam managed to laugh. 'Let's just hope they're at the gatehouse, aye.'

Lucy nodded.

'I did at one point think that maybe we should split up,' he said, 'to be more efficient, make better use of the short window of time we have. But, then I though, no.'

'No!' Lucy asserted in complete agreement, shaking her head nervously. 'Terrible idea.'

Sam hoisted the bag of tools onto his shoulder. 'Come on then, let's get this over and done with.' He stepped through the gap and readied himself, then started to make his way down the stones to the water…

The bag of tools also swung towards the side of the pool as he dropped away, as though there was a large magnet buried within the masonry. Sam couldn't help finding fascination in the fact the tools didn't just fall from the bag into the water, but he shook it away, needing keep fully focused on their mission.

He leaned towards the inky surface, and carefully pushed his face through the film… He opened his eyes, but he could see nothing, just blackness? Then he realised, the sky this time was lightless, it appears to be night. He pulled back out.

'It's dark?' he said, turning to Lucy.

She frowned. Then her brow softened. 'Of course, everything is *opposite* to here, so it'll be midnight there.'

'Damn it!' Sam muttered.

'No, it's okay, it might actually help us?' Lucy suggested.

Sam tweaked the corners of his mouth and seesawed his head in contemplation. 'Maybe. You might have a point…' He looked down at the still, onyx surface with mild uncertainty, contemplating their options. 'Okay. Let's do it.'

He grabbed a torch from the bag, and pushed his face through again, this time, allowing his eyes a few moments to acclimatise…

The dank decay of the other world gradually resolved into view as his pupils widened to the darkness, revealing a greyscale of overgrowing landscape and crumbling architecture existing in a morbidly silent world. A world that had never courted laughter, birdsong or the midnight calls of foxes.

He hung still for a few moments, looking up at the handrail silhouetted against the flat-grey sky, unable to see or hear anything untoward, so quietly, he passed through.

He dipped his hand back into the fluid, and indicated to Lucy to follow

Her body eventually split the fluid and rose through the film. She saw Sam crouched behind the handrail, scanning the grounds for anything they wouldn't desire to encounter… She joined him.

'Can you see anything?' she asked in whispered tones.

He shook his head. 'No, it seems to be clear…' He took a last look around. 'Come on.'

He rose from behind the safety of the railing, and climbed over. He offered a helping hand to Lucy, all the time keeping a vigilant look out. She swung her long legs over and dropped onto the steps.

'Hang on there a sec,' he said, quietly stepping away and lowering the bag of tools into the thick undergrowth at the base of the staircase. He quickly grabbed the other torch before covering it over. 'Here,' he said, handing it to Lucy, 'only turn it on if you absolutely need to – okay?'

'Okay,' she agreed.

Sam held still, gazing up at all the windows, but he saw nothing. 'Come on,' he whispered, 'let's go…'

They made their way through the grounds, keeping their eyes peeled for any kind of movement: the hasty passing of a fleeting child darting through the darkness, or the contorted limbs of a rage-filled entity striding its fury towards them.

Although cloaked in darkness, they could still see a subtle luminance emitting from the concave sky above them. 'Is there a moon, above all that?' asked Lucy.

'I don't know,' he answered, 'but I doubt it.'

Lucy studied the clouds again. 'So what makes the light here?'

He joined her in looking skyward. He thought she'd asked a very good question, and as clever as he was, he was unable to muster a single theory to push forward.

They eventually rounded a cluster of hedges and saw the gatehouse ahead of them. They crouched low in the foliage, allowing the frigid atmosphere to settle into total silence before they crossed…

'It doesn't look like there's anyone there?' Lucy whispered.

Sam shrugged. 'We'll have to take a look anyway.' Lucy nodded in agreement.

They rose, cautiously creeping across the overgrown lawns that more resembled meadow than grounds to a stately home, and made their way towards the house, scanning the widows for any signs of movement.

Lucy climbed the steps and tried the door, it was still unlocked. 'Sam,' she hissed under her breath, swinging the door into the lobby. He stepped up to join her, and they both made their way inside…

Lucy crept through the lobby area and leaned her face into the drawing room. 'Jill…? Jack…?' she called, but there was no response.

Sam moved to the base of the staircase. The steps climbed

away from his tentative feet into total darkness, like they were being swallowed by the house.

He took the torch from his pocket and switched it on, swinging the beam up towards the landing area.

The light's blinding beam reflected off the midnight mist hanging in the air, turning the shadow into a glaring white fog.

He began slowly climbing the creaking steps, swinging the beam around the murk, picking off details of the stairwell.

As he neared the top, his torchlight illuminated a side table he remembered seeing in the stables.

A lone, black figure suddenly darted across the landing in front of him. His hand shook and the torch fell from his startled fingers.

He scrambled to pick it up again, fumbling his panicked hands towards the swinging beam of the rolling light.

He managed to take it up again, and swung the trembling beam back up the stairwell. It fell on the features of an ashen face peering down at him, his lip curled over his teeth, and he stumbled back a few steps. He steadied his hand and directed the beam back to the top – the face was gone.

'*Lucy…!*' he hissed, anxious eyes glued to the landing.

She appeared at the bottom of the steps. 'What is it?'

'I-I saw something,' he replied, swinging the light back up towards the landing. The beam illuminated a different face, staring down at them both, eyes wide, looking frantic.

The face suddenly rose and burst forwards out of the darkness, thundering down the stairwell towards him.

Sam faltered back, his torch light stuttering across the charging figure.

It reached out towards him, and clapped its hands across the end of his light.

A small sliver spilled from between the cloaking fingers,

and Sam could see, in the under-light of the faint, orange glow, Jill's face just inches from his own.

'Oh Jesus Christ!' he whispered, slumping forwards in relief. He switched off the torch and dropped it from the cup of her hands, sliding it into his pocket. 'Bloody hell, Jill!' He despaired – instinctively wrapping his arms around her.

She stiffened in his arms the same way Jack did the day before, but then allowed the joy she felt at seeing them again show. She folded her tiny arms around him, clinging tight.

He took the torch from his pocket again, and turned it on, cupping his hand over the lens to douse the light.

'You came back,' she said, beaming, the surprise in her voice palpable.

'Of course we came back, we *said* we would.'

She looked him in the face, a look racked with gratitude. Sam could tell, in her world, no one had ever kept a promise before, and in reality, neither of them were probably aware of what a promise even was.

Lucy carefully climbed the stairs to join them, half feeling her way through the gloom, half trusting in her familiarity of the space.

'Was that Jack?' asked Sam, nodding his under-lit face towards the top of the steps.

Jill nodded. 'Come with me,' she instructed, turning and making her way up to the top floor. They followed…

They walked along the landing and turned into what, on the other side, would be Lucy's room. Lucy's face lit up. 'It's *my* room,' she muttered excitedly to Sam, as they entered the dimly lit space.

The children had placed a few candles about the room, and hung heavy blankets across the windows to stifle any light.

Sam recognised many of the scavenged objects he'd seen blanketing the loft space at the Hall; they'd obviously brought them across to add some sense of familiarity to the room. He smiled.

The children were sitting on a heavy-set, brass-framed bed, tarnished to a deep powdery-brown.

Lucy wandered in behind Sam and looked about the room, fascinated by seeing the mirrored version of a space so wholly familiar to herself. 'So, you've moved here then have you?' she asked.

The children nodded with what Lucy was sure must be the first show of any emotion resembling joy that she could remember either of them exhibiting.

Lucy ambled about the space, inspecting the details of their decorating. 'Did you know,' she said, turning to face their watching faces. 'On the other side, where we're from, this would be *my* room,' she explained. The children's faces lit up, seeming to find genuine joy at the tenuous connection.

'So listen,' Sam interjected, trying to maintain some level of focus, 'we've got a plan. We're going to try and get you two out of here.'

The children looked to each other, then gave a less than convincing nod in response. 'What? You would rather stay here? In this shithole?' Sam snapped. 'You'd rather stay in this damn place, hiding away like mice from some bloody creature that wants to do you harm. Well, do you!?'

'Sam! *Control* it!' Lucy snapped, seeing his anger beginning to fray again – and so soon. 'They know *nothing* but this world! And nothing of *our* world!'

She turned her attention to Jill, as the apparent stronger of the pair. 'You have to trust me, *us*, this *is* the best thing for you both. This place,' she said, looking about the room, 'you don't realise it yet, but this place is horrific, it's terrifying, and you *need* to trust us on this – okay? It's for the best, for you both.'

Jill forced an anaemic smile. 'Okay.'

'I'm sorry,' said Sam, shamed by his loss of control. But neither he nor Lucy had any idea of the sheer levels of unconstrained, thunderous fury the two children had had to endure through the entirety in their sad little lives. Lives where the closest thing they'd experienced to love, was managing to successfully hide from the hate.

Sam stepped in. 'Look, I don't know how the hell to judge what a day is in this place? But we're going to come for you tomorrow. I assume it'll be dark again like it is now, but we're not really sure, so just *stay here.* Don't leave for anything, okay?'

He reached into his jacket pocket and pulled out cakes and sandwiches he'd made for them. 'Here, I brought these for you to eat.'

The hungry children instantly dived on them, trying to work out what the clingfilm was.

Jack managed to break though first, and took an eager bite. His face twisted out of shape and looked up at Sam with what can only be described as disgust.

'Erm, yeah. Trust me, they're fine,' he said, 'better leave them for an hour or two, and I have a feeling they'll taste just amazing.'

'Two hours?' Jill asked. 'What is – "two hours"?'

'Oh God, yeah, I forgot,' he despaired. 'Erm? Two hours issss…?' He abandoned his attempt. 'Look, just leave them till later, and they'll be fine, alright? Trust me.'

They agreed.

Lucy started to toy her fingers through her hair again, her eyes searching about the room for a mirror. Sam rolled his eyes. 'Right, we have to go. We'll be back tom…' He sighed. 'We'll be back when it goes dark again. Just wait for us.'

Sam turned to gather Lucy up. 'Come on you,' he ordered. He stopped and shone a parting smile back at the children. 'See you real soon…'

They both left the house and made their way tentatively through the grounds, keeping a watchful eye out…

They reached the clearing again, and darting across to the staircase, Lucy began clambering over the handrail.

'Hang on,' whispered Sam, taking a step back from the ornate railings.

He looked up to check the windows were clear of prying eyes, but he could see nothing.

He carefully covered the end of his torch, and quietly turned it on.

The air was deathly quiet. Sam allowed a sliver of light to escape through his fingers, then began searching for the snake and venom design he'd seen hidden among the intricacies of the other handrail…

He found it. It looked exactly the same, except the venom on this occasion was fronting a different symbol. He shuffled across and twisted his eyes to see what it was… He saw it was also an 'Ankh', but this time, it was inverted. He now felt certain his theory must be correct.

Sam searched his pocket for a stick of chalk and shuffled in closer. He leaned back and began to study the railings, marking where he'd need to cut to allow the children to pass…

A hand suddenly thrust though the bars and grabbed the end of the torch.

Sam jolted at the sight of Lucy's face pressed hard up against the railings, illuminated red by the torch light passing through the skin of her fingers. She had a finger pressed hard across her lips, begging him to be quiet.

She turned terrified eyes towards the house. Sam slowly rotated his head to see what she was looking at…

The doors were open, but there was no one stood in the opening. Then Sam saw movement. A dark mass hunched on the floor of the doorway. It started to crawl forwards into what little light there was.

Sam felt the torch start to shake in his hand. He slowly moved his thumb to the switch, and turned it off.

The figure crawled towards them, sniffing the ground, then turned its face skyward to smell the air.

Sam stiffened. He recognised it, it was the same emaciated figure that had come for them the first time. He could hear it breathing. It began extending its bony limbs down the long staircase towards him.

Sam slowly dropped a hand to the ground, his panicked fingers feeling around for a stone. He took one up in his hand.

He watched, breath held, waiting for the Thing to turn its gaze away.

It continued striding towards him, sniffing, tasting the air.

It turned briefly towards the opposite side of the staircase, sniffing the stagnant air. Sam took his chance, tossing the stone skyward over the entity, but as it left his fingers, it almost stopped dead in mid-air.

The rock began a creeping arc through the dank, midnight sky, all the time, the figure still sniffing out the intruders hiding within the obsidian blackness.

The Thing began stretching its sinewy limbs down the staircase towards him once again. Sam tried shrinking back from the advancing horror, his frantic eyes scanning desperately for a place to run. He cowered as close to the twisting bars as he could, attempting to merge within them.

There was a sharp *clack* from the top of the steps as the stone slowly recoiled off the sandstone slab. The entity spun round violently, and scuttled up the staircase towards the sound…

Sam rose on quivering legs, and leaped silently over the railing, dropping down next to Lucy. They both watch as the Thing examined the pebble as it slowly spun through the air.

Sam waved a bladed hand to Lucy to make her way to the pool. She shuffled forwards, carefully aligning her feet, then crept silently down the wall, lowering herself through the pool.

Sam turned back to take one last look... The arachnid figure was right behind him, face leering through the tangle of railings.

Sam faltered back and began to quake. He attempted to back silently towards the pool, the creature sniffing the air, thrusting its face between the bars towards him... It sensed he was there, hiding in the dark.

Sam quietly turned his crouching body, carefully aligning his feet with the first steps on the path back to his world, all the time, his anxious eyes locked firmly on the abomination searching him out.

Suddenly – he burst into urgent strides down the wall.

The entity exploded from its placidity, emitting a stinging, sonorous scream towards his fleeing prey. It clambered violently at the bars, but seemed unable to climb over, held fast by the same invisible force that had held the children back.

Sam dropped away from its thrusting reach and deafening wail, striding long and urgent.

He pressed his whole body into the ebony milk – sinking through it into blinding sunlight.

FOURTEEN

TO PLUCK FLOWERS FROM DEAD SOIL

WITH LEGS TREMBLING, Sam just about managed to stumble across the stones to safety. He saw Lucy across the way, bent double, vomit splashing from her gaping mouth.

'We've got to get them out of that place!' she coughed – still retching, 'we have to get them away from that – that – *thing*!' She heaved another stomach load of her revulsion onto the ground.

Sam walked across and gently rubbed her back, Lucy could feel his hand shaking through her spine. 'Oh Christ, Sam, what are we going to do?'

He fortified his tattered resolve. 'Get them out of there,' he said – more determined than ever, 'then we'll concrete over the pools, and burn the bastard place down.'

Lucy swiped the back of her hand across her mouth, and stood upright. Her stomach felt tight from convulsing. She clawed her fingers across her gut. 'We're doing it tomorrow!' she proclaimed. 'I can't go another night without sleep.'

Sam agreed. 'We'll get them out, don't you worry. Tomorrow it is.'

They both left to find Hilly, to fill her in on everything that had happened…

Hilly sat on her bed in the core of the story, listening, her knees pulled tight to her chest, shielding herself from the horrendous details of their last visit… 'Do you really think you can get them away from the monster?' Hilly asked.

Lucy and Sam glanced at each other, trying not to exhibit their very real doubts. 'Yes,' said Sam, forcing razor-sharp determination, 'we *will*.'

Lucy pondered Hilly's slightly naive use of the word 'monster'. She'd not herself thought of the wiry figure precisely in those terms, the seething hatred she'd felt emanating from its very core had somehow felt incredibly human in its spiralling levels of detestation and loathing, and because of that, neither she nor Sam had considered monster a word they would naturally chose to describe it. But there was no doubting how veraciously the word fitted.

'So, will I get to meet them?' asked Hilly.

Sam smirked, slightly confused by the question. 'Well of course you will. What did you think, we're going to hide them away and refuse ever to let them meet anyone else?'

Hilly thought about his mildly cynical response. 'But isn't that kind of what's already happened to them?'

Sam was stumped by the poignancy of her words, however accidental that poignancy may have been, they doused the flames of his sarcasm. 'I suppose you're right. I guess in a way, it is kind of a prison for them. It's easy to forget that I guess. I'm sorry.'

They all sat quietly in contemplation of the terrible lives the children had been forced to live. 'What do you think they're doing right now?' asked Lucy.

Sam shrugged. 'I dunno, eating I hope. The food should taste passable by now.'

'You don't think that creature could find them, do you?' asked Hilly.

Sam shrugged again – failing to mask his doubts. 'Well. Let's hope not.'

Again, the three of them sat in quiet contemplation. 'Could you describe it to me? The monster?' requested Hilly.

Sam sagged, resenting being asked to relive the most terrifying event he'd ever had to face. But he *was* her brother, and he realised that if the shoe was on the other foot, he'd certainly be asking her to do the same. So he tried. 'You're much better with words than I am, but I'll have a go.'

He closed his eyes and dropped his chin to his chest, taking himself back to the base of the staircase in the other world... In his mind, he's was looking up at the house, it's dark, and he can see the creature in the doorway, crawling slowly towards him.

'There's something slightly human about it, but I'm sure it is not human!' he explained. 'Its face – it's strange, it's full of anger, but somehow, it looks lifeless at the same time. I guess that's because I can see no emotion in its eyes.' His brows furrowed. 'But it hates me... I can *feel* that, its hatred fills the air whenever it looks at me. But I don't think I've done anything to deserve it.'

'I think it hates everything,' interjected Lucy, 'haven't you felt there's some sort of resentment inside it?'

'Yes! I *have*. That's the right word, "resentment".'

'But what does it actually look like? You know, physically?'

'A bit like a spider,' said Lucy, 'but as Sam said, in some ways, it's also kind of human, but its arms and legs are thin and spindly, and it crawls around like an insect.'

'But I've seen it run, too,' Sam interjected, 'like we would. But yeah, Lucy's right, it is totally like an insect.'

Hilly screwed her face up and pulled the bed clothes tight around her neck. 'It sounds horrid.'

Her brother smirked ironically. 'Yeah, and then some.'

Lucy's mind drifted… 'I wonder if it's another demon, like the one I saw in the library?'

'Maybe,' Sam responded. 'At first I thought it might be that magician guy, Mallette, but, nah.'

Lucy clutched a hand to her stomach, not sure if the aching she was feeling was hunger, or the after effects of vomiting her fears so violently. She concluded it was probably an amalgamation of both. 'I need to get back and make an appearance,' she said, 'else Mum'll start getting suspicious, and start watching me wherever I go. And until we've got Jill and Jack out from there, I can do without that.'

'Alright,' Sam agreed…

*

The light, once again, descended into night, revealing a crisp sky blanketed with stars. Lucy sat in the kitchen alone, rushing to finish her dinner.

She rose from the table, still chewing the last mouthful of food, and slotted her plate in amongst the rest of the dirty dishes crowding the sink.

Immersed in thought, she threaded herself into her favourite red cardigan… 'I'm just popping out to see Sam and Hilly,' she shouted to her mother, who was standing ironing while watching telly in the living room, 'I'll clean the dishes as soon as I get back, okay? I won't be too long.'

She shut the front door and galloped down the steps before her mother had a chance to instigate any unwanted interrogation. She made her way down the bank towards the Fletcher's house…

Lucy exited the trees and strode energetically towards the cottage. She heard Sam in his father's workshop, she recognised the particular way he tended to mumble to himself when he did anything that required concentration.

The door was hanging slightly ajar, so she peered in, then slid through the gap into the light. 'Whatcha doing!' she shouted.

He lurched into full Moro reflex, tossing a screwdriver up into the rafters. He spun around to the fanfare of the tool clattering back to earth. 'Shit, Lucy! What are you trying to bloody do to me.'

She giggled like a naughty child. 'Sorry, I couldn't help myself.'

'Well, try!' he replied.

'I've been so worried about tomorrow, I thought I'd cheer myself up by making you jump. Anyway, what's wrong with you?' she asked. 'I thought you'd find it funny.'

'Yeah, well I didn't, you great plonk!' He shook his head and laughed. 'Bloody pillock.'

She laughed along with him. 'What are you up to?'

'Oh, not a lot. Just checking there isn't anything else we might need for tomorrow's rescue attempt.'

Lucy stepped up next to him and began picking through the objects scattered across the worktop. 'I just keep wanting to wake up and find this has all been nothing but a bad dream.'

'Yeah, I know, same here,' he said, 'but unfortunately, it isn't.' He nudged her with a matey shoulder. 'So, we'll just have to do what we can to fix it, aye.'

'*Can* we fix it?' she asked, toying with a box of screws.

The corners of Sam's mouth twisted with indecision, and he shrugged. 'I don't know? But this Mallette didn't exist until he was born, so I guess it's not unreasonable to imagine he can be made to go away again.'

Lucy put the screws down. 'Let's hope so.'

Sam drew a folded piece of paper from his back pocket and handed it to Lucy. 'This is the plan for tomorrow, it's not overly complicated or anything, but read it a few times later on, so we're both singing from the same song sheet.' It was a term his father used a lot, but it was the first time he'd ever had a chance to use it himself.

'Thanks,' she said, slipping the piece of paper into her pocket.

She turned to face him, and wrapped her arms around him. The close proximity took him aback.

He put down a roll of wire and reciprocated the gesture, engulfing her in the gentlest embrace he had ever given anyone.

She could feel the warmth of his cheek against her ear. 'I love you,' he whispered – barely audibly.

Lucy allowed the words to float through her mind for a time, before pulling back from the hold, and looking him square in the eye. 'What did you just say?'

Sam stuttered out of the moment, 'I-I just – you know. You're my friend and all that, and – and I wanted to tell you that, that I love you.' He winced an embarrassed smile.

Lucy was surprised to find herself feeling disappointed by his response. But she was *sure* the words were delivered with true intent, and she discovered herself hoping that they were. 'Look, I'll see you tomorrow,' she said, 'if we get this done, we can start trying to forget about that place.'

Sam nodded. 'Okay, poop,' he said, wishing he had the nerve to tell her the trueness of his feelings.

She hovered expectantly before him, waiting to see if he had anything else to say… but he offered nothing. She sagged… 'Well, goodnight then,' she said, turning to leave.

Sam extended a hand towards her, aching to call her back. But he swallowed his emotions, and watched her weave through the gap into the warm, night air…

*

Helen stood at the kitchen sink washing the breakfast pans, stooping to look out of the window at the sky... It was the first morning of recent times where she's been presented with a blanket of cloud. But they seemed thin to her, and she was sure the sun would eventually burn them away.

Lucy pushed her breakfast around her plate like a croupier, her stomach squirming at the uncertainty of what the outcome of the day would be.

She attempted to force herself to eat something, alive to the need to keep her strength up for the sake of Jill and Jack. She managed to dry swallow a few mouthfuls, but she'd only managed a few hours' sleep during a night of doubts: duvet pulled up tight to her neck, both side lights blazing, but at least the night passed free of the nightmares that had plagued the one previous.

She scooped the rest of her breakfast into the bin, and agitated a sponge around the plate.

She checked the clock, and rushed upstairs to get herself ready, ready to meet Sam at Hobswyke...

*

A nervous Lucy eventually reached the hall, but Sam was nowhere to be seen. She'd purposely contrived to arrive late so she wouldn't have to be alone with the house, but her efforts appeared fruitless.

She crunched across the gravelled clearing towards the sweeping staircase, scanning for signs that she wasn't alone.

She deliberately tried avoiding looking directly at the house for fear of catching sight of something watching her from behind one of the grime-tinted windows, thankful at least that it was broad daylight, and not the dead of night.

'Sam?' she called, listening for a reply, but nothing.

She turned her attention to the house, and noticed the main doors to the Hall were hanging slightly open. She stumbled back, tripping over her feet, feeling certain that they were closed the last time they were there.

She looked around, wondering who, or *what* could have opened them.

An unquenchable curiosity pulled her reluctantly up the long staircase towards the entrance, her eyes locked on the opening, blinkering herself from catching sight of any of the windows watching her approach.

Her gaze drifted up to the lunette above the doors, the horned cherubs hiding behind their heavenly counterparts appeared to be studying her with interest, peeking mischievously through drawn bows and fans of tiny feathered wings, watching her slowly climb the steps towards them. 'Stop it!' she snapped – her imagination beginning to run wild.

She reached the doors, shuffling her feet nervously along the gritstone step toward the parting…

Her approach was halted by the reciprocating slap of rushing footsteps echoing from inside the room. She stumbled back from the sound, its volume becoming alarmingly loud.

Sam burst from the doors, shocked at seeing Lucy right in front of him. '*Shit!*' he cried, rearing up sharply.

'God almighty!' Lucy complained. 'What the *hell* are you trying to do to me!'

'Sorry. Sorry,' he apologised – his countenance sheepish.

'What were you doing in there?' she asked, leaning around him to peek inside the marbled room.

'Nothing. Nothing at all. I-I was just looking around to check.'

'Check what?'

'I don't know, I guess I was trying to familiarise myself with the layout of the Hall again, just in case we have to go back in there, when we go across.'

He turned and looked in through the open door. 'You have to remember, I haven't been in Hobswyke for years, and I'm not as familiar with the place as you are.'

Lucy sensed him not being entirely honest with her, but struggled to make out in what way.

'Come on,' he urged, 'I think the sooner we get this done…' He turned, and pulled the large doors closed, then joined Lucy to make their way down the staircase.

He could feel her suspicions scolding his ear. 'Ahh good, you wore dark clothing,' he said, trying to distract her from her burning curiosity, 'so you *did* get my text then – excellent.'

Lucy couldn't quite make him out, so decided to let it go, there being far more important matters looming on the horizon to deal with.

Sam tightened the straps on his rucksack in readiness. He wore camouflaged cargo trousers and the darkest green top he could find.

They stepped up to the break. Sam took his copy of the plan nervously from his pocket and spun to face Lucy like a soapbox orator.

'So, we're going to do this kind of the same way we did it yesterday, okay? I go first to check it's safe to pass across, then you follow.' Lucy nodded. 'We check to see if the coast is clear, then we jump over the handrail and make our way to the gatehouse.' Lucy nodded again, Sam slid his finger down the page to the next row of bullet points.

He continued, 'We collect the children and make our way back to the bushes across from the front of the Hall. I leave *you* and the kids there to hide and wait for me, then *I* go round to the far side of the Hall and set up the diversion.' He turned a look over his shoulder to his rucksack. 'Then, hopefully, while that *thing* is distracted, I can quickly cut through the handrail and get us all out of there.'

'Sounds good,' Lucy confirmed.

Sam folded the paper and slipped it back into his pocket, drawing two miner's style head torches out of the same pocket and slipping one around his head. He handed the other one to Lucy. 'I know it's not particularly fashionable, but put this on, just in case we need to use our hands.'

She examined it to see where you turn it on, then clipped it around her head, feeling for the switch to check it worked...

Sam took his place in the break. 'Are you ready then?'

'Yes. Believe it or not, I actually am!' she chuckled, nervously.

'Come on then...'

Lucy watched as Sam made his way steadily down the wall, hopefully for the last time.

He dipped his face through the ebony film, then waved her through.

Lucy rose from the pool into darkness again, but this time, it felt different, the air she drew into her lungs was icy cold and crystallised with frost.

Sam was already crouching behind the handrail, taking a look around... She rose up the wall and joined his side.

'*Jeeesus* it's cold,' she complained, rubbing her hands over her arms. Her eyes were transfixed on the breath drifting in slow motion from their mouths, hanging almost motionless in the frosty air, before gradually melting away into the darkness like salt crystals in water.

Sam's frozen breath had built up around his face. He swiped his hand through the air to clear his line of vision. Lucy copied him.

'Come on,' he whispered.

They both silently clambered over the handrail and

crouched on the other side. 'Wait there,' he said, quickly stepping across to lift the tool bag clear of the undergrowth. He was relieved to find it still there, and placed it carefully down adjacent to the planned escape route.

They both scanned the lightless windows for anything resembling a face pressed up against the glass. But they saw nothing, and finally set off for the gatehouse…

The frost-encrusted grass crunched beneath their tentative footsteps, it sounded loud in the static air. 'I hope they're okay,' said Lucy.

'I'm sure they'll be fine,' he replied, 'try not to worry.'

Lucy's eyes scanned the landscape as they made their way across the grounds. How different everything looked coated in ice-white crystals, giving the place a magical look, it helped counter the natural air of foreboding that normally sullied the atmosphere. She shivered.

Sam heard Lucy's jaw chattering, and dropped back to be level with her, wrapping his arm around her shoulders. 'Is it the cold? Or are you afraid?' he asked in whispered tones.

She stammered a laugh. 'Both!' Sam chuckled.

They eventually reached the gatehouse and began climbing the steps, then they stopped; the door was hanging wide open.

They looked at each other with hardened eyes. 'Maybe they'd been out and forgot to close it again?' said Sam.

Lucy twisted a look of doubt back at him. 'That doesn't sound like them, they always seem so careful.'

They stepped tentatively through the door, looking and listening for signs of movement.

They made a cursory scan of the kitchen, then the living room. Nothing seemed out of place.

They started slowly up the staircase, their cheeks wincing at every *creak* that stabbed through the silence. Sam shrouded the end of his torch again, half expecting to see two tiny faces appear on the landing – but the faces never came.

'Where *are* they?' Lucy muttered.

'I don't know. I told them to stay here?'

They stepped quietly onto the landing and tiptoed towards Lucy's room. No light was spilling from the open door.

Sam rounded the frame and shone his hand torch into the gloom of the bedroom, painting the walls with the disk of light, their eyes transfixed as it meandered through the space. It drifted along the wall and across an old piece of furniture topped with dust-laden ornaments. Past a painting hanging crooked from the peeling wallpaper. They saw a cluster of unlit candles, and balls of discarded clingfilm.

Sam swung the torchlight to the centre of the room. Crumpled sheets hung off the side of the unmade bed, and cushions lay scattered, but there was no sign of the children?

'I *told* them to wait here,' Sam whispered, stepping in and looking around.

'Something's not right,' Lucy hissed, shaking her head, 'something's happened.'

A loud *crack* emitted from the corner of the room. Sam spun his light towards it. It fell on a large, bow-fronted wardrobe.

The beam began to shake. Lucy extended her arm and placed a reinforcing hand on his shoulder.

They both shuffled slowly towards the corner. Sam frantically painting the light around all of the darkest crevices.

The wardrobe suddenly shifted towards them. They shied away – startled.

Lucy started to pant with panic. The wardrobe shifted again, the floorboards creaking beneath the weight.

Sam snapped his head around to spot the door, readying himself to run.

'*Lucy?*' came a muffled voice drifting from deep within the shadows.

Lucy baulked at the sound of her own name… 'J-Jill? I-Is that you?' she asked.

They both shuffled guardedly towards the corner of the room, holding each other's hand. They tentatively peeked behind the wardrobe… Jill and Jack's anxious faces peered up at them, squeezed in tight between the furniture and the wall.

Sam handed the torch to Lucy, and heaved the wardrobe aside, the children crawled out into the room.

'What are you doing behind there?' asked Lucy.

Jill was looking suspiciously about the room. 'Was that you, before?' she asked.

'Before? What do you mean "before"?' Lucy replied.

Jill looked towards the door. 'Did you only just come in, or were you here before?'

'Well, no. We've only just arrived, just now…'

Jill shot petrified eyes back at Jack. He dropped to the ground and ducked behind Jill's legs. 'I-I think, *Him* was here!' she whispered. 'I think he was looking for us.'

Jill began to shake visibly. Lucy dropped to her knees and pulled the fear-drenched children hard into her.

Sam turned and crept cautiously towards the door. He rolled his face out into the corridor… He peered into the liquorice blackness cloaking the passage, listening intently for any sounds: the passing of a breath, the scraping of a nail, the creek of planted footsteps – but he could hear nothing.

'Okay, we're going!' he insisted. '*Now!*'

He flicked on his torch, and guided them along the passageway. They made their way quietly down the staircase to the main door. Sam held up a hand like a SWAT team operative, ordering them to wait.

He wiped a window clear with his sleeve, and peered through it, looking for movement outside.

He shook his head. 'Nothing,' he muttered, 'come on.'

They all made their way down the steps into the freezing air, dropping onto the path. They began making their way back across the grounds towards the Hall…

The sound of eight feet fracturing ice-glazed blades of grass seemed deafening within their attempts to move undetected. They all tried different ways to land a tread, but nothing seemed to silence their passage.

Sam turned to address the children as they walked.

'So, listen. I have to cut the railings so you can pass through. That's what was stopping me from getting Jack out the last time,' he explained to Jill. 'They seem to create some kind of force field that holds you both here.'

Jill took hold of Jack's hand, and gave his fingers a squeeze. She smiled into his worried eyes, somehow knowing that this unexpected detour to the path of their lives was for the best.

The amber-eyed children were starting to enjoy not only the company, but the attention they'd been receiving of late, a variety of attention neither of them could ever remember having received before. It felt nice to not be alone for once, and on the receiving end of these new things called 'kindness', and 'compassion'.

Sam turned again, and began explaining how the stepping stones worked. They nodded their understanding.

They all finally reached the row of bushes that faced the Hall from the far side of the clearing. 'Okay, you've got to stay here with Lucy, I have something I need to do first before we can get you out of this place.' The children indicated their understanding.

Sam peered out through the branches to check the house was free of watching faces... He felt certain their presence there remained undetected.

'Wait here,' he said, flinching a comforting smile towards their expectant faces. He turned to face Lucy, and pressed a heartfelt kiss against the soft pillow of her lips, just in case things went wrong, and he never got the chance again.

She smiled back at him, and flashed her eyes. 'I'll see you soon,' she asserted. 'There'll be another one of those waiting for you.'

He smiled, and nodded, then set off around the back of the hedgerow towards the far side of the Hall, weaving through as much undergrowth as he could to help travers unseen...

He came to a break in the bushes. There was about a thirty foot clearing to cross, right in front of the long windows of what on the other side would be the east wing.

He suddenly felt very detached from the others, a desperate sense of his own isolation.

A throb of his quickening heartbeat pounded in his ears as he crouched among the frost-encrusted branches.

'Come on!' He gritted his teeth hard. 'Pull your *shit* together!'

A feeling like he was drowning beneath the pressure of the tasks he'd set himself engulfed his faltering confidence. Tasks with no viable option to back out of.

After a time, breathing deeply, he managed to gather himself back together, reigning in his considerable anguish.

His head was now shrouded in a thick cloud of frozen breath. He swiped it away from his face, then directed laser-focused eyes across the clearing to the next explosion of undergrowth.

He sucked in air through his clenched teeth, steeled himself, then darted across the clearing…

Thirty feet felt like a mile in light of his exposure, but he eventually reached the far side and ducked in among leaves.

He took to a knee, and allowed himself a few moments to pacify his shaking ardour… 'Come on, come on, come on, come on, come on,' he muttered, breathing hard to clear the cluster of knots in his gut.

He scouted the grounds again. All still seemed to be clear. He set off again with revitalised resolve…

He spied an area of open ground in the distance that seemed perfect for his needs, a wide open space visible from the back of the Hall.

A crescent of trees surrounded the clearing – a wall of twisted wooden pillars to aid hiding his movements.

He skulked around behind the gnarled trunks and ducked behind the one in the centre.

He scooped the rucksack of his back and swung it to the front, opening it, and emptying the contents onto the ground.

He peeked around the trunk to make sure he was properly masked by the tree, then turned on his head torch.

Sam took a folded tarpaulin from the pile, and stuffed it back in his bag, then carefully unfolded a heavy, foil roasting dish, and placed it on the ground.

Covering his torch with his hand, he peered around the tree again to check the house… It still looked clear.

He dropped his hand from the light and tore open two boxes of firelighters, and emptied them into the foil dish.

Carefully, he took up a cluster of rockets that he had left over from the last bonfire night. He'd shortened the sticks and extended all of the fuses.

He took up the tray, and ran out into the clearing, placing it down on the grass, and began pushing the sticks of each rocket into the ground around the perimeter of the dish, draping each extended fuse over the edge of the foil.

Sam breathed deep, and struck a match, touching the slow-dancing flame to one of the firelighter blocks...

The flame eventually caught, and started slowly crawling over the rest of the cubes.

Sam could smell the benzine fumes rising from the dish as the orange glow began to flair in slow motion and expand across the tray.

Quickly gathering his things, he ran back to the tree. He shoved everything back into the bag, closing it up, and threading it over his shoulders...

He picked up a couple of rocks, and walked defiantly back into the clearing. He took aim, and tossed them hard towards one of the larger windows.

They left his hand and slowed, spinning gradually through the air towards the waiting pane of glass.

He turned, and sprinted for the hedges, snaking his way back through the undergrowth towards where he'd left the others...

Sam arrived back and ducked down beside them. They all jumped at his sudden appearance.

'*Shit,* Sam!' Lucy fizzed. She took a calming breath. 'Everything okay?'

He pressed a finger to his lips to silence her, and pointed towards the sky, instructing them to listen with a tap to his ear... They all hung motionless, staring at the ground – waiting.

Suddenly, the silence was shattered by a crashing sound from the far side of the Hall. 'Let's go!' Sam instructed, rising through the leaves and sprinting towards the stone staircase. They all followed suit.

The main doors suddenly smashed open. They all froze, and dropped to the ground, lying utterly motionless in the chilled darkness.

Elongated limbs extended out of the shadows of the entrance, unfurling into the freezing air. The creature emitted a shrill scream into the night, and exploded from the door towards the far side of the hall.

It cascaded past them, just meters away, and scuttled off into the distance.

They all lay motionless until it was out of sight, then jumped up and sprinted for the steps.

Sam skidded to a halt and whipped the top of the tool bag open, grabbing the grinder.

He strode urgently and with conviction towards the railings, and turned it on, but nothing happened? He cycled the switch again, but the tool remained motionless.

Bewildered – he turned to Lucy. 'There's something wrong with it?' he hissed. 'It was working just fine in the workshop?!' Then he paused, and looked down at the grinder…

He felt a low-frequency vibration through his fingers, then the cutting disk began slowly rotating, gradually gathering speed. 'Oh shit!' he cried. 'Of course, it won't work here!'

He stuffed the grinder back in the bag, and took out the hacksaw.

A loud fizz rose slowly into the sky behind them. The children turned to look, as Sam began frantically sawing at the bars.

They watched as a rocket hissed skyward towards the blanket of oppression capping their world, then the sky lit up to the tune of a slow motion expansion of sparks and fizzing particles. A few moments later, a thumping wave of sound passed through them all, startling the children.

The light illuminated the plumes of iron particles floating

gently away from every frantic stroke of the hacksaw blade.

Sam finally made it through one of the heavy handrails, and dropped the blade down to a thin, twisting pillar beneath it, and began thrashing the saw again, his shoulders flooding with lactic acid.

Another slow-motion fizz reached for the sky, followed by an explosion of colour to mask the sound of the cutting.

Sam pumped the blade with everything he had, and with a clatter, the blade dropped through yet another railing.

He flexed the bars apart to free the saw, then shuffled across a few feet and began to cut down the other side.

There was another eruption of light above the Hall, another sonic wave expanding past them, echoing around the surrounding trees like a Gregorian chant.

Crackling particles spread and floated towards the ground, illuminating a long, seething figure watching them from the far corner of the house.

Jill screamed and threw herself in front of Jack. He began sobbing and scurried behind her legs.

Sam turned to look what the commotion was, and froze. He pressed his back up against the railings, and cursed.

The entity dropped to the ground and began striding towards them with conviction, then stopped, rotating its hateful gaze slowly towards the Hall.

Sam turned to see what was distracting it, and gasped! '*Noooooo!*' he screamed as he watched Lucy running for the house.

'Keep cutting!' she wailed. 'Don't you dare try to follow me, just *fucking* do it!'

She sprinted and leapt over the splintered fragments of what remained of the doors hanging off their twisted hinges, then turned, locking her eyes on the panel beneath the side table on the far end of the room, racing towards it with all the speed her legs could generate.

There was a thunderous crash right behind her, followed by a piercing scream that filled the entire room.

Her lip curled hard against her nose as she fought an impulse to cry.

She reached the table and dropped to her knees, sliding underneath its derelict opulence and slapping into the wall.

She could hear the thump of the thing barrelling towards her, wailing its anger at her audacity in invading its world.

Lucy fumbled desperately around the edge of the panel, not daring to look behind her. 'Come *on*!' she screamed. The reciprocating *slap* of approaching footsteps growing deafening.

The cover finally popped from the wall, and she tossed it behind her. It slid imperceptibly along the ground as she crawled in through the hole, fumbling her fingers at the torch on her head to turn it on.

She heard the thing step on the panel just as she managed to struggle to her feet, and begin rushing through the passage.

The skeletal figure clattered through the opening into the tunnel, scrambled to its feet, and began unfolding itself towards her. She screamed a scream that shredded her vocal chords!

She ricocheted through the narrow passageways, attempting to blinker herself from the horror following close behind, attempting to traverse its claustrophobic proportions as efficiently as she could, trying to keep one step ahead of the creature's advancing reach.

She sprinted through the narrow corridors, leaping and swinging through the pipework assault course.

Lucy turned to look behind her, the beam from her head torch stuttering across its face. It looked drawn and emaciated, with paper-thin skin sucked tight to its skull, sunken eyes burning her back with bristling loathing.

The horror of seeing its face kicked her legs into a higher

gear, and she sprinted from the frantic cacophony of smashing limbs clamouring right behind her shoulders.

She spied a fork in the passage ahead, and wondered which way to turn? The right hand branch looked much tighter, so she dived for it, smashing her right shin hard against a wooden baton.

Struggling to her feet, she limped away from the wailing figure trying to scramble through the hole. As thin as it was, it was still too big to slip through easily.

Lucy hobbled along the tunnel, turned a corner, as was met by a dead end! 'Oh shit, please! No!' she begged the seclusion. She started to weep. 'Nooo!' she cried, feeling desperately around the walls for any avenue of escape. The wailing began to louden – the thing was through, and on its way!

'*Oh my God!*' she sobbed through a tear-glazed face, sinking helplessly to the floor in acceptance of her end.

Then she noticed another timber panel spanning a hole next to her left knee. She erupted from her resignation, and hurled her shoulder hard against it, knocking it into a room. She crawled through into the candle-lit library!

There was a deep, thrashing rumble from somewhere behind the panelling, the thing fast approaching. Her panicked eyes scanned the room for a place to hide…

She swung her arms wildly through the pillars of candle wax caging her beneath the shelving, and hobbled across the room to the altar. She crouched down behind it, just as the first wiry limb began extending into the room.

She clapped her hands across her mouth, attempting to stifle the sounds of her heavy breathing, leaning across to peer around the stone… She could see the creature crouched by the hole, studying the room, sniffing the wax-infused air. It started to crawl into the space.

Lucy pulled back behind the altar. Her shoulder caught something hanging down. She quickly snapped her fingers around it to stop it swinging, then gently released a slim, leather strap.

She looked at her fingers. There were thick films of coagulated blood coating her digits!

She lifted her eyes along the cord, they rose to meet the face of a dog looking back at her. It's head hung limp off the edge of the ceremonial-stone, its throat cut.

She had to wrap both hands across her mouth to muffle her scream! Its blood-filled eyes stared lifelessly down at her, she turned away from the horror.

Lucy suddenly realised the creature was now just on the other side of the altar, creeping around its perimeter, looking for *her*. It lifted its face from the floor and sniffed at the fresh blood coating the stone.

Lucy shuffled around the base to keep on the opposite side from it, trying not to disturb the dozens of pet collars littering the ground.

She continued to circle the altar, keeping hidden from the beast, then noticed she was adjacent to the hole in the wall. She decided to make a run for it.

Stooping low, she dashed across the floor to the waiting tunnel, slinking through and taking a quick peek back inside the room… The thing didn't appear to have seen her.

She started to make her way back along the passage, shin bone stinging, trying to avoid treading on anything that might make a sound.

She gradually sped up her escape as she got further in and away from the room, until she was as close to a sprint as she could manage with a messed up leg.

She checked behind her, but couldn't see anything following, and turned back to the front, just in time to see the water pipe before it cracked her hard across the forehead. She landed on her back, barely conscious…

Her mind and vision swirled in a mist, eyes rolling in their sockets…

She could hear distant screams drifting through her scrambled thoughts, the core of which was the pain. The sharp, stinging pain.

The screams grew louder, and more piercing. Her eyes rolled down from beneath her fluttering lids, and she groaned back into reality…

The air was heavy with the livid howls of the advancing monstrosity. Lucy shook herself awake and staggered unsteadily to her feet.

She charged for the tight gap again and fought her way through. The thing lunged and wrapped its long bony fingers around the heal of her trainer, just as she managed to snap it out of reach.

She started climbing uneven rungs of pipework and timber that she recognised rose to Jill and Jack's old haunt.

The creature finally managed to force itself through, and started following her up the wall.

She screamed with panic at the sight of its contorted features rising from the dark, the sound of her fear fanning the flames of its boiling desire to tear her limb from limb.

Lucy's hands flailed towards the hole into the loft space as she stumbled through it, lashing her feet towards the thing's advancing grasp.

Staggering to her feet, she made for the other hole, ducking through just as the entity clattered into the loft space.

She rattled along the tight passage towards the other set of rungs, the monster bursting into the crawlspace behind her, and unfurling its tortured limbs in the direction of her escape.

She panicked, and her feet slipped off the damp pipework. She plummeted down the shaft, bouncing off the sides as she dropped away.

She landed awkwardly in a heap at the bottom of the chimney, her legs buckled beneath her. She was winded, her lips gulping at the air for breath like a hooked fish.

Lucy turned her dazed expression up to a blurred image of a drawn, skeletal face crawling down the shaft towards her...

A pair of hands suddenly extended through an opening behind her shoulders, and dragged her through the hole, she looked up, her vacant eyes seeing Sam's out-of-focus features looking down at her.

He dragged her clear and quickly kicked the tray of burning firelighters in through the hole. Jill and Jack ran forwards, tossing armfuls of dry kindling on top.

It caught, and slowly erupted, shooting slow-dancing flames up the shaft towards the screeching monster.

They helped Lucy to her feet, and carried her out of the coal store into the frozen air. 'Are you okay?' asked Sam.

She nodded, weakly. He hooked her arm around the back of his neck, and led her away.

They made their way around to the front of the house. Sam leading them all through the smashed doors into the entrance hall.

'Why are we going in here!?' slurred Lucy – still feeling scrambled. 'Why aren't we going to the pool?'

'I didn't managed to cut through the bars in time, I *had* to come and help you. But don't worry, I have another plan.'

He guided the three of them into the dining hall and slammed the doors behind him.

'Drag some furniture in front of *that*!' he ordered. Jill and Jack complied – pulling any pieces of furniture they could manage to move with their tiny frames across to the doors. Lucy shook her head clear, and stumbled across to help them.

Sam sprinted to the far end of the long room and strained to take down a large mirror from the wall, but he couldn't quite lift it. 'Lucy,' he shouted, 'I need you to help me.'

She shoved a side table against the doors, and limped to him on legs close to collapsing beneath her. But she summoned her remaining strength, and powered through.

'You have to help me get this down,' he cried, trying to heave the heavy mirror off its mountings.

She threw her shoulder beneath it, and lifted with everything she had left… The mirror popped from its hangers and they lowered it to the floor. Sam spun it around, and started dragging it towards the corner of the room. 'What are you doing?' Lucy asked. 'Why aren't we trying to get out of here?'

'*Shhhhh!*' Sam hissed, impatiently. 'What do you think I'm trying to do, will you just try and bloody trust me for once.' Lucy could see his anger begin to fray again, and decided not to antagonise him by asking anymore questions.

There was a loud bang from the doors. The children screamed, and winced back from the haphazard stack of furniture.

The creature was throwing itself wildly at the barricade, fingernails scratching manically at the wood.

Lucy watched Sam give the mirror a final shove into the corner of the room and look down into it. A look of amazement expanded across his face.

He swung his rucksack off his back, ripped the tarpaulin from it, and snapped it open.

Lucy limped across to the mirror and looked down into the reflection… But there was no reflection to be seen, at least not of her! Then she realised, she could see into Hobswyke Hall, just like looking through a window. She recognised the paintings, and the tapestries, hanging inverted on the walls beneath her amazed gaze. It was just the way her mother had described in her dream.

Lucy found it difficult to believe, but there it was, undeniable, lying at her feet in front of her.

Sam tossed the tarp across the mirror, completely covering the glass. 'Jill, Jack!' he shouted. 'Come on, we're leaving. *Now*!'

The entity had managed to force a small gap between the doors, and was halfway in, frantically clawing its gangly limbs through the narrow sliver of access to try to get to them.

The children ran to Sam. He pulled them in close and turned to grab Lucy.

He led them across the sheet into the centre of the mirror.

The entity finally managed to clamber over the stacked furniture, and slapped onto the ground, it rose and started to scuttle along the floor towards them.

Sam pulled them all in tight. 'Shit, Lucy! I hope this works!' he begged.

The creature broke into a full sprint straight towards them. Sam stamped a foot hard onto the glass, shattering it beneath them. They all began to drop through the floor, enveloped in the sheet. Everything went pitch black, and they all plummeted into total weightlessness…

FIFTEEN

A WHOLE OTHER WORLD

A PLUMMETING SACK-FULL of the unknowing drifted weightless for what felt like forever, clinging tightly together, tangled into a ball of limbs and torch-lit faces floating ethereally through a place unfriended by light, except what they'd brought with them.

Time seemed almost to have stopped. Sam turned his eyes slowly up towards the open end of the tarpaulin, the beam from his head torch catching shards of fragmented mirror spinning slowly in the open end of the enveloping sheet, falling along with them through whatever it was they were all passing through. But he could see nothing else, just the tumbling shards spinning and colliding in total darkness… Then he noticed a bright spot far in the distance. He couldn't make out it if it was going away from them, or they from it, but it continued to shrink into the *nothingness* until it was just a pinprick of light amidst the fragments of glass…

The shards began to accelerate their spin, and started drifting down towards them. They could all feel some form of gravity begin to load their limbs with weight.

The acceleration began increasing alarmingly. Time quickening.

Sam raised his arms and began trying to gather the edges of the tarpaulin tightly together, cocooning them from the jagged fragments hitching a ride.

The perceived speed continued to increase. 'Hang on!' Sam shouted, sensing that their fall may be nearing some kind of climax, else they may just continue to accelerate until their speed passed that of light itself, and their molecules just froze in the aether – locked together in a timeless state for all eternity.

They could began to hear a *tinkle* from the fragments of glass around the plummeting sack. The area around their feet started to glow light-blue, some kind of light source approaching from what they perceived to be beneath them.

Sam tightened his grip around the gathered tarp, and wrapped his free arm around the others.

The blue light suddenly intensified, illuminating the entire sack. They all instinctively braced.

There was an almighty *crash*! A brief impact jolting through their legs. They hung momentarily weightless, before the pull of gravity swung down through their shoulders, and they all thumped down onto something solid.

They remained static in their tangle of limbs, processing what they had all just experienced, trying in vain to relate it to something they may have felt before, but none of them succeeding.

'Is everyone okay?' asked Sam.

'We think so,' answered Lucy, speaking for the rest, her arms engulfing the children – their expressions a mixture of excitement, relief, bewilderment and hope.

Sam tentatively released the ends of the sheet… He'd been gripping it so hard his hand had cramped into a claw.

He heard pieces of glass sliding off the tarpaulin as he released it, and landing on what he desperately hoped to see. 'Be careful of the glass,' he said, slowly spreading the ends of the tarpaulin apart with his hands like the head of a flower.

Sam's face broke into a smile, then a grim, and he tentatively released a laugh laced with more relief than he can ever remember feeling in his entire life.

They all peered through the opening to see what so amused him… Lucy's face also brightened, and she joined in the relief-fuelled manic laughter, folding the sheet carefully away from the children, and rising triumphantly into the dining room of Hobswyke Hall.

Sam staggered to his feet. He pinched himself, checking he wasn't dreaming.

Lucy turned a face incandescent with joy towards him, wilting a look of gratitude into his red eyes and flinging her arms around his neck. She pressed her soft, round lips hard against his, it was only the second time in their entire lives their mouths had touched. Sam – riding on the joy of the moment – never wanted it to end…

Lucy pulled out of the hold. 'You saved us!' she cried. 'You did it! You fucking did it!' Her smile relaxed. She welled with ultimate gratitude and looked deep into his soul. 'You saved *me,*' she muttered into his adoring gaze, 'you saved my life, Sam…' She embraced him again, dropping her chin on his shoulder.

Lucy felt that Sam was shaking his head. 'No, Lucy… Any thanks goes to *you.* You were incredible, and *I*, and these two, will *never* know how ever to thank you. You're one brave lady.'

They squeezed their relief into each other's weary bones, their eyes slowly morphing back to turquoise and chestnut-brown.

Sam hoisted Lucy into his arms, and carried her across the sea of broken glass. They looked back at the shattered mirror pushed into the corner of the room. So that's what you were up to in here before.' She smirked. 'Bloody hell, Sam, you're amazing – do you know that? You think of everything.'

They turned to the children who were wandering about the room, drinking in the warmth of the light and atmosphere of their new world.

Jill was staring up at all the portraits lining the walls. Row upon row, stack upon stack of images of other people. Different faces from different eras, many more faces than she'd ever been given a chance to relate to in her life. She found the experience overwhelming.

Lucy limped up behind her, and rested her hand on her shoulder. 'Who are these people?' asked Jill.

'*These,* are my ancestors,' she explained. 'An ancestor, is someone who has been a part of your family in the past. They're people I'm related to, but who are no longer with us – if you understand.'

Jill looked confused at Lucy's description, having never had anything similar in her life to compare it to. But she was happy just to gaze in wonderment at the wall of faces, trying to imagine what it would be like to meet each and every one of them.

Sam dropped to a knee to inspect Lucy's leg. 'May I?' he asked, looking up at her – making gestures to lift the leg of her trousers.

She smiled at his unwavering adherence to manners and the rules of etiquette, despite all they'd just been through together. She nodded. 'Of course,' she said.

Carefully, he rolled up the hem of her trouser leg, and sucked in air at the amount of heavy bruising mottling her skin. 'Bloody hell, Lucy!' he cried. 'Are you sure you're going to be okay?'

'I'll be fine,' she assured him, shaking the trouser leg down again. 'Don't worry about it, I'll heal.'

Sam stood again. They both looked over at the fascinated children. Jill was leading Jack around the room by his hand. 'So what do we do with this pair now?' asked Sam,

Lucy began to laugh. 'I have absolutely no idea.'

'Well, don't worry, I've sorted something out, at least for now,' he explained.

'Like what?'

'Like never you mind.' He grinned, then it softened. 'Come on, I'll show you.'

He looked across to the kids. 'Jill, Jack,' he called, 'we're going to take you to a place where you can stay, just for tonight, okay?'

Sam spun a look back towards Lucy, and beamed at her with more than a little excitement. 'Wait until they see sunshine!' he whispered.

Lucy's eyes widened. She stepped away and stooped to glance up at the sky through one of the windows, the earlier cloud had cleared, and the sun was out in full force. 'Oh my God!' she exclaimed – her face brightening at the thought of the joy she knew she'd feel just watching their reactions. 'Crap-in-hell, Sam! Come on!'

They collected the kids, and made their way out of the dining room and across the marbled floor.

The children spun in wonderment at both the differences, and the familiarity of the house.

They all arrived at the main entrance. Sam stopped and turned to face them. 'Now, are you two ready?' he said to their expectant faces. They both nodded, but neither of them knowing what it was he was referring to.

He stepped to the doors, gave the handles a theatrical twist, then swung them wide open, unveiling the full, unbridled beauty of a sunlit day.

Two tiny faces widened to the vision, overwhelmed by the

beauty of the sight that met their eyes. They wandered out into the warmth and the breeze, serenaded by the joy-filled birdsong saturating the air of the purest of summer days.

A tear of happiness snaked down Jill's cheek at a sight she never imagined could exist, Jack loosing her hand and galloping down the steps. He stopped half way, and looked at the railings. He turned a look up towards Sam and pointed to the gap.

Sam nodded. 'That's it,' he confirmed, 'that's how we found you.' The boy beamed, and continued to bounce down the staircase.

He stopped at the bottom and froze, looking out at the vista of hills stretching far to the horizon.

Jill dropped down the steps to join his side. They both looked out, observing 'distance' for the first time in their lives.

Sam and Lucy watched, sharing in their experience, and finding new-found appreciation of the beauty of the world into which they were lucky enough to be born.

Lucy turned to Sam. 'Come on then, Samuel,' she said, affectionately squeezing his hand, 'show me this idea you've had for the kids.'

*

They all made their way across the grounds towards the far side of the estate, tiny heads on tiny bodies spinning like meerkats at all the far off details that never existed in their world.

Sam gestured to the group to wait by a large, splintered Yew tree. He trotted out onto the lawn that dropped away towards the stables, lolloping with feigned nonchalance down the bank, scouting the area for any unwanted faces… The coast looked clear.

'Come on,' he called, turning back to the others who were

skulking behind the fractured truck of a tree. He waved them through.

Sam kept a keen eye out while they all rushed across to the stable block. 'The third one along,' he called to Lucy – she nodded her understanding.

Sam caught them up, and strode ahead to stable number three. He walked the bolt from its staple, then parted the door slightly.

He turned to front the children's intrigue. 'Now, listen. This will only be temporary, okay? It'll just be for now, at least until… Well… until.' He opened the door and the children stepped tentatively inside…

They were presented with a freshly swept stable cleared of all dust and cobwebs. A heavy, brass-framed bed they already knew had been placed against the wall at the back, made up with fresh bedding and flanked by two side tables, each topped with a chintz lamp that filled the room with warm light.

There was a small fan heater set on a thermostat to correct the chill that the star-encrusted night would inevitably bring. And two chairs sat neatly beneath a small table reeking of newly applied furniture polish, all sitting atop a freshly beaten rug, laid over the concrete to protect their feet.

'Did you do this, Sam! It's fantastic,' Lucy mewed, clasping her hands together beneath a smile.

The table top was strewn with an eclectic mix of all things edible: sandwiches, fruit, cakes, crisps, chocolate bars and biscuits. And there were two flasks – one labelled 'Soup', the other one 'Tea'. There was even a bowl of sugar and a small jug of milk set between two freshly washed mugs.

'Blimey, Sam!' Lucy said, nudging him. 'I never had you down as such a nester!' She beamed at him, fondly. 'It's amazing.'

Sam attempted to play down his efforts. 'Well, of course, I

wasn't actually sure we were ever going to get to use it,' he said, 'but, we managed it, thanks to you.'

'No,' she insisted, '*we* did it, together. It's *us*.'

More than a little excited, the kids wandered over to the bed. Freshly washed garments lay folded neatly into two piles. Jill turned quizzical eyes back at Sam.

'Oh yeah, those are just some clean clothes for you to put on, you know, if you want to.' He pointed to each pile. 'They're just some old jeans and T-shirts of mine that are too small for me now – they're for you Jack. And there's a couple of Hilly's dresses for you Jill. Or there's a pair of her jeans and a loose top too, if you'd prefer that.'

Jill lifted one of the dresses into the light, her eyes flooded with smiles. The only form of attention she's ever received in her life before this, was when she was the recipient of spitting hatred. The kindness overwhelmed her, and she collapsed where she stood and began to cry, slumped on her buckled legs, clutching the dress tightly in her tiny hands. She was overcome by the tide of kindness, and the relief she felt at escaping the prison of her life.

Tears ran freely down a happy face. A face smiling at finding there's another world, and another option. A world motivated by kind intentions and manned by people with an ability to care.

Jack knelt down next to her, and wrapped himself around his sister, they both took time to share in each other's relief…

Jill eventually struggled to her feet, Lucy stepping in to help her up. The young girl wiped her eyes dry and looked up at Lucy. 'Who is Hilly?' she asked, holding the dress out.

Lucy's brow brightened. 'Of course, you haven't met Hilly yet, have you,' she said. 'Hilly is Sam's sister,' she explained, pointing across the room. 'I *think* the same way that Jill is to you, Jack? Is she your sister?'

He shrugged and nodded in unison. 'I think so,' he said, sensing that that was somehow right.

'Well, you look so alike, I think you *must* be.'

Lucy's phone vibrated. She pulled it from her pocket, there was a voicemail symbol flashing on the screen. She tapped it...

'You have one new message. New message – Beep!'

'Lucy? It's Grandma. I'm sorry to bother you my love, but there's some things I need to tell you. Your mother told me that you had spoken to her. I don't know what your motivations where in telling her, but I guess it's probably better that she knows... Anyway, I don't want your mum knowing what I have to say, so I was wondering if it would be at all possible for you to come over and visit me on your own sometime? It would be nice to see you anyway. Let me know if you're able to come.

Love you... Bye.'

Beep! You have no more messages, and no saved messages.

Lucy stared down at her phone, looking mildly troubled...

'Lucy?' said Sam – concerned. 'Is everything okay?'

'Listen,' she said, 'there's something I've got to go and do.'

'Is everything alright?'

'Yes, it's fine – there's nothing to worry about.' She turned to the children who were now perched on the edge of the bed. 'Are you two going to be alright on your own?' she asked. They nodded.

'Don't worry,' Sam assured her, 'I'll sort them out. I'll introduce them to the joys of tea. And I can show them where the garden toilets are so they can wash up, and – well, whatever else they might need to do. But we shan't go into that.'

Lucy smirked. 'Okay…'

She turned to the children again. 'I'll see you both tomorrow, alright. Now it's going to get dark soon, that's normal here too, so don't be afraid. But when it gets bright again – like it is now – we'll be back to see you, and we'll work out how on earth we're going to make people aware of your existence.'

Sam smiled at the new arrivals, then at Lucy. 'I don't know where it is you've got to go, but good luck,' he said, 'it's been a hell of a day.'

She laughed at the level of understatement. 'Hasn't it just.'

'I'll be leaving myself in a bit,' he said, 'I've got to help my dad mend some fencing.' He looked at the kids. 'But I'll *also* be back to see you tomorrow, and then you can meet Hilly… *Oh!* And you might want to wait a while before you eat any of that. Then it'll probably taste alright.'

Lucy stepped in and hugged the children. 'See you soon, kids,' she whispered, placing a kiss on top their heads. She turned and hugged Sam, then parted to find out what it was her grandmother had to say…

SIXTEEN

TRUTH BE KNOWN

'I'M JUST POPPING to the shops,' Lucy called to her mother, 'do you need me to get anything?' She prayed that the answer be 'no', to save the inconvenience of actually having to visit a store.

'You're popping out?' her mother asked. 'Do you want me to come with you?'

'*No*, Mum!' she griped, 'I have to get used to driving on my own at some point.'

'Okay, okay. Just be careful, alright. There are some nutters on the road. The keys are in my bag. And erm, no – I don't think we need anything.'

'Thanks, Mum,' Lucy said, grabbing the keys and making for the door.

Lucy strode to the car, texting her grandmother en route:

> *I'm on my way, I won't be long. Just let them know at the door that I'm coming, I don't think visiting ends for a few hours, but let them know anyway, just in case.*

I'll see you soon, love you. L X

*

At the end of a thought-filled drive, Lucy finally arrived at Furnhurst Gardens. She turned in through the gates and made her way along the drive to the visitors car park.

She hardly remembered anything of the journey, too wrapped up in wondering what it was her grandmother had to tell her. But she knew it must be in some way related to Hobswyke, because she wanted her to come alone. But other than that, she really had no notion what it could be…

Lucy rapped on the door to her grandmothers suite. 'Come in,' sang a voice from inside the room.

Lucy walked in. Her grandmother was sitting in her usual chair looking out of the window, watching the remainder of the day fade out.

'Hi, Nan, how are you?' Lucy asked.

'I'm fine, dear,' she said. She stretched up to deposit a kiss on her granddaughter's cheek. 'Thank you for coming.'

'That's okay – I was intrigued,' said Lucy, with an excited shrug. She walked over to the kettle. 'Tea?' she asked.

'Please, dear, that would be lovely.'

Lucy sat and handed the mug over. 'So, what did you want to talk to me about?'

The old woman took a sip of her drink, then settled back into her chair. She looked intensely at Lucy, eyes full of contemplation. 'Last time you were here, you were going to tell me something, but your mother walked in on us. What was it?'

Lucy dropped her eyes to the floor, deciding how much she was willing to tell, and how much she'd be wise to keep to herself… 'There are things I don't want to tell you yet, Nan, because, if I'm honest, I don't think you'd actually believe me.'

Her grandmother loosed an almost mocking laugh. 'Let me tell you something,' she said, 'you'd be unpleasantly surprised what I'd be willing to believe about that house.'

Lucy squinted at the old lady's words, wondering what she could possibly have meant by that. She found herself contemplating spilling everything. 'I think I know where Mum was when she went missing.'

The old woman's sepia eyes flashed. 'What…? Where?' she asked.

'Well, you know Sam – Peter's son? He discovered…' She stopped herself, aware of how utterly ridiculous what she was about to say would sound.

Her grandmother nodded encouragement. 'You can tell me.'

Lucy sighed… 'He discovered, a passageway to another place, a *secret* place,' she explained. 'It's a portal that leads to another world, a world that's a lot like ours. Well, actually, it looks almost exactly the same, but it just feels different. It feels, somehow, rotten. And we think it must have been created by Antoine Mallette.'

Her grandmother sat motionless, listening, apparently unmoved by the revelation.

Lucy was surprised to find she wasn't being looked upon like she belonged in an asylum, so decided to test the waters a bit further .

'Okay. Well, we've *both* passed through into this *world*, and we found things on the other side that I really don't want to talk about yet, but what I *do* know, is that I'm pretty certain it must be where Mum was lost for all that time.'

Violet turned her strangely calm gaze to the window again. The sky grew dark, dusk just setting in.

'I know how it sounds, Nan. I *really* do,' Lucy insisted, 'but I'm being truthful, we went there, this place is *real*.'

Violet sighed a deep sigh. 'Nothing of what you've said sounds unbelievable to me, not under the circumstances.'

'What circumstances?'

'I wasn't entirely honest with you the other day, about how long your mother was missing.'

'Nine or ten years wasn't it?'

The old lady snorted an ironic laugh. 'Just over twenty!' she replied.

'What!' Lucy fizzed.

Violet shut her eyes and nodded her shame in not being wholly truthful. 'Your mother appeared back in our lives only a few months before you were born, but two decades *after* she went missing.'

'Oh my God!' Lucy mumbled.

'But the reason I'm not doubting your tale, is for one reason in particular.'

'What reason's that?'

Her grandmother averted her gaze to the wall, making sure she had the facts straight in her mind. 'Helen, *and* Thomas, both disappeared. Then one night we heard the crash, and we found your mother sitting amongst the glass shards of the mirror she'd decided to break – for whatever reason? I guess that's something we'll never know?'

The detail didn't pass Lucy by, but she kept her lips buttoned tight. 'But you told me that already?' she said.

'I know I did, but what I *didn't* tell you, is that when we found her, she looked no older than you do now.' She turned to examine Lucy's face, studying her apparent age. 'Mmm – Maybe even younger?' she muttered.

The old lady shuffled in her seat to get more comfortable. 'Well, it didn't even occur to us at the time that she'd been missing that long. I'm afraid when you reach a certain age, *ten* or *twenty* years can tend to feel a lot like *one*. But after we'd thought about it, and checked her records, we realised that she was in fact twenty-seven years old! But, she looked every bit like a young teenager?'

Lucy stood and teased the curtains closed, to keep the conversation private, the room now much brighter than the darkening skies outside.

She sat again. 'Go on.'

'So, here's the *weirdest* part!' her grandmother said, leaning in closer to Lucy and lowering her voice to a more clandestine level. 'While we were cleaning and dressing her wounds, and putting her into fresh clothes, and feeding her, and cutting her hair – she started, ageing!'

'Ageing?' asked Lucy.

'Yes. Ageing… Right in front of our eyes, as *God* is my witness, she aged… I mean, don't get me wrong, it was almost too gradual to notice. But we suddenly realised that she somehow looked older, and more mature than when we'd first found her… At first we thought it was all in our imagination – well, you would, wouldn't you. But as the hours passed, we realised that she was *actually* ageing.'

She leaned back into her chair again and sighed. 'And by the next day, she looked every bit the age she was supposed to be.'

Lucy gazed in disbelief at the weirdness of the story. She knew her grandmother to be a wholly honest person, not prone to flights of fancy, and in the light of all that happened of late, Lucy felt no reason to doubt anything she'd being told. But still…

'You won't tell your mother any of this?' her grandmother asked. 'You see, she doesn't actually know.'

'What do you mean, "she doesn't know"?'

'We never told her, as far as she knows, when we discovered her, she looked twenty-seven years old… *You*, are the only person apart from me who knows *any* of this, so this time, *don't* tell anyone, most of all Helen!'

Lucy pondered the pressure of the knowledge she now held. 'Okay,' she agreed.

The old lady's brows crimped. 'No. Hang on. There is one more who knows. I nearly forgot.'

'Who is it?'

'Peter… Peter Fletcher.'

Lucy reared back. 'Peter knows?'

'Yes, he does… You see, Peter was a Hobswyke orphan too. We fostered him when the place shut down, and when he was old enough, we gave him the lakeside cottage, and he worked the grounds as caretaker. He, knows *everything*. We told him so there would *always* be someone in Helen's life to keep an eye on her.'

A crackling voice come over the speaker system:

> *Visiting time is now over. Please can all visitors make their way to the exit or we'll have to come and eject you from the building and I'm sure none of you really want that do you? Because we will use handcuffs. So get out now, just get out.*
>
> *Thaaaank yoooooou.*

Lucy smirked. 'You have the comedy receptionist on tonight.' Violet rolled her eyes.

Lucy gathered her things together, trying to absorb all she'd learned. 'I have to go now, Nan, but *thank* you! For your honesty.'

Violet smiled. 'It was nice to get it off my chest for once. Now *please*, remember what I said. And *stay* away from that house.'

'I will. I promise... I'll see you very soon.'

She kissed the pensive old lady, and made a move to leave. She looked back from the door to part on a smile, but her grandmother was frowning at the ground, wearing a subtly pained expression.

'Are you okay, Nan?' asked Lucy.

'You know...' the old lady murmured, 'my great grandmother once told me something, something I found interesting at the time, but that didn't really mean much to me then.'

'And what was it?' Lucy asked.

She sighed a troubled sigh. 'She told me that when the Claybournes originally took over the house and grounds, they'd changed the name left over by Antoine Mallette. The place was originally called "Hobs*wicket* Hall".'

Lucy also found interest in the snippet of history, but failed to see any relevance.

The old woman looked across at the girl leaning against the open door. 'It didn't occur to me until now, until you told me *your* tale, but "Hob's – Wicket" are old English words, they mean "Devil's Gate".'

Lucy hung stunned in the relevance of the name, a blatant clue pinned defiantly to the house by Mallette for the world to notice, and for all to apparently miss – until now, that is.

Lucy nodded her understanding.

'Stay away from the house, for me,' Violet pleaded.

Lucy crimped a thoughtful smile, and left, closing the door gently behind her...

SEVENTEEN

NEW ARRIVALS

LUCY TURNED IN THROUGH the majestic stone pillars standing guard either side of the entrance to Hobswyke drive. She pulled in next to the gatehouse and parked.

The engine fell silent, and she sat quietly in her thoughts…

She pondered Peter's part in it all: was he a traitor? A spy? Or is he more like an ally – keeping careful watch over her mother as a kind of guardian? She struggled to form an opinion with which she felt comfortable.

She adjusted the rearview mirror towards herself, and attempted to imagine her face ageing ten years in the space of a handful of hours. *What would it feel like?* she wondered. *Would I even notice it happening if I couldn't see my own reflection?*

A frantic rapping on the side-window ripped her from her daydream, her heart leapt from her mouth.

Her mother presented a concerned face to the glass. 'Where have you been?' she cried – her voice muffled by the glass.

Lucy grabbed her bag and popped the door. 'Sorry, Mum, I lost track of time.'

'Where did you go?' her mother reiterated. 'I've been worried sick!'

'Well, you know. I thought I'd drive around for a bit, to get used to it,' she said, faking exasperation.

'I tried ringing you, but it just kept going straight to voicemail... I was about to call the police!'

Lucy took her phone from her bag, pretending that she hadn't actually turned it off. 'The battery must be flat,' she said, pretending to press the buttons. 'Yeah, look, the battery's dead.'

Lucy laughed affectionately at what she perceived to be a love-fuelled overreaction. 'Oh, Mum! If you're like this when I just pop out for a bit of a drive, what are you going to be like when I get a motorbike?'

'You are *not* getting a bloody motorbike!' her mother asserted.

Lucy laughed, then began to choke... She clasped her hands tightly around her neck. 'Oh God! Help me!' she gurgled. 'Please! I – can't breathe!' She staggered around in front of her mother. 'You *must* loosen those apron strings!' She flopped her tongue from the corner of her mouth and made a series of gargling sounds.

Her mother just looked on unamused. 'You should feel lucky that you have a mother that cares,' she complained.

Lucy giggled, linked her mother's arm, and started escorting her to the house – working hard to hide her limp. 'Come on you, you *worry-a-holic*, I'll make us some tea.'

*

Darkness descended and Lucy lay in bed, curled up on her side. She wondered what the children were doing, and if they were fine on their first night in a strange, new place.

She'd been attempting to concoct possible ways to herald

the existence of the two new additions to their world. How much to tell, how much to keep silent about? But she was unable to think of a single way that didn't involve having to spill every single bean from the metaphorical tin.

She tried putting it to one side for the night, exhausted by what had in reality been a number of extremely stressful days.

She shut her eyes...

The bulge of Lucy's corneas began to dance beneath her lids, sinking away into a dream-state, pulled down, down, down by her exhaustion, sinking away, far away from the real world...

She found herself standing in the centre of the marble floor of the entrance hall of Hobswyke. She could hear music playing ethereally behind the doors of the ballroom.

She wandered through the dank atmosphere of the unlit room towards the muffled song, the sound of her footsteps echoing around the darkness.

There was light shining beneath the doors, occasionally broken by the passing shadow of something, or someone inside.

Lucy stepped onto the fan of light, turned the handles, and swung the doors open...

They revealed an old gramophone heavily laden with spans of wafting cobwebs, spinning a warped record beneath its pin-sharp needle. The disc bled to the tune of the scratches as the horn blasted its grainy waltz into the space.

Pairs of faceless dancers rotated about the room, their fixed frames gliding eerily to the crackling melody.

Lucy twisted her head down towards the floor, she could see no feet beneath the gowns, they floated about the room to the muffled tones drifting through the air.

She rose again and came face to face with her mother leaning into her, peering into Lucy's eyes, a deviant smile stretched wide below a faraway gaze that seemed devoid of emotion.

'You can't come in here, little girl,' her mother said, as

though addressing someone far in the distance, 'you're not old enough to be in here. You're just a child,' she mewed.

A deadpan smile slowly extended across her face, stretching wide until it reached her ears. 'You're just a child, and you're not welcome, so you have to go now, see. So, *get out*!' she whispered, aggressively, gently closing the doors…

They banged shut. The music ceased. The light beneath the door fell dark.

Lucy stood alone again in the obsidian silence, her breathing the only sound she could hear echoing throughout the cold, empty space.

A woody crack behind her broke the tension, she turned from the doors to find the cause of the sound.

She saw her mother sitting with her back to her at a dressing table on the farthest side of the hall, illuminated by a single candle slow dancing to the thumping beat of Lucy's heart. She was leaning forwards, making long sweeping passes with her hairbrush down towards the floor. Slow, mesmeric strokes hypnotising Lucy with its consistent rhythm.

She walked slowly across the leaf-strewn acreage of marble towards her mother's arched back, watching the hypnotic sweep of the brush…

'Mummy…' she called as she neared her. But her mother failed to hear her calls. 'Mummy?' she called again.

The brushing ceased mid-stroke, pausing for a beat, then her mother sat upright… She was headless, a clean-cut neck rising from the elegant sweep of her shoulders. Lucy staggered back, pressing a fist hard into her teeth.

The body began a creeping turn to look back at her, the severed neck twisting to front her interruption. She threw her hands across her eyes, and turned her back on the vision, stumbling away from the creak of the seat as she heard her mother stand…

The doors to the library began opening before her. She felt drawn to the orange flicker fanning across the marble as they slowly swung apart. She wandered into the room…

All of the books that lined the walls were ablaze, a hellish furnace of flames licking around every shelf in half time. The altar glowed devil-red at the core of the immolating room.

Black bony fingers extended from behind the sandstone block, crawling over the edge like arachnid limbs, feeling their ways towards the intruder.

A silhouetted face peered over the edge at Lucy, all she could see were the eyes looking at her. The digits tightened, scraping chipped nails along the blood-soaked sandstone…

'Luuuuuuuuucyyyyyyyy…' it called, watching her, taunting…

'Lucyyyy…' it sang again.

She stood, frozen to the spot, quivering eyes staring in fear.

The fingers danced, the thing began to rise into the light. It had a face, the face of her grandmother.

'Luuuuucyyyyyyy?' it sang mocking, slowly shuffling around the block of stone, extending its protracted arms out in her direction. 'Lucyyy… Are you listening to meee…?'

Lucy wanted desperately to leave the dream, but she didn't know how. Her grandmother crouched low and started to scuttle towards her, her face fixed with a wicked grin. 'I saw your mother,' it taunted, 'I saw her change. As *Satan* is my witness, she got older, right in front of my eyes.'

The thing shut its eyes tight, then opened them again. The eyes had gone, leaving hollow cavities weeping thick tears of coagulating blood.

It started to chuckle cruelly, continuing to advance towards Lucy's petrification.

'We watched her, me and your grandpa,' the thing said, turning a look to the far side of the room.

Lucy's mortified gaze followed the thing's. Her grandfather was grinning at her from behind the glass of the long-cased clock, waving at her with black, emaciated fingers of bone and sinew.

She snapped her head back to her advancing grandmother. 'Yesssss. We both watched her growing much, much olderrrrr…' she mocked. 'Ah! Look! It's happening to *me* now…' it mumbled.

The skin of the thing began sucking slowly onto its skull. 'I'm ageing, Lucy,' it said, in its deadpan voice. 'I'm ageing right before your eyes. And there's nothing you can do to stop it.'

Lucy backed away into the marbled room, passing her headless mother who was now standing by the doorway facing her.

'Look! Look, Helen,' it cried, 'I'm growing old, just like you.' Her skin suddenly rotted down to slime, teeth tumbling from receding gums. Her mother's skin started to drop off too, slapping onto the floor like wet flannels.

Her grandmother started to screech at Lucy through its toothless face. 'I'm dying, Lucy. I'm dying because of you! And when I'm dead, you'll be next, and there's nothing anyone can do to…'

Lucy jolted awake! 'Holy shit!' she slurred, cupping her face in her hands.

She sat up in bed and took a few calming breaths. She'd never had nightmares as bad as these before.

She took a sip of the water she kept on the side table. The words from the dream continued to swirl around her thoughts, replaying like a stuck record…

She suddenly jumped from the bed, and looked to the clock – 4:18am. She stared through the illuminated numbers, replaying the words from the dream…

She put the glass down, felt around in the dark for her clothes, and quickly got dressed…

Clothed and booted, Lucy made her way into the bathroom and straightened her hair in the mirror, and waited a while, trying to judge how long it would usually take her to pee.

She placed her hand on the flush in readiness, then pressed down hard on the handle, unleashing a torrent of water into the pan. The noise filled the bathroom.

She quickly opened the door and snuck downstairs, masked by the sound of the rushing water.

Quietly, she left the house, tiptoed down the steps, and away along the path…

She made her way through the night, serenaded by the rustle of the leaves and the lunar breeze.

Eventually, she neared the stable block, nervous of what she might find waiting for her. She made her way tentatively to stable number three, and pulled lightly at the handle, but it was locked from the inside.

Lucy didn't know what to do, was she being ridiculous? She needed to know.

Her fingertips tapped lightly on the door, and she presented an ear, listening for signs of life. She tapped again, and heard sounds from inside.

'Jill…? Jack?' she called, there was a noise from right behind the door. 'Are you in there? It's Lucy, can you let me in?'

After a considerable pause, there was a clack from the lock, and the door swung loose in its frame.

'I-It's open,' said a voice, but not a voice she recognised.

Gingerly, she pulled the door towards her. Something scurried away into the shadow. Lucy flinched back, fearful of the dark.

Her shaking hand grabbed the phone from her pocket. She swiped to the torch function, and tapped it, directing the beam into the room… 'Jill…? Jack…? I-Is that you?' she asked, her voice shaking.

The light passed a mound of empty food wrappers on the table, the back of a chair, then flashed across two faces cowering behind the bed. There was a familiarity to the features, but the faces looked different. Older, more mature in their essence.

'Something's happening to us!' said a voice, still tinged with the innocence of a child, but carrying a far deeper tone.

'Jack, is that you?' Lucy said.

The voice sobbed, 'Yes.' He sounded petrified.

Lucy rounded the end of the bed to take a better look… The children had aged, both now wearing years visually closer to Lucy's! 'Listen, I know you're both frightened,' she said, straining to not display the fear she was herself feeling, 'but this thing that's happening to you, happened to someone else I know. It's just something to do with coming through to this world.'

She stepped tentatively closer, and crouched before them, Jack was cosseting his sister, her exaggerated limbs curled tightly into a foetal ball.

Lucy shuffled closer, and gently placed a comforting hand on Jill's knee. 'It's okay, Jilly, I think whatever is happening, has probably finished now.' Lucy could only pray that she was right.

She backed away from the bed, coaxing them to follow. 'Come on, let me see you. Don't be afraid.' She looked about the stable and considered turning on a light, but decided it wouldn't help her in her cause.

She swiped her phone and typed a quick message to Sam…

Jack rose tentatively from behind the bed, splaying a hand towards Jill to stay hidden. He wandered apprehensively into the room. Lucy leaned across to switch on one of the lights… The lamp flicked on, illuminating the undeniable fear in Jack's face.

He shied from the sudden brightness, his only knowledge of any changes being his increase in height, and Jill's commentary on what had been happening to his face.

He was wearing the old clothes Sam had given him, but the jeans now sat high on his shins and were tight to his legs, and the T-shirt clung to him like a second skin. Lucy could see every malnourished rib showing through the cloth.

He looked understandably bewildered and afraid, to the point that she could sense he would rather be back in the other world right now, than endure what was happening to him.

Lucy stepped in and looked up into his face with fond, but pitying eyes. 'Look at you,' she whispered in the most optimistic voice she could carry – addressing his new features. 'Look how tall you are,' she said, 'and look, Jack, you're so handsome now,' she asserted, still talking to him like he was a child, which in reality, wasn't far from the truth. She smiled genuinely into his abashment. 'Pleased to meet you, "Jack",' she said, hands gently cupping his face.

Lucy turned her attention to Jill, reaching a hand out towards her. 'Come on. Come here, let me see you too.'

Jill peered up at her brother from behind the bed, then back to Lucy… Reluctantly, she raised her arm and wrapped long fingers around Lucy's encouraging hands.

Lucy pulled her to her feet, and guided her into the light. She turned and look at her, and began combing the hair back off her face with her fingers, brushing it clear of her features like she was a doll. Lucy's eyes lit up.

'Jilly!' she simpered. 'Oh my word, you have one of the most beautiful faces I have ever seen.' She examined the meek visage looking back at her, trying to see past the film of grime still coating her skin. 'What a gorgeous girl,' she sang, 'I wish *I* looked like you.'

Lucy stepped back to drink in their new bodies. 'You've *no* need to be afraid, okay? I know this is going to sound sort of ridiculous, but in a way, what's happened to you is actually kind of normal.' She realised how stupid that sounded, but also knew – with a level of certainty – the truth in what she'd said.

Lucy started to laugh, she couldn't help herself. The dress Jill had on still seemed to fit reasonably well, despite her increase in size. But Jack on the other hand looked as though his clothes had been painted on. 'Come here you,' she said, still chuckling – glad of the opportunity for levity to break the awkwardness, 'let's see if there's something larger among this lot.'

She led him across to the pile of clothes on the chair in the corner, and began holding them up to his bewilderment one at a time…

The stable door slowly creaked open. Sam crept in.

He saw Jill standing awkwardly in the insipid dim light, and walked across to her. 'I got your message,' he said, 'what's happened? Is everything okay?' Jill turned a confused look across to Lucy in the corner.

Sam continued to gaze at her, waiting for a response…

He made a sudden lumbering lurch back away from the girl's confusion. 'What the hell!' he cried. 'Who the hell are you?'

Lucy and Jack started to giggle. Sam turned towards the laughter, and saw Lucy helping Jack into a baggy T-shirt.

He returned his bewilderment back to Jill, and recognised Hilly's dress. 'What's going on!?' he cried.

'Sam,' said Lucy, 'it's fine. Something's happened, and it's really nothing to be afraid of. Let's just sit down, and I'll try to explain. My nan has told me *everything*…'

EIGHTEEN

A STRANGER COMES KNOCKING

LUCY PACED THE STABLE regaling the trio with everything she'd learned. Three confused and fascinated faces gazed back at her from the edge of the bed.

Sam sat awkwardly between Jill and Jack. He had a job resetting his perception of Jack, no longer a frightened child to be guided, now a boy he needed to make efforts to bond with.

And Jilly, she seemed far more softly feminine than before, a demureness to her demeanour that he'd not seen in her until now. He watched her face as she listened to Lucy's explanations. Although free of the paint and embellishments Sam found it common to see adorning a female face, there was an undeniable level of prettiness to her delicate features that he'd only really ever seen in Lucy before.

He had much to come to terms with in a short space of time, as did they all.

Lucy finally ceased wearing a groove in the rug, and turned to face the bed. '...So I reckon you were right, Sam. Time *does* seem to run slower over that side, but if you come through to *our* world, it seems that you catch up on the years you've managed to cheat passing.'

Although Sam was the original compiler of this theory – a theory that seemed to be unequivocally confirmed by pretty much everything surrounding him – he struggled to wrap his head around any of it. 'Is this mad to anyone else?' he complained.

'No, it's mad,' Lucy confirmed.

'…So, what now?' asked Sam.

Lucy shrugged.

Sam sat in silence for a time, realising he had to be strong for the sake of all of them. He lifted himself from his thoughts and wrapped his arms around the shame-laden shoulders of Jilly and Jack sitting either side of him, giving them an affectionate squeeze. 'Are you two going to be okay?' he asked.

There was a short pause, then they both nodded in unison.

Sam inspected their hair. 'I guess we need to get you two cleaned up a bit,' he suggested. He turned to Lucy. 'My dad's going to be out most of the day, I think we should give these two a scrub.' He looked at them both. 'Personally, I'd be absolutely fascinated to see what they actually look like under all these clods of earth,' he said, flavouring his words with lighthearted sarcasm.

Lucy laughed sympathetically. 'That's a great idea, why don't we do that…'

*

They waited until eight, giving Sam's father time to leave. Luckily, he had to make an early start.

They all made their way across the grounds until they reached the cottage by the lake. Sam signalled the group to stop, and walked on ahead to check his father's car had gone… It wasn't there. 'Come on,' he called.

Jill and Jack wandered towards Sam's house, they recognised it from the other side, but how different it looked in bright sunlight.

Once again, the birds sang boisterously from the surrounding trees, filling the fresh morning air with optimism. Jack looked to his sister, and smiled.

'It's beautiful,' Jilly proclaimed – the first words she'd spoken since the transformation. Her voice seemed soft, and sweet natured.

The two new inhabitants seemed to have switched roles, a detail that hadn't escaped Sam and Lucy.

Jack seemed to be the one now leading the two of them through their experience, attentive and protective of his sibling. And Jill, now decidedly meek in her manner, seemed far more needing of a shoulder to lean on. A complete reversal, but the girl inside was still recognisable.

Sam rolled his eyes. 'Of *cooourse*,' he muttered, finally seeing the light, and realising what was happening.

'Look how much stronger *he* is,' Lucy whispered, as they observed the twins interact.

'I know, it's amazing isn't it, the change in them both. Look how he watches out for her.'

They all entered the house, invited in by Sam. He closed the door behind them and called to Hilly.

They all heard a thump from her bed above, and she ran from her room and came bounding down the staircase, stopping midway.

'Hilly, this is Jill and Jack,' announced Sam, then presented a paddled hand towards the staircase, 'and this, this is Hilly.'

Hilly looked more than a little confused. 'I… I thought you said they were—'

'They *were*,' said Lucy. She sighed. 'Come in the living room with me, and I'll explain what's happened.'

A short time later, Lucy and Hilly finally joined the rest upstairs, Hilly now in possession of the latest bizarre details of the unfolding narrative. She hovered unsure in front of the new arrivals. 'Hello,' she said, smiling. 'I'm sorry, I didn't know what to expect.'

Jilly and Jack smiled back at her, just happy to see another friendly face.

Hilly wasn't sure of the form, so she just lunged in and gave them both a hug – feeling that after listening to so many tales of their exploits, that she almost knew them. On this occasion, the show of kindness was gratefully received with far less awkwardness than they'd managed before.

Sam led Jack to his room. 'Come on, you, let's find you some bigger clothes.'

Lucy and Hilly escorted Jill into the bathroom…

Ten minutes later, Jill was kneeling on a folded towel at the side of the bathtub, leaning over the side, Hilly and Lucy massaging thick suds of shampoo in though her matted hair.

'Now, you need to keep your eyes closed,' Hilly advised in a matronly tone, 'or they'll start to sting.' She was having what felt like an inappropriate amount of fun using Jill as a doll to be played with.

They rinsed her hair, and began conditioning it. Jill was unsure what to make of the processes they were inflicting on her. She'd never washed her hair before, let alone had it done *for* her by two overly excited, giggling females.

They gave it a final rinse, and quickly towelled it dry, before ushering her into Hilly's room and attacking her with a hairdryer…

The hairdryer eventually fell silent, and Lucy scooped the freshly washed hair clear of Jill's face.

Both Hilly and Lucy's expressions dropped. 'Oh my God,' muttered Hilly, 'look how much like you she looks?'

Innocent eyes, glowing vibrant turquoise looked back at Lucy, she could almost be fooled into thinking she was seeing her own reflection. 'What's wrong?' asked Jill.

'Nothing,' Lucy replied, but feeling it *was* something significant. *Is Jill the parallel-world version of me?* she thought to herself, finding the thought an unnerving one to contemplate.

'Dear God, she looks like you!' said Sam, who'd appeared in the doorway.

'I know, we were just saying the same thing,' she responded, 'crazy isn't it.' She turned to Sam and mouthed to him. 'Is she me? A *version* of me?'

Sam crimped the corners of his mouth and shrugged. 'Oh! Yeah!' he remembered, swinging his body open like a gate, revealing Jack standing behind him, wearing clothes that actually fitted. 'Ta-daaaa!' he cried.

'That's better,' said Lucy, 'does that *feel* better?' she asked.

Jack nodded. 'Yes, much better, thank you.'

Lucy considered a question she'd been meaning to ask, but for whatever reason, hadn't felt able to until now.

'Come here,' she said, patting the bed next to Jill. He crossed the room and sat. 'Do either of you remember where you came from?'

'What do you mean?' asked Jack.

'I don't know?' she said, giving her line of questioning a rethink. 'Do you know, or do you *think*, you originally came from *this* world, *our* world?' she asked, looking about the room.

They look at each other, then shrugged again.

'Okay… Well, what's your earliest memory? Is there anything you can remember from when you were very small?'

Jack strained to think back that far. Jill watched, leaving it to him to answer for her. 'I just remember, *Him*, used to bring us food,' he recalled, 'he used to speak to us once, when we were small, even though it was mainly shouting. But he became more hateful towards us the older we got.' He looked down into his lap with sadness in his eyes. 'It's like, like he hated us, and we didn't know why?' He shook his head. 'He used to try to hurt me, but *Girl* – sorry, *Jill* would put herself in front of me, and *Him* would hit her. So one day, we hid from him, and began looking after ourselves. But it just made *Him* more angry.'

Sam and Lucy listened intently, fascinated, but finding his words uncomfortable to hear.

Jack continued. 'He changed: the way he looked, the way he acted, the way he treated us. So we decided we needed to hide from him completely, until we had nothing else to do with him, *except* hide.'

'Why do you call yourselves "Girl" and "Boy"?' asked Sam.

'That's what *Him* used to call us, when he shouted at us,' said Jill, finally joining in the conversation.

'Well, you're safe now,' asserted Lucy. She looked back towards Sam. 'We've finished in the bathroom, if you wanted to show Jack what to do.'

'Come on, Jack my lad,' said Sam, 'let me introduce you to both the chore, *and* the joy of showering, then maybe we can give that hair a bit of a trim.'

'Noooo!' cried Hilly – who'd always harboured a liking of long hair on a boy. 'Leave it as it is, it suits him.'

Sam frowned at his sister's awkward display of attraction, and led Jack away to the relative safety of the bathroom.

While Jack got accustomed to the sensation of hot water on his skin, Sam warmed the oven and slid in a tray full of sausages. Sam seemed to do the majority of the food preparation in the house, his father having a tendency to incinerate most things he'd ever attempted to cook…

Now, with the two new arrivals clean and clad in fresh clothes, they all sat around the table to eat.

The new additions inspected their plates, more with fascination than anything else, intrigued by what was in fact, the first hot food they'd ever had placed before them.

The steam rising from their plates carried the aroma of the food into the air, neither of them realising it had a scent before.

Sam began eating in an exaggerated manner, demonstrating what to do. The new arrivals picked up the cutlery, and clumsily began mimicking has actions…

Jilly fumbled with the knife and fork, slicing a piece of bacon and dipping it in her egg – the same way Sam did – and wrapped her hunger around it.

The flavour of the bacon exploded across taste buds that had never been stimulated by anything more exciting than an apple before. She closed her eyes to focus on the new experience.

Lucy was just happy to sit and observe them enjoying their new world. She smiled fondly, then joined them in demolishing the food…

They all finished, Jack wiping his plate clean with a slice of bread and butter the same as Sam.

'Does all food taste like that?' asked Jill.

'Pretty much,' answered Sam, 'unless my dad cooks it, and then it just tastes like the remnants of a house fire.'

They look at him confused.

'My dad. He's a terrible cook,' he explained. 'If you ever end up eating any of *his* food, you'll know what I'm on about. Then you'll probably run off and jump back through that bloody pool,' he laughed.

'What are we going to do about that?' asked Lucy.

'What do you mean?'

'Well, the railing's still broken for a start,' she replied.

Sam gave it some thought... 'Hm, we should at least wire it back in place or something, at least for now,' he suggested, thinking it all through. 'We need to lock the house up too, but I don't know where the keys are?'

'*I've* got them, they're back up at the house,' Lucy said.

'Okay. So why don't we give these two a tour of the grounds for a bit. We could have a picnic over by the far side of the lake if you like. Your mum doesn't often go over there.'

'Sounds good,' said Lucy.

'Then after that, maybe it would be best to take them back to the stable. I don't think we're ready to tell anyone about them just yet, do you?'

'No,' Lucy agreed, 'maybe tomorrow though.'

Sam nodded. 'Okay. Agreed. Then after that, we'll go and get the stuff together to fix that railing in place, then we can go over to yours to get those keys, and we can finally lock the place up tight.'

Lucy concurred...

*

The three of them spent the afternoon showing the new arrivals around the grounds, explaining the way life is in the new world. They soaked up all they were told, eyes glowing with wonder at how amazing everything sounded in contrast to the toxic existence they'd been forced to live up until now...

They drank in the sights, sounds and palpable optimism of the world they now resided, unsure of the future, but ultimately, knowing they were in a better place.

By late afternoon, Jill and Jack had grown accustomed to a 'smile' being their primary expression, and happiness the default feeling in their hearts...

Lucy and Sam eventually deposited the new arrivals back at the stables, handing them a bag full of food for later. 'We have to go now, we have some things we need to do up at the house,' they explained, 'but we'll see you again tomorrow, okay?'

The twins nodded. Jilly looked across at Lucy with a heart bursting with gratitude. She trotted over, enveloping Lucy in a hug. Sam followed suit, stepping up to Jack and giving him a pally squeeze of the shoulder.

They left and dropped Hilly off at the cottage, collecting what they'd need from the workshop, before setting off for the gatehouse to collect the keys to Hobswyke.

'How in all that's holy are we going to spring those two on your mum and my dad?' asked Sam.

Lucy loosed a clueless laugh. 'I was foolishly hoping you might have some thoughts on that, but obviously not… I guess honesty might be the only way?'

'They'll lock us up,' he said, snorting a solitary laugh.

They exited the tree-lined path that climbed to the gatehouse, just in time to observe Sam's father turning his Land Rover round by the main gate.

They both ducked into the greenery and watched.

'What's he doing?' whispered Sam, 'he was supposed to be away all day today? He told me he wouldn't be back till late.'

There was a ligneous slam from the house, and Lucy's mother trotted down the steps from the front door and climbed in with Peter. They drove away through the gate onto the main road and disappeared off into the distance.

'Where would they going at this time of the day?' queried Sam.

Lucy's confusion showed in her face. 'God knows. I can't imagine.'

'Well let's grab those keys, and get this done while they're not here. It might actually be a blessing that they've both gone out.'

*

Lucy darted into her room and rummaged through her rucksack, her fingers chasing the jangle of the keys around the bottom of her bag... She finally managed to scoop them up, and folded them into her hand...

She trotted back downstairs. 'Hang on,' she said, stepping to the phone, taking up the handset to see who her mother last called. There was only one number indicated – Peter's mobile. 'She called your dad.'

'When?'

She looked to the clock on the wall. 'About two and a half hours ago.'

She then checked for any incoming calls... Again, there was just one number indicated – her grandmother's mobile, and it came in just before the call that was made to Peter.

Pensive, Lucy placed the handset down again. 'Nan called,' she said, 'is that where they were going?' she wondered.

'Maybe? Would that be unusual?'

Lucy seesawed an indecisive head. 'I'm not sure? I guess not.'

Lucy snapped the keys up again, and made for the door. 'Come on, let's get it done.'

*

They picked up the broken section of railing and offered it up to the gap. Sam bent the bars around, trying to flex the buckled panel back into something close to its original shape.

'There,' he said, 'that's pretty close. Just hold it still for me while I get a couple of fixings on it.'

He rummaged in his bag of bits, and drew out some tying wire and side cutters. He snipped off a few of lengths, and started twisting it around the bars.

Ten minutes of work later, and Sam tossed the cutters back into the bag. 'That should do it,' he said, stepping back to inspect his handiwork.

'You can't tell,' said Lucy. Sam agreed.

'Come on then,' he said, grabbing the bag. 'Let's lock up this hellhole, and get away from here once and for all...'

Lucy contemplated the term 'hellhole'. *How apt,* she thought.

They climbed the steps and approached the oppressive doors. Sam looked at Lucy. Did you really see something in the library,' he asked, 'on this side?'

She blinked and nodded. 'Yes. It was horrible,' she said. 'I never want to see anything like that again.'

Sam took the keys from her, sliding the most extravagant one into the lock. 'Let's never come back here,' he suggested, like they were making a pact.

'*Deal*,' she agreed, happily.

Sam turned the key in the lock for what they both hoped would be the last time. A loud, hollow *clank* rang out through the entire house, chiming their intention to never again revisit the place.

Lucy pulled Sam into her, and placed a kiss on his mouth, partly to seal their intentions, and partly allowing herself to succumb to a long-felt urge.

Sam floated on the taste of her breath and the softness of her mouth, sailing on the sea of his dreams made real...

She leaned back, and attentively wiped the lipstick from

his mouth with her thumb. 'Come on you,' she said, 'let's go.'

Lucy took hold of Sam's hand, and they set off for home. She stopped them midway down the stairs. 'Hang on,' she said, turning to the pool. She took the keys from her pocket, and studied them in her hand… She stepped to the railing, and extended her arm out over the water. 'Do I?' she asked.

'What if your mum asks where they are? Wouldn't that be a problem?' he asked.

Lucy thought about his reasoning. 'I guess you're right.'

She folded the keys back into her hand. 'I'll hang them back under the sink, and then try to forget they exist!'

They set off again, making their way across the gravel towards the lawn. The light had begun to fade, the day passing quicker than either of them had realised.

A viscous *sloshing* emanated from the pool, bony fingers breaching the surface tension of the obsidian liquid, and rising towards the rapidly darkening skies.

Twig-like digits of bone and sinew began to feel around the carvings, clawing for the feel of featureless stone. The fingers found what they sought, and lay flat against the disk. Sinewy arms tugged at the handhold, held fast by a bastardisation of gravity, lifting a drawn, emaciated face through the splitting onyx into a whole new reality.

It skulked up the wall to the back of the railings, its cadaverous eyes leering through the bars, searching for something it resented losing.

The thing extended its elongated limbs over the handrail, stepping down onto the other side. A hacksaw fell from its skeletal hand and clattered on the steps.

It sniffed at the air. There was a flicker of recognition in its gaunt face. The creature turned its squint, lifeless eyes towards the lawn that drop away from the hall, and started towards it…

NINETEEN

COMETH THE ICE MAN

JACK RETURNED from yet another visit to the table, clutching two cake bars. He rejoined his sister on the bed and handed one to her.

'Are we going to be okay?' Jilly asked.

'I think so,' he said, 'they seem really nice, don't they.'

'No,' she replied, 'they *are* really nice.'

He smirked. 'Yes. Yes they are...'

They unwrapped their cakes, and took a bite in unison. 'I'd be happy to live in *here,* forever,' Jill said, looking about the dingy stable.

'Me too,' he agreed, laughing at how sad that would probably seem to anyone from this new world. 'Did you see where they live! The nice things they have?' He turned saddened eyes down at his lap. 'Why couldn't we have lived here, instead of – of *that* place?'

'I don't know,' said Jill. 'Hey!' she barked, optimistically. 'Now we do.'

Jack allowed a smile to douse his sadness.

The door of the stable began to rattle against its frame. Jack ceased chewing, and shoot an urgent look across to his sister…

The door rattled again, this time with far too much intensity to just be the wind.

Jack turned to face the door, and shuffled in front of Jill.

The door started to shake, the deadlock clattering in its staple.

Jack's adrenalin spiked. He readied himself to throw all he had at anything coming through the door.

'Jack? Are you there?' asked a voice filtering through the wood. They recognised it, it was Sam's.

The twins released their collectively held breaths. Jack lunged from the bed and slid back the lock.

The door swung out into the night. Sam and Lucy's theatrically happy faces appeared around the edge. 'I hope we aren't disturbing you?' asked Lucy. 'We were sort of passing, so we thought we'd come and check on you both, and see that you didn't need anything. *Do* you need anything?'

Jill watched Lucy's face from the bed, fascinated by the compassionate gleam in her eyes. She nodded quietly in response to Lucy's question.

'What is it, Jilly?' asked Lucy. 'What is it you need?'

Jill wore a look of sad submission. Lucy walked around and sat next to her. 'What is it, my love?' she asked. 'What's the matter?'

Jill looked hesitant. 'W-Why are you helping us?'

Lucy baulked at the absurdity of the question. 'What do you mean?' she asked, straining to imagine a reason why they *wouldn't*.

'Well. Why *would* you? You don't really have a reason to?'

Pity tugged lightly at the corners of Lucy's mouth. 'Yes we do,' she asserted, 'it's because we care. And besides, we have no other choice now do we. We've both kind of grown to love you.'

A single tear broke free from Jill's glistened eye, and meandered down her cheek, the saline taste of her gratitude wetting the corner of her mouth.

Lucy wiped the tear clear with her thumb, and caressed her face. 'It's going to be okay,' she murmured, 'we'll never let anything hurt you ever again. That's a promise.'

Lucy could plainly see the pain of the lives they'd both been forced to live, just by the lost expression behind Jill's eyes. She stood to join Sam back at the door, and noticed Jack's eyes were also a cerulean blue. She felt surprised that she only just noticed. Being female, it was the kind of detail that rarely passed her by.

'Well, we'll see you both tomorrow,' she reassured them, 'so sleep well, and sweet dreams.' She looked to Jill. '...Love you,' she whispered.

Jill beamed her gratitude.

They left through the door, and waited until they heard the lock slip back across, then made their way up the bank towards Sam's house.

Lucy began to sob. She'd allowed herself to absorb too much of the sadness she saw beyond Jill's eyes.

'What's wrong?' asked Sam – a cursory question, as he already knew the answer. Lucy was apt to feel the emotion she saw in others. She'd always been an ultimately compassionate person, able to feel every stab of pain and suffering she could see worn desperately across the faces of others. Sam considered it must be both a gift, and a curse, and in equal measures.

He wrapped his arm around her shoulders, and gave her a squeeze, a reminder in pressure form that he was there for her.

They reached the top of the green, and turned to step through the break in the fence that cut onto the path.

Sam stopped, turning his attention to an area of the lawn shaded from the moonlight by the limbs of a sprawling oak.

He leaned in, attempting to see through the murk… He sensed something lurking beneath the umbrella of the shadows, crouched to the ground, watching them pass.

'Hello?' he called, in a voice laced with disquiet… but there was no answer.

'Is everything okay?' asked Lucy, who was wondering where he'd gone.

'Yes… It's fine,' he muttered – still peering into the darkness and sounding anything but convincing. He turned back to join her, and smiled to waylay her concern. 'It's nothing,' he said, 'just my imagination running riot.'

She linked his arm, and they stepped through the dilapidated fence. Sam darted a last look back over his shoulder, shaking his head clear of the notion.

They finally arrived at Sam's cottage, but his father's Land Rover was nowhere to be seen. 'Are they not back yet?' asked Lucy.

'Apparently not?' he replied. 'Maybe they're up at your place.'

Sam swung the workshop door open and began replacing the tools they'd borrowed. Lucy stepped up to help. 'Maybe we need to get my grandmother involved, you know, in revealing Jill and Jack?' she suggested. 'I think Mum and your dad are more likely to listen to *her*.'

Sam ceased tidying to consider the idea… 'It's not a bad thought,' he said, 'by what you've told me, she does seem to know quite a bit about what's going on with that place already.'

He finished redistributing the last of the tools, and they turned and left.

'So, I'll see you tomorrow?' said Lucy.

'Yep, see you tomorrow.'

Lucy leant forwards on pointed toes, and placed a kiss lightly on his cheek, then turned her abashment away, and began to saunter up the path.

Sam watched her snake away through the woodlands until she was no longer visible, and turned to go inside…

Lucy ambled with zero conviction along the tree-lined path that climbed to the gatehouse, smiling wryly to herself at how happy the new arrivals seemed, and how readily they were both taking to their new environment.

A wave of rustling leaves ran the gauntlet through the tunnel of trees, hissing past Lucy to the tune of a whistling breeze racing along the path.

She watched the ripple fizz past and disappear up the bank, until the air fell silent.

The sharp *crack* of a fracturing branch split the silence from deep in the gallery of twigs behind her. She spun around and looked down into the gloom of the unlit path… She peered into the darkness, listening…

Another wave of wind-agitated leaves fizzled past Lucy's scrutinising, filling the air with its white-noise hiss.

Lucy listened intensely for any sound alien to the fizz of the whispering vegetation. 'Sam, is that you?' she called – but there was no reply to be heard above the gossiping leaves.

Uneasy – she turned back up the bank and speeded up her walk…

She finally exited the trees just in time to see Peter drive down the lane from the gatehouse. She heard the *slam* of the front door. 'Where on earth have *they* been all this time?' she murmured into the night.

Lucy slowly climbed the steps to the entrance, and presented an ear to the door. She could hear her mother inside, calling her name. She swung the door open, trying to act nonchalant. Her mother pirouetted round from midway up the staircase, her face racking with concern. 'And where the hell have you been?' she asked in a decidedly assailing manner.

'What do you mean? I've been out,' she replied. 'And anyway, I could ask where *you've* been all this time?' she spat in retaliation.

Her mother flushed a look manifesting far more guilt than Lucy. 'Nowhere, I-I just had some things to do.'

'What, with Peter?'

'Her mother stuttered at the mention of Peter. 'Y-Yes, with Peter…' she snapped, slipping her coat off and hanging it over the banister. She made her way into the kitchen and headed for the fridge.

Lucy's curiosity peaked at her mother's out-of-character behaviour. She watched her from the lobby.

Her mother took a half-empty bottle of Pino from the door of the refrigerator, and poured herself a glass. Lucy frowned, her mother rarely ever drank on her own. 'Is everything alright?' Lucy asked.

'Of course,' Helen jabbed – agitated. She took a seat at the table. 'Why wouldn't it be?'

Her mother clocked the harshness in her own voice, and set the glass down. 'I'm sorry,' she mumbled, 'I shouldn't talk to you like that.'

'That's okay.'

'It's just…' She paused. 'Is there something, *anything* you would like to talk to me about? Or-Or tell me, or ask?'

Lucy frowned, wondering what prompted such a question. 'Well – there was one thing I wanted to ask you,' she said, plying her words with butter softness.

'Okay… Go on?'

Lucy drew a chair out and took a seat opposite. She sat,

silent, composing her question. 'When I was born, was it just me? Or, or did I have a twin? You know, that maybe didn't make it?'

Helen's whole face gasped. '*What?* No… Of *course* not.'

Lucy's eyes crimped with suspicion. 'You *would* tell me if I did,' she said, 'you know, if I would have had – say – a brother?'

Helen stared back at Lucy's expectant face. 'What are you talking about?' she said. 'What on *earth* has bought *this* on?'

Lucy fought to hide her scepticism, her mother's apparent bewilderment failing to ring true. She decided to push no further, and shook her head to mark the end of her attempts at interrogation. 'I guess it's nothing,' she said, 'don't worry about it.'

Lucy stood and made her way up the staircase to her room.

Helen watched her leave, feeling dismayed… 'Lucy?' she called, but Lucy didn't respond.

The bedroom door clacked shut.

*

Lucy lay motionless in her contemplation of the day that had been. She had much to mull over, and truths to try and discern from apparent curtains of deception.

If Jill *was* the other-world's version of her, where did Jack fit in? Was her mother lying? *Did* she in fact have a brother that didn't make it through the birthing process? Or did it, but everyone – for some reason – is hiding it.

She realised they might be answers she'd be better off attempting to extract from her grandmothers lips, her mother's mouth seeming impenetrably buttoned up tight.

She was pulled from her thoughts by the chatter of squirrel claws scrabbling over the rooftop. She smiled, happy to be distracted from questions she couldn't yet answer. 'Knock it off,' she shouted, 'don't you lot have beds to go to? Or nests? Or whatever it is you tree rats call home!'

The sounds of scratching claws were replaced by the subtly laboured creaks of her mildly wine-dosed mother climbing the staircase… She reached the top, and Lucy sensed her hovering outside her door, she lay perfectly still, not yet ready or desiring to talk about the matters that lay uneasy on her mind.

Her mother's shadow eventually departed the slither of light beneath the door, and the landing went dark.

Lucy listened to the gentle brush of her mother's bedroom door skimming the carpet as she quietly shut herself away for the night, hailing the end of her day…

Lucy continued lying perfectly still, the moonlight filtering through her curtains. She could hear the groan of the floorboards next door, following the creak-pattern of her mother's set routine: her walk to the bedside table, and the click of the switch as she flicked on the light, then the slow walk back across to her dressing table, stepping hesitantly as she fumbled to unclip her earrings. She hovered there for a time, thumb nailing the clips and catches of the rest of her jewellery, and the porcelain *chink* as they were dropped into the china pot she kept them in.

The chair from under the table was drawn out, and she could hear her begin to undress, draping her clothes neatly over the back of the seat.

The routine now usually went one of two ways – either she'd walk three paces to the chest of draws and take out a fresh nighty, or six to the side of bed to dig out the current one from beneath the duvet. She heard three paces and the draw slide out, it must be time for a fresh one…

In time, her mother climbed into bed, and shuffled to get comfortable. There was the second click as she flicked off the lamp, and the house finally fell still and silent.

Lucy embraced the stillness, a most welcomed, and stark contrast to the turmoil of the day. Her lids grew leaden.

She woke to the scratch of the squirrels returning for a repeat performance, clawing over the roof tiles. 'Come on guys, give it a rest,' she complained under her breath.

She heard them again, scratching across the slates, but it was not the usual scamper that she was used to hearing, the *scrit* of the claws seemed much slower than she was used to.

The roof suddenly groaned beneath a loading of weight far greater than that of any tree-dwelling rodent. Lucy jolted fully awake!

The roof complained again, this time, right above her head. She peered from under her bedclothes towards the ceiling, following the sound, as whatever was on the roof crawled towards the eves.

She jumped from her bed, and shied back from the sound. It was now right above the doors that opened out onto her balcony. She sensed the weight leave the roof, and whatever it was now scraping down the outside wall.

She saw a shadow pass behind the curtains, lowering silently onto the raised terrace behind!

Lucy stood in the dark, prone, apprehensively watching the drapes hanging over the doors. There was a hesitant squeal from behind the curtains, amplified by Lucy's inflating fears, cleaving through the silence like a saw through skin. Something was turning the handle!

Did I lock it?! she said under her breath. She thought she did. But she couldn't be sure?

The squealing ceased, and everything went quiet again… A new sound replaced the squealing, a hollow, scratching sound. Short, sporadic bursts. Resonating through the glass of the doors. Lucy stood frozen, glued to the floor.

She broke free the bonds of her fear, and began shuffling towards the noise, trying desperately to think of just *one* untroubling thing that could possibly be making such a sound. The scratching continued…

She extended a trembling hand towards the curtains, and parted them slightly with her fingers. Tentatively, she offered her eye to the gap…

Her pupil flicked around through the parting, trying to pinpoint the source of the sound. The scratching started again, her eye snapped to the source, and dilated! She saw a single, sinewy finger levering the putty from around the glass with its chipped nail.

She shook, shrinking back from the door, face tight with fear. She began sobbing uncontrollably. 'Please, God, *no!*' she whimpered. The scratching intensified.

Lucy looked about the floor for her trainers. She spied them, and quickly slipped them on.

She fought hard to force back the tears that begged to run free, desperately needing herself fully together and 'with it'.

The scraping stopped… Lucy held a breath… The silence sat for what felt like an eternity.

Lucy started to shuffle back towards the moonlit drapes, watching for signs of movement.

She parted the curtains again, and offered up her eye… A drawn, emaciated, skeletal face was staring straight back at her, its bulimic lips drawn back from calcite teeth. She screamed!

The thing drew back, and threw itself violently at the glass. It shattered into the room, sending slithers of glass spinning into Lucy's face! It began smashing itself repeatedly against the window, buckling the netting of lead strip that had held the panes of glass solid for three hundred years.

It reached its arm through one of the holes, and tried grabbing for Lucy, ripping the curtain from the rail. They fluttered to the ground, unveiling the full horror: The *thing*, the *entity*, the *monster* was now in *her* world, and it knew where she was!

It twisted its face against the lead-netting, trying to force its way in. Lucy looked around. She grabbed her phone and a bottle of scent from her chest-of-draws, and thundered from the room.

'Lucy! What the bloody-hell is going on?!' screamed her mother from the comfort of her bed.

Lucy didn't answer, all she could think about, was getting the thing away from the house, and away from her mother.

She careened down the staircase, grabbed for the lock, and rattled through the main doors, clearing the steps in one leap, darting a look up towards her balcony. The thing was already clambering down the wall towards her. She screamed and instantly upped her pace.

Helen burst into Lucy's room, slapping at the light switch, faltering back away from the sight of the shattered window that greeted her confusion.

Lucy sprinted down the bank, away from the visceral wail chasing her.

Her legs pumped as fast as they could. She could feel the hems of her pyjamas whipping at her ankles, the juddering reciprocation of her panicked breaths filling her ears.

She turned down the tree-lined path, and made for the fork. The thing followed.

Helen stumbled from the house just in time to see a dark, arachnid shape scuttle into the shadows of the trees. '*Lucyyyyyy!*' she screeched.

She ran back inside, and grabbed the phone from its base. She scrolled to Peter's number, and frantically began stabbing her finger at the *call* button.

Lucy could sense the thing was gaining. She twisted the lid off the scent bottle and began splashing some of the contents behind her as she thundered down the bank.

She reached the fork, and hooked a left towards Hobswyke, flicking a glance behind her as she rounded the bend. The thing was now only fifty yards away and gaining fast.

She hurled the scent bottle up the path and ducked through the gap in the hedgerow. The bottle spun through the air, sprinkling its contents up the lane.

Lucy dropped to the ground, lying flat against the dew-laden grass, and held her breath…

The creature clamoured round the corner and slowed to a crawl. It dropped on all fours, and began to creep slowly along the path, sniffing the droplets of scent that peppered the tarmac.

Lucy cowered in the grass, crouched as small as she could make herself trying to melt into the earth.

She held the hand that had been holding the bottle as far away from the thing as she possibly could, for fear of it picking up the scent.

The creature raised its nose skyward and sniffed at the air. It turned in Lucy's direction and extended its paper-thin nostrils towards her. They flexed at the breeze.

Emotionless eyes peered out into the darkness, searching out the girl who dared to invade its world… It turned away again, and with a hollow half-scream, set off up the lane.

Lucy drew a breath, and waited until she was sure the thing had gone, then rose gingerly from the grass, and edged back out onto the path.

She looked up the lane, but could see no sign of the cadaverous beast. She took a breath, and turned to make her way towards Sam's house. She stopped herself, realising that she didn't want to risk leading the thing to him.

She re-evaluated her options, then stepped back through the hedgerow and began making her way across the lawn towards an abandoned farm situated on the farthest side of the grounds. It'd been lying empty for decades, and she felt sure it would be a safe place to hide.

She took her phone from her pocket, and typed a message for Sam:

MALLETTE'S HERE!!! He's chasing me!

I'm making my way to the old farmstead to hide, can you meet me there with Jill and Jack, I think he might easily find them at the stable.

Please hurry… I'm afraid.

She continued across the field, turning the occasional look back to check she wasn't being followed.

Her phone rang out, the shrill jingle filling the frigid, night air. Her panicked fingers scrambled to swipe it silent again.

An excruciating shriek erupted from the trees behind her, and the thing exploded through the undergrowth and began barrelling across the grass towards her.

Her bones turned to gossamer, and with a whimper, she sprinted for the far side of the field, not daring to look back, sucking in petrified breaths through gritted teeth…

She finally reached the gate. It hung, twisted off its hinges, the wet, rotted wood pulled from the rusted bolts by the softness of its decaying fibres and the forces of gravity.

She stumbled over it on panicked legs, breaking it free of its final fixings. It thumped onto the ground sending Lucy careening across soil, baked solid by the relentless beating of the sun's radiation.

She staggered to her feet again, and ran into the cobbled yard. It was encircled by an eclectic mix of derelict buildings: the farmhouse was on her right, brick-built animal pens to her left, and ahead of her, an old timber barn with a large hayloft above it.

Her eyes flickered about the space, trying desperately to make a decision where best to run…

She heard wheezing, anaerobic breaths fast approaching the gate. She shuddered, turned and darted for the house.

Lucy skidded to a stop and squatted by the door. She stretched up to try the handle – it turned. It wasn't locked. She strained to open the door as quietly as she could, stepping inside, and with a nudge, closed it quietly behind her…

She found herself in the kitchen, and nearly started to gag on the fetid stench of mildew and damp rot clouding the air. She pulled the neck of her pyjamas up, over her nose in an attempt to filter the throat-burning atmosphere.

Lucy heard a sound outside, and crouched down beneath a window. She slowly lifted her eyes above a sill encrusted with twenty years of dust and the desiccated shells of dead insects.

Peering out from the grime-streaked glass, she saw *'It'*, crouched in the centre of the courtyard.

She studied the creature, hunched in the white-light of a full moon. It was the first chance she'd had to properly see it since they'd first encountered it. It seemed to have on some form of clothing, but it was difficult to see where it started and ended: damp, thread bare, and heavy with dirt and grime. It shuddered with rage, and strode across the cobbles. The parchment-thin skin on its legs rippling atop clustered strands of malnourished muscle fibres, racking the length of its tortured bones. They twitched and flinched with every stride it made in its search for Lucy.

She dropped down again, and anxiously scanned the room for options, then, reached up carefully slipping the latch on the door.

Keeping low – she hurried across the kitchen and ducked through into the living room, and crept to the window to check the whereabouts of *the thing*… She saw it, still in the yard, but now, it had turned and was making its way towards the house!

'Shit!' she spat, looking around for any avenue of escape. There was a back door ahead of her, and she could only prey it wasn't locked.

Fleet feet ran across the damp carpet, the soles of her shoes slapping against the waterlogged pile. Gingerly, she twisted the handle, and the door popped free from its frame. She exhaled her relief, pulling the handle towards her… The oil-starved hinges *cracked*, shattering the silence.

There was a heavy thud from the far side of the kitchen. The thing was at the door, trying to break through.

Lucy gripped the handle, and heaved it towards her. It graunched open, announcing her location to anything within a half-mile radius.

The thumping behind her intensified. Lucy ducked through into a yard overun with coils of thick-bramble and horsetail. She had no other choice than to try and manoeuvre through them.

She weaved carefully through their tangle, flexing loops of thorn-encrusted bough clear of her bare arms and face with hesitant, pinching fingers, threading her way through the rings of woody teeth. The thumping continued, intensifying, but the door was still holding fast.

Lucy could see she was nearly through, and bent the last coils back away from her face.

There was a splintering crash from inside the cottage. Lucy shuddered at the savagery of the sound! She panicked.

Throwing caution to the wind, she made a run for it, snagging her forearms as she burst from the razor-sharp thicket.

She turned and snapped a look behind her. It wasn't through the door yet.

Lucy sprinted along the back of the house, and around the side, past small brick-built outbuildings. She spied the cobbled courtyard ahead of her, and made a frantic dash for it.

She exited into the opening, desperately searching for a new place to hide, spying the animal pens across the way, and started towards them.

Lucy heard a seething, hollow, breathing on her left from the far end of the cottage. She froze, and turned to look… The *thing* had run back through the house and was now standing by what remained of the main door of the cottage, watching her.

Hot, liquid warmth trickled down her thighs, and she had a feeling she'd left her own body.

It extended itself slowly towards her. She felt unable to move, glued to the ground, frozen in fear in the flat, light of the moon.

The creature suddenly stopped advancing, and crouched, squinting its emotionless eyes as if examining her… It twisted its gaze, studying its prey…

Its angular face stretched wide, and it raised a limb, thrusting a needle-straight digit towards her. '*Hellllll…*' it hissed.

Lucy managed to unfreeze her legs, and turned to run, sprinting away to the animal sheds.

She flicked a terrified glance behind her, the emaciated figure was still standing there, watching her run, and Lucy was sure she saw what looked to be a look of confusion on its moonlit face.

She clambered over the railing and dropped inelegantly into a maze of rusted gates and fenced-off pens. She struggled to her feet, and meandered deep into the unlit labyrinth, trying to lose herself in the confusion of steel tubes.

She spied a darkened corner, and made for it, stumbling over the last of the gates and sinking into the gloom.

Lucy sat huddled, and scooped a few armfuls of the damp, rotted hay carpeting the floor over her, hoping the stench would mask her fear-scented skin.

She watched from her tenebrous hiding place, barely daring to draw breath…

A long, slender shadow began to lengthen into the pens. The *thing* – silhouetted by the cold, lunar glow – crept hesitantly into sight.

It stopped shy of the railings, crouched, and sniffed the steel… Lucy noticed a moment of recognition in its gaunt features, and sank lower into the moulding hay.

The creature leaned in, scanning the darkness for Lucy, the scent of her fear hanging fresh in its nose.

It clambered over the railing like a cellar spider, unfurling its limbs into the maze of animal pens.

Lucy stiffened, trying in vain to sink through the floor. It smelled the next set of bars, and clambered over them…

The creature methodically unravelled it gangly limbs through the maze of steel towards Lucy's hiding place, searching her out through the pitch-black, moulding atmosphere. Methodically, it reeled in the distance between them. Lucy sat utterly helpless, and started to make peace with the realisation that this was the end of her time in this world.

Serious contemplation of rising into the creatures waiting arms grew strong in her mind, as if in accepting her fate, she could at least feel in some part that she ended her days on her own terms.

The creature climbed over the final set of railings and lowered itself into Lucy's pen. She shut her eyes, and exhaled her desire to carry on living, releasing the last of her considerable fight, awaiting a destiny that she'd run out of avenues to escape from…

'*Oi!*' yelled a voice from the far end of the shed. The thing rose into a shard of moonlight, and turned to see what dared to interrupt its search.

Sam, Jack and Jilly were stood at the furthest end of the pens, shocked at seeing the creature in *their* realm, but their desire to save a friend overwhelmed any fears they may have had, and counter-intuitively, they called to it – taunting. 'Hey, you, over here,' they screamed.

It leered at their arrogance, baring blackened teeth, chattering its broiling anger.

Lucy saw her chance, and crawled quietly away behind its averted anger. She saw a gap in the rotted timbers and slid under the fencing and struggled to her feet, running from the shed into the freshness of the night air.

Sam, Jack and Jilly saw Lucy slink away and hovered, observing the skeletal figure looming in the shadow, but it just stood, watching them watching it.

Sam felt perplexed. The *thing*, the *creature*, *Mallette*, or whatever best described it, seemed far less relentless in its disposition than it had been on their first encounter.

'What do we do now?' asked Jill.

'I-I-I don't know,' replied Sam, 'I'm afraid my plan ended when I shouted "Oi".'

The thing began to clamber over the railings in their direction, like the spider from hell that it was, eyes locked solid on the three of them. 'Boyyyyy…' it wheezed – rivers of drool running from its mouth.

Jack shied from his old moniker, the other two followed suit.

They all turned and ran, making their way hastily around the back of the shed.

They could hear the creature begin thundering over the railings to follow, the clatter of its bony limbs ringing loud through the miles of hollow tubing.

They turned the corner at the end of the building, and saw Lucy waiting for them over by the doors of the barn, frantically waving at them to follow…

They sprinted to the entrance to join her side, just happy to see her alive. They all entered a vast space filled to the rafters with antiquated machinery: early tractors, industrial bandsaws, threshing machines, reversible ploughs, balers, flails, all sharing a time-inherited coating of powdery brown rust.

'We need to hide,' whispered Sam. They hurriedly made their way further in, prompted by the sounds of the rapidly advancing beast.

They weaved deep in amongst the museum of obsolete equipment, snaking through the lanes running between each city-block of abandoned machinery.

They all split up and hid…

Sam stepped up onto the front of a tractor. He rolled his face from behind the radiator grill, and watched the entrance.

The thing's twisted shadow extended through the doorway, its twisted limbs extending into the barn, peering suspiciously around the frame. It could smell them all through the lingering aroma of old grease and coagulated oil.

It sunk down onto its hands and crabbed sideways into the shadows, twisting its face close to the ground, seeking a telltale glimpse of feet beneath the acre of forgotten apparatus.

All four of them stood perched on different objects, lifting their feet clear of the ground. Sam looked across to Lucy. 'Are you okay?' he mouthed.

Her brows crumpled. 'No,' she mimed in response, looking close to tears.

Sam wrapped his fingers around one of the tractor's

cracked tyres to steady himself, and crouched between his bent knees, twisting his head down to peek through the maze of steering linkages he was balanced on… He could just about see the creature's gangly limbs crawling through the machinery graveyard towards them. It looked to be heading straight towards Jack's hiding place.

Sam noticed a few old bolts scattered on the ground, and leaned out to grab one.

He quietly rose again to look over the tractor. He could see a clear path to the entrance. He looked about the room, seeking an escape option, and saw one.

He extended his arm back, then hurled the rusting chunk of metal towards the doors…

It cracked off the planking at the far end of the shed. The emaciated creature screeched at the sound, turned, and scurried back towards the noise.

Sam dropped down off his towing-point perch, and beckoned the rest to follow. They followed suit, and meandered silently through the labyrinth of rusted tin ware towards a ladder Sam had spied in the unlit corner of the room. It seemed to rise into the hayloft above and, in the scheme of things, it seemed their only option.

Sam led the way, and the rest followed, gingerly feeling their way up the rot-softened rungs in total darkness.

Sam stepped off the ladder into the loft, and helped the rest through the hatch one at a time. Carefully, he lowered the wooden trapdoor across the hole, and they all took a breath…

The loft space was illuminated by a thousand shards of light shining through its pepper-pot roof. 'I'm sorry, Sammy,' whispered Lucy, 'when you called me, it heard my phone and followed me here. I didn't have a chance to let you know to stay away.'

'Oh *shit*, I'm sorry,' he said. 'I-I didn't think!'

'It's not your fault,' she said. She looked about the loft space. 'What are we going to do now?' she asked, but Sam looked as bereft of ideas as she was.

He chewed nervously at the side of his finger, trying to formulate any kind of plan to get them all away from the wiry insect-from-hell relentlessly pursuing them… The other three looked on in anticipation of an idea.

He dropped down and peered between the planks of the hatch, but could see nothing.

'Can you see it?' asked Lucy.

He shook his head. 'No, it's not there.'

'So, what do we do?' she asked, praying he had a suggestion.

Sam stretched up and looked around. He saw a door at the far end of the hayloft, there was a handrail just visible beyond the frame. He concluded it must be a staircase.

He extended his chin towards it. 'There,' he said, they all looked. 'We'll make our way down and hope it doesn't see us, then I think we need to go and get help.'

Lucy nodded. In her mind, the existence of the entity had been kept a secret from the adults for far too long now. 'Okay, I agree.'

They all rose and started creeping across the cavernous loft space towards the door, the damp floorboards making surprisingly little sound – the moulding timbers too soft to creak.

Sam noticed a large knothole in one of the planks, and sank down to peer through it. He rolled his eye around the hole, looking for any signs of the thing below, but could see nothing of the creature, it seemed to have left. He breathed a deep sigh of relief. 'I think it's gone,' he said.

He stood to rejoin the others, and they made for the door. 'Go,' he whispered to Jill and Jack, ushering them through towards the staircase.

A set of long, sinewy fingers wrapped the frame of their escape route, and the wretched, meatless aberration crawled from the unlit stairwell into the room.

Lucy let out an impotent scream! Sam froze. Jill and Jack stood petrified in front of the tall, willowy figure looming menacingly in the doorway before them, its grime-stained skin and the filth-encrusted rags barely visible in the near-lightless entranceway.

Its protracted limbs spanned the frame like a web, cutting off their means of escape. They all erupted into a sprint for the hatch. Sam arrived first and dropped down to open it, but there was no handle top-side! He pawed at the edges of the plank panel with desperate fingers, but couldn't hook them under enough to lift it.

The entity stepped from the shadows into the loft space, the thousand needles of light illuminating its emaciation. But somehow, it looked different. Its limbs seemed softened, not so taught with rage as they were before. It crept through the isolated islands of darkness and light towards them, crouched low.

Sam continued in vain to get any kind of purchase on the trapdoor, but failed.

The thing twisted its gaze at the terrified huddle at far end of the attic.

Sam abandoned his attempts, and stood to shield Lucy, a shard of light illuminating his face.

The thing recognised him, and bared its charcoal teeth, letting out an ungodly screech and making a lunge in his direction.

Jack stepped in front of Sam. 'No!' he yelled. The thing stopped. Its face relaxed out of its anger, lowering its emaciated lip back across its grinding teeth.

It watched Jack, just staring at him, studying. The sight of Jack's face seemed to subdue its fury, Sam even fancied he saw a weak spark of humility hidden deep within its black, sunken eye sockets.

The entity leaned its fiendish face forwards into a shard of light. 'B-B-Boyyy,' it croaked, with its withered, fibrous vocal chords. It twisted its skeletal face like a dog reacting to a new sound, then took another step closer. They all crystallised with fright. The entity saw the fear in their faces, and backed away again a half step.

'What's it doing?' Lucy whispered, her diaphragm quivering, feeling close to fainting. 'Why isn't it coming for us?'

It strode gingerly forwards into yet another beam scything through the perforations of the roof. The four of them drew a collective breath. Its face was changing, looking subtly more human than it ever had before – far less animal, more comparable to a man.

With uncharacteristic curiosity, it rotated its face like a curious dog, examining Jack. They all saw the recognition in its face, but it seemed curious about the changes it saw in Jack now he looked older.

Another move, the light cutting across its eyes – they were framed with confusion, and displaying more sadness than the hate and resentment the four of them had become accustomed to facing. But whatever the look they now had, it was a look that was a far cry from the loathing and dead-eyed hate that once there was.

Jill peered from behind her brother's protective gate. The creature caught a glimpse of her face, and took an urgent step towards her, extending a tentative arm. '*Girllll*,' it wheezed, its voice still metallic, but now, softer. Its voice seemed strangely laced with a perceivable amount of regret, almost apologetic in its grainy whispered tone.

Jill ducked back behind the protection of her brother's

outstretched arms. The creature dropped its clawed hand again, appearing oddly dejected.

Lucy looked askance from the back of the huddle, confused by the peculiarity in the creature's behaviour, finding it near impossible to read its intentions.

The creature turned its eyes back to Jack. They seemed to be pleading to him. There was a subtle sense of desperation in its countenance, they could all see it trying to fight through its long-worn lividity.

It crept apprehensively towards Jack's palpable uncertainty, reaching out to him. Jack didn't feel as much inclination to back away as before, fortified by the perceivably pathetic nature of the tortured creature reaching out for him.

Sam watched, as emaciated, cadaverous fingers advanced towards Jack's face, wondering at what point to push Jack aside and make a grab for the twisted, skeletal arm.

He looked around to see where he could push him, then snapped his eyes back to the advancing hand... His eyes widened. The fingers, they seemed to be foreshortening, receding, shrinking back away from Jack's face as the creature advanced towards him. Then they all saw it, the entity's entire gangly physique seemed to be morphing, changing, transforming from its furious gait to something far less threatening. '*Look!*' Sam hissed. 'Look at it, it's, it's changing.'

'B-Boyyyyy... Giiiirl...' it wheezed, pawing desperately at the two of them with its shrinking limbs.

Jilly and Jack could see something they barely had memories of, manifesting in front of their eyes. A vague shadow from their past, earlier life, almost banished from their rejected memories. It was the only thing that could have been considered a *positive* in their sad little lives.

The creature's fingers finally managed to reach out and touch Jack, but only because Jack resisted pulling away.

The hand now looked decidedly human, a tenderness and curiosity in the way it moved. The entity lifted its gaunt face to look up at the boy, its sunken eyes acting as wells for the tears of regret it seemed to be shedding.

'Father?' said Jack.

The thing dropped to its knees, and wrapped itself around him.

'*Father*?' muttered Sam, under his considerably confused breath.

Footsteps thundered up the staircase. A silhouetted figure shone a blinding light through the entrance into the loft space. 'Lucy! Sam? What the *hell* is going on in here,' the silhouette shouted. Lucy recognised the voice, it was her mother. 'What *is* all this?' she insisted.

She strode towards the gathering, shining the beam of the torch around all of the protagonists. The thing scuttled away from the light and cowered into the corner.

She walked towards the huddle, flashing the light in all of their faces. 'Is someone going to tell me what is going on?' she yelled – shocked at seeing unfamiliar faces. She'd always thought she knew all of her daughter's friends, but she didn't recognise these two.

She shone the torch directly into Jack's eyes. He squinted, and raised a hand to block the stinging light.

Helen's whole face fell open. She leaned to the side to see around his hand. Jack blinked into the light.

She lowered the torch slightly to stop him squinting. His face straightened, and Helen gasped. She clasped her hand to her mouth.

'Mum? What's wrong?' asked Lucy. But her mother was too shocked to hear her. She just stared at Jack as if nothing else existed.

She stepped towards him. 'T-Thomas?' she asked.

Jack stepped back from the apparent stranger, shaking his head.

She stepped towards him again. 'I-Is that you…? Is that you, Thomas…?' she said again.

'H-H-Helen?' croaked a voice from the unlit corner of the loft. She spun the beam towards the voice. A gaunt, skeletal figure edged tentatively from the shadows towards her. Helen shied from the hideous figure, her face racked with revulsion. Then she halted her retreat.

A shard of moonlight cut across its pitiful eyes, she recognised the intention behind them. They were eyes she hadn't look into for nineteen years.

'Oh good God in heaven,' she simpered, 'Thomas!'

Lucy watched on – shocked to hear her mother say the name. That this cruel entity that had terrified them so utterly, could have possibly grown from the boy her grandmother had described to her.

Helen edged towards him, but he shied away, embarrassed by what he'd become.

She examined him with the warmth of the torchlight. He looked thin, desolate and meatless. 'Oh my God, what on earth happened to you?' she wept. She stepped to him, dropping to her knees, and engulfed him in her relief at seeing him again.

Her fingers could feel the bones through his paper-thin skin. She reran every dream and fleeting thought she'd ever had of him, finally coming to the realisation that those dreams, were in fact memories.

The rest of them watched Lucy's mother holding the wretched man, a man who'd only existed in her dreams for the past nineteen years. Then Helen's brow furrowed, and she turned the torchlight back to Jack, then to Thomas again. Her face displaying her confusion at how much like her memories of Thomas Jack looked. Then the light fell on Lucy and Jilly watching from the back of the huddle and, for a split second, she was unable to tell them apart?

'What's going on?' she simpered, her saline eyes emptying down her face. 'Who… Who *are* you?'

'Th-They're ours,' Thomas croaked from the umbrella of the shadows he skulked in. 'They're our children.'

He looked to Jilly and Jack. 'Boy, G-Girl *Th-This*, is your mother.'

Another set of footsteps thundered up the staircase, and Peter Fletcher appeared in the doorway. 'I got your message, what's happening…?'

TWENTY

THE JOURNAL OF LUCY CLAYBOURNE

July 5th

After nearly 18 years, I finally met my father… and it was the last person I would have expected, or wanted it to be. But the hope I'd always held close to my heart can't change the realities of my life, so I find myself in a position where I need to try to accept them…

I guess I've always been in possession of the knowledge that I might one day discover the identity of my father, but I confess to having never imagined the possibility of having a sister and a brother too! I don't know who it was more of a shock for, me or my poor mum?

It's almost funny, I heard of Thomas for the first time just a few days ago, when Grandma described a child to me from her past. What a twist to my strange life that she was actually speaking of the man who would eventually be complicit in conceiving me.

Peter arrived at the barn a short time after Mum. I have never seen a man look so confused in all my life. If it wasn't for the enormity of the situation, I think I could have allowed myself to laugh. Poor thing, but Peter's been amazing in helping sort things out tonight.

We got something for Thomas to eat, he's so thin. Peter likened him to a POW? I didn't know what that was at first, so had to look it up, apparently it means 'Prisoner of War'. I didn't really know what that was either, so I searched for some pictures. I can now see where he's coming from… I find it so sad sometimes to see how shitty humans can be towards each other… It makes me realise that often, 'we' are real monsters.

We were all up most of the night trying to unravel everything. Sam seemed to already have most of it worked out in his amazing mind. I sometimes wish I had half of his brain, mine doesn't seem to work all that well!

Mum and Thomas can't recall how they actually got trapped in the other realm, but they somehow managed to learn how to survive. Then when they became of age, Mum must have got pregnant. First with the twins, then with me. And that's when Mum must have accidentally created, or discovered, a portal back into this world.

Sam said, 'Imagine how you would be in that place, if the only meaningful thing in your life suddenly left you.' He reckons the resulting resentment and anger must have manifested as a physical change over the years, turning him outwardly into the monster that he'd become inside. What a strange and messed up world it is through there!

Hilly's frightened by him, but I'm not surprised, the way he still looks, and together with the tales we've been telling her. But he does now at least look human. I'm just glad she never saw him before!

Do I keep calling him 'Thomas', or will I ever one day

ever call him 'Father', or 'Dad'? I guess that one will be answered in time.

Everyone else is trying to sleep now, I'm not sure how successful they'll be, this has all been so very bizarre, a bit like a dream... But I've needed to write this down as a way to draw a close to my day.

I'm going to try to sleep myself now, I hope there are no more surprises waiting for me, I don't think I could handle that.

I guess I'll write everything that we've learned in my journal tomorrow, after I've slept some...

I'm just going to tape some cardboard over my balcony window, and sleep in the spare room tonight, then it's time to draw an end to this weirdest of days...

July 6th

Amazingly, I managed to sleep. Mad, considering how much of the last few days I've been rerunning through my mind.

I'm going to go and check on the new arrivals, and see how they're all doing.

Peter gave Thomas a place to rest at his for the night, Jack and Jilly seemed more than happy to remain at the stables. It's funny, I think they actually like it there!?

But Holy Shit! I have a sister, and a brother... and I now know who my father is. That's crazy!

I'll go and get something to eat now. Peter is going to try and do something to fix my window sometime today. I guess I'll write more then...

What a horrible morning! What was that word Mum used? 'Harrowing'? Anyway, me and Mum quickly ate something, then we went over to Peter's to check on Thomas. Apparently, he slept in their spare room, but UNDER the bed!

I've never cried so much in my entire life, both of us did. To see how thin my father is in the light of day, and how ill he looks. It amazes me how differently I perceive him now, now I know his true nature. To me, he looks pitiful and pathetic. That word seems cruel, but I'm afraid it fits.

Hilly is still wary of him this morning, hiding behind me as we were talking. I think it'll help when he eventually puts some weight on. But bloody hell he's tall. He's well over 6 feet. Peter reckons he must be 6 foot 3, or 6 foot 4?

Mum said she's started to remember a lot now, maybe seeing him again has kick-started her memory? Thomas seems reluctant to talk about it all, and who can blame him, he's been trapped in that terrible place for 40 years! That's more than twice the time I've been alive. And I doubt any of his memories would be happy ones.

It's funny watching Peter's face while we're talking about what's been happening, it must all sounds so unbelievable. I know it would to me if I hadn't actually seen it myself.

Sam and Peter are going up to Hobswyke later today to weld the railings back in place. I hope Sam doesn't get too freaked out at having to go back there.

I love Sam, I don't think anyone has ever been there for me as much as he has over the last few days. My feelings for him, I guess, have got much stronger. I think about him a lot, all the time in fact, and with nothing but extreme fondness...

SHIT! Peter is a mess! He came back with Sam after fixing the railing back in place, and apparently, Sam showed him how the stepping stones work. It seemed his dad didn't handle it well.

Sam then pushed his phone through the liquid and took a picture. He showed it to his dad. He FREAKED! I think this whole experience is going to mess with us all in some way. I just hope it doesn't affects anyone long term!

Me, Jilly and Jack all hugged when we saw each other. We've hugged before of course, but this time, we held each other as brother and sisters, and it did feel different. It felt amazing!

I pulled Sam into the huddle too, I could see he was feeling left out. As far as I'm concerned, he's as much of a brother to them as anyone. As for me, I can no longer look upon Sam that way, like I might have before. If I'm to be honest with myself, my feelings for him are now very different. Few people on this planet are as wonderful as Samuel Fletcher, and that's something I can no longer ignore.

Mum spent much of the day with Jilly and Jack. She says she has some vague recollection of them as babies, before she accidentally created the portal back to this world. I guess the shock of breaking through the mirror and falling through that awful blackness back into Hobswyke would be frightening enough to give anyone amnesia! But it was lovely to watch her being with them. She has 19 years to catch up on, and she seems determined to give it to them all in one, heartfelt hit!

I've just realised, I'm the youngest of the three of us, by about 1 year... That feels a bit weird!

July 7th

We're going to go and see my nan tomorrow, she wants to see Thomas, and of course, the grandkids she never knew she had.

We have much to sort out over the next few weeks. Grandma says she still knows a few people high up in government, and she thinks there are strings she can pull to create paperwork for the new arrivals, without too many questions being asked. I hope she's right!

I'm just going to pop out and meet up with Sam before the day ends. He says he wants to see me, and yes, I'd like to see him too...

TWENTY-ONE

SOMETHING THEY MISSED?

'HI, SAMMY,' Lucy warbled, as she strolled down the lane. She could see Sam ahead of her sitting on the stump of a felled tree, keenly awaiting her arrival.

'Hey,' he replied in a relaxed voice, smiling, 'you alright?'

'Yep. I'm good – I think.'

He smirked and nodded knowingly. 'Thanks for coming out for a bit,' he said, 'there's been so much happening lately, I've not had much chance to get you alone.'

Lucy laughed, coyly. She'd felt the same way. She struggled to not flush crimson pink. 'I know. It's been difficult,' she empathised, 'shall we walk over to the lake?'

'Why not? That'd be nice…'

Sam rose from the stump to join her, offering her an arm to loop, and they set off…

'Your dad's been good today,' said Sam, 'in good spirits, if you can imagine such a thing.' But Lucy didn't answer, she just gazed through the pavement passing beneath their saunter. 'Lucy? Are you alright?'

'Hm? Oh. Sorry,' she said, 'it's just that I haven't called him

"Dad" yet. It just sounded – I don't know – odd.'

'Sorry,' he said.

Lucy seemed distracted by her thoughts. 'Nooo. No it's fine,' she insisted, 'it *is* actually something I think I'm going to have to get used to – eventually.' She smiled across at him to let him know she was fine with it. 'I was also just thinking about what we're eventually going to do about everything. Where they're all going to go?'

Sam's brows flickered his confusion. 'Surely, Jilly and Jack—'

'Oh yeah,' she said, knowing where he was going with his comment, 'they'll most probably move into the gatehouse with me and Mum. In fact, I think Mum'll insist on it. And if she doesn't, *I* will.' 'Mind you, have you seen the way she is with them?'

Sam laughed affectionately. 'She's acting like a new mother.'

Lucy smirked. 'We mock, but it's not that far from the truth, is it?'

'Yeah, I guess you're right…' he said, softly smiling. 'So, it's just your father then, really.'

Lucy inhaled and loosed a clueless breath, and nodded. 'Yeah.'

'Well, he's fine to be at ours for now. Him and Dad are actually really getting along. Thomas even seems to have some vague memories of my dad as a child, when they were both orphans.'

'Really?'

'Yeah,' he said. 'We've all learned so much about each other over these last few days. It's been kind of crazy…' They continued to saunter along the path. 'How's your grandma now by the way? It must have been quite a shock for her.'

Lucy took a deep breath a sighed. 'Yeah. She's fine. She's strong.'

Sam agreed.

'We're going over to see her tomorrow, so she can finally see him. It's been nearly forty years you know.'

'I know. It's hard to get your head around.'

Lucy looked across at him. 'That's where they both went the other night – your dad and my mum – when they disappeared off together. They went to see my nan.'

'Is that true?' he asked.

She nodded. 'Apparently, Nan got worried about what I'd told her, and decided to let them know what we'd been doing, and what we'd found... I guess she was just worried about us, so I can't really blame her.''Guess not.' He laughed. 'I'm surprised they believed her. It must have sounded insane.'

They both turned off the path and made their way across the green towards the lake shore, then saw Jilly and Jack were already there, sitting on one of the benches that looked out over the water.

'Look who's here,' muttered Lucy, lifting her chin towards the water's edge, pleased to see them out and about on their own. 'Hello, you two!' she called.

They both turned smiles to their arrival. 'Hello,' said Jilly in her soft, timid voice.

Lucy leaned over the back of the bench and wrapped her arms around the both of them. 'Whatcha doin'?' she said, brightly.

Jill and Jack looked at each other, and frowned.

'What – are – you – doing,' she reiterated, without the yank accent.

'Owww...' they said in unison.

'We were just enjoying looking around,' said Jack, 'it's so lovely here.'

'It's not bad is it,' said Sam, turning to drink in the view they were both admiring. He lolloped to the water's edge, crouched, and started flipping pebbles, looking for one that was round, flat and smooth… He found one, stood, and hurled it side-on… It skimmed across the millpond stillness of the lake, kissing the reflected sky with a succession of bright splashes. He counted as it bounces across the water… 'Eleven!' he cried with a strange sense of triumph.

Jack rose from the seat and walked down to join him. Lucy took his seat next to her sister, shrugging tweely and nudging Jilly with her shoulder.

Jack crouched next to Sam. 'Do you want a go?' asked Sam. 'You need to find one that's flat, a bit like this one here.' But Jack didn't seem interested. He just picked up random pebbles, held them up, and dropped them, watching the speed of their fall.

'Ah. Yeah,' said Sam, 'I'd forgotten about that.' Jack looked to him for answers. Sam attempted an explanation in the simplest terms he could. 'The way the stones fall *here*, is, I guess, how they're supposed to fall. There's something about the other place that makes things move much slower. Slower to fall, slower to burn, slower to splash, that kind of thing. Do you understand?'

Jack shrugged.

'It's a thing called "time", and it's running much slower through there.'

Jack nodded, finally gleaning some understanding, however vague. 'It's always been a bit like that,' Jack said, 'things moving slowly, compared to what I see here.' He dropped another pebble, and watched it click against the other stones. 'But recently, it's been getting even slower than it was before. But I didn't realise that wasn't normal. Until now.'

'Even *slower*?' said Sam.

'Yes. The things like that,' he said dropping another rock, 'the *time* thing, has recently been getting slower than it ever was.'

Sam thought about Jack's words… 'I wonder why?' he said, thoughtfully, out into the distance. 'What could be making that happen?'

Lucy and Jilly watched the boys from the seat, already at a place where they could share a comfortable silence. 'What are they talking about?' asked Jill.

Lucy huffed a theatrically dismissive shrug. 'Boy stuff,' she responded. Jilly laughed. Lucy turned to face her. 'How's your dad doing now? *Our* dad. *Thomas* I mean… How's Thomas doing?'

'He's fine, I think?' she said. 'It's nice to see him the way he is now. I think we'd forgotten that he ever existed – because of what he'd become.'

'I can imagine,' said Lucy.

Sam walked up to join them. 'Well, I have to say, I find the name *Thomas* decidedly less intimidating than, "*The Master*",' he said, with a levitous air of sarcasm.

Jack rose from the stones and turned to Jill. She looked back at him, there was apprehension in their faces, and confusion hanging in the air between them.

Sam's brow furrowed at their reactions. 'What? What have I said?' he asked.

Jilly shook her head with a modicum amount of confusion. 'The Master, *isn't* Thomas,' she explained.

'What?' Lucy said. 'But I thought you said—'

Jack looked puzzled too. 'No. *The Master* is the other one. The *magic* one.' He looked visibly nervous just to be talking of him.

Jill took up the baton, lowering her voice as though they were in a crowded room full of their enemies. 'The Master is the one that brings the animals through the mirror,' whispered Jill, nervously. 'Those ones he uses to *wet the stone*.'

Sam stepped in closer. 'His name,' he said, 'this, *man*. Is it Mallette?'

Jilly flinched at the mere mention of the name, then covered her mouth with her hand. She nodded, then the nod became a frantic shake. 'Yes, but you shouldn't say his name!' she whispered insistently through her fingers.

'But why didn't we see him?' asked Lucy.

Jack looked decidedly pained and as reluctant to talk of Mallette as his sister. He ducked nervously into the huddle and whispered, 'Because… he's not always there,' he explained under his breath. He looked around nervously like a frightened bird, then leaned further in. 'He mostly lives in the mirrors.'

Both Sam and Lucy pulled peculiar faces in unison.

'We have to stop talking about him!' insisted Jilly. 'He's – he's not a good person.'

'Okay. Okay…' said Lucy, 'we're sorry. We won't say anymore.' She took Jill's hand and cupped it into her own, and smiled.

But Sam had many questions he wanted to present, and fresh answers he *needed* to know. But he pulled them all back inside for the sake of the new arrivals, and held them fast.

*

Sam and Lucy arrived at the lakeside cottage after escorting Jack and Jilly back to the stable.

Sam had been quiet, looking a mixture of pensive and apprehensive. 'So, what do you make of all that then?' he asked.

Lucy shook her head and slow-blinked. 'Shhh, it's not our problem anymore. We're out of that place, and so are they,' she said, glancing in the direction of the stable block. 'Let's just all try and forget about it, for the sake of the kids.'

Sam looked back at her soft, calming features, wondering if he'd ever be able to act like nothing had happened… He eventually smiled. 'Okay. I guess you're right. I will try.'

'Thank you,' she said, affectionately.

Sam huffed a snigger. '"Kids?"' he said with sarcasm. 'You do realise they're older than both of us!'

Lucy laughed, nodded, then look deep into his eyes. She rose onto her toes, pulled him in close, and kissed him with far more tenderness than she ever had before.

Sam could feel her body pressed against his, the rise and fall of her breathing. A wave of affection exhaled through her soft mouth and he freed himself to receive it… The kiss became a hug, and they hung for what felt like a lifetime in the happiness of their embrace… 'I love you, Sam,' she muttered into his grateful ear.

The words completed Sam's life. 'I love you too,' he whispered. His response tightened her hold, and she dropped her head affectionately onto his shoulder.

They eventually unwrapped themselves, and gazed into each other with smiling eyes. 'So, I'll see you tomorrow?' she said.

Sam smiled. 'I'd love to.'

Lucy turned to make her way home. Sam watched her leave, his innards feeling like they've been stirred with a spoon. 'Bye,' he called up the lane.

She twisted a look back over the delicate sweep of her shoulder. 'Bye…'

*

The day had been a long one. Sam sat up in bed with his back against the headboard. He was staring at the wall opposite, his thoughts filled with nothing but *Lucy*, his face wincing the occasional smile as he leafed through his fondest memories.

He was struggling with the concept that the most beautiful person he'd ever encountered had proclaimed her love for him.

But he gradually found himself able accept it, and believe in its truth.

He pulled back out of his thoughts, and took his phone from the bedside table. He swiped the screen and tapped his picture files. He scrolled through the thumbnails until he saw one of Lucy, and tapped it…

He swiped through his photos, never realising until now, just how many of the pictures on his phone were of her. He paused on each one, finding something in every image to smile at. 'You're amazing,' he muttered fondly into the Rolodex of images of her beaming face.

He continued swiping through the gallery of his life, until he happened upon the photo he took through the pool to show his father.

His expression puckered, repulsed at the image, and the memories it birthed. He turned his face away, but his eyes remained locked on the picture.

He pondered Lucy's desire to try to forget about 'that place', and tapped the image. The trash can symbol flashed up in the corner of the screen. He hovered his thumb above it, trying to find the inner strength to delete the one and only photographic evidence he, or any of them had, of the strange world they'd discovered.

He withdrew his thumb, closed the photo file, and turned the screen off. He sat in the disquiet of his failure to delete the image, reasoning that he didn't need to delete it, he'd just avoid looking at it.

But curiosity crushed his resistance, and he lifted the phone again, swiping to the picture files and reopening the image.

He dragged the picture larger on the screen and leaned into it. The memories of their rescue flooded back. The sheer horror they'd faced, and the unbridled joy they'd felt at succeeding. He was amazed to realise just how much the memories had faded over the course of just a couple of days .

He dabbed his finger on the screen again, bringing up the trash can option for a second time. He presented his thumb to tap it, then stopped. His brow darkened. He lifted the phone closer to his face. He studied the photo through concerned eyes. 'What on earth?' he muttered.

He zoomed further into the image with a spread of his fingers, and looked again. He could see a figure silhouetted against the dusky sky, crouched on the roof of the mansion. He expanded the image as large as it would go. He could see the hunched figure clearer now, its eyes glowing bright red. It seemed to be looking down towards the pool, straight at the camera.

Sam shuddered, quickly swiping the image away, and urgently opened the phone function.

He scrolled to Lucy's thumbnail, and presses it. He lifted the phone to his ear and darted a look at the time on his bedside table: 1:29am. He quickly tapped the call off again. 'Damn!' he said.

He loosed a frustrated sigh, and fought to calm himself... 'You can show her tomorrow,' he told the solitude of the room, 'what's the rush?'

*

Lucy lay slumped in her bed with her knees pulled up tight, resting her journal on her legs to bring it closer to her eyes. She was just finishing her final entry for the day.

She rotated her gaze fondly as she wrote the last few words, before flamboyantly tapping the pen at the end of the sentence.

'There. Finished,' she said, snapping the book shut. She leaned her head back against the marshmallowy softness of her stack of pillows, and stared thoughtfully through at the ceiling. A reminiscent smile licked at the corners of her mouth…

She opened the journal again and flattened it out on her knees, taking the lid of the ballpoint between her teeth and drawing the pen out. She presented the nib to the last word of the very last sentence and wrote, the pen hovering millimetres above the page. She lifted contemplative eyes and stared across at the wall opposite. She smiled, and dropped her eyes back to the page, drawing a heart next to the word '**Sam**' and skewering it with a meticulously detailed arrow.

She shut the book again, kicked the duvet off her legs, and rose from the bed. She walked over to her chest of draws and deposited the journal on top of it.

She took a moment to check herself in the new antique mirror her mother had bought for her. She peered at her reflection. 'Well, goodnight then,' she said to the face looking back at her, 'but let's not make this *goodbye*,' she said with a thespian air, 'let's make it *au revoir*.'

She smiled lightly, and ran her fingers around the peaks and troughs of the carved, wooden frame. The silvering on the outer edges of the glass was mottled and heavily foxed. 'Like laughter lines worn proudly on a face that's lived a life of happiness,' she muttered…

Lucy turned, walked back across the room, and jumped back into bed. She pulled the duvet up around her neck and leaned across to turn off the bedside lamp. The light clicked off, and the room fell into darkness, save for the sliver of moonlight on the wall opposite.

Lucy shuffled to get comfortable, and settled… The house fell silent, and still, not a sound to be heard…

The mirror lorded over Lucy, sitting high and proud on top the chest of draws, echoing the world that lay before it…

A dark smudge appeared in the reflection of the moonlit room, manifesting in the farthest reaches of the negative space.

The smudge began to shimmer, and muddy, then began moving slowly forwards towards the glass. The smut swirled like an angry cloud, and thickened into a writhing, smoky mass, its growing force distorting the reflection. A churning mass floating ethereally towards the back of the mirror, its smoky tendrils slowly curling inwards, beginning to solidify, resolving into a scant silhouette of a heavily cloaked figure.

The entity continued to drift until it hovered just behind the window to the world beyond. It lifted bony hands from beneath the cloak, and presented them to the crystal boundary to Lucy's room.

A face rose from beneath the hood, and opened its eyes. They flashed incandescent like a searing furnace, the edges of its smouldering sockets quivering in the haze of the heat flaming from its hateful gaze.

The entity rolled its face against the glass, and looked down at Lucy asleep in her bed. A desiccated lip quivered back from chipped, calcite teeth. They shimmered in the livid heat emanating from its mouth.

'*Je viens pour toi…*' the figure hissed, it's breath on fire, the bristling anger in its voice ringing through the glass. '*Je viens pour toi…!*'

Wrathful fingers dropped away from the mirror again, leaving bloody fingerprints behind. It sank away from the glass, melting into the reflected shadows of the room… And as quickly as it had come, the thing was gone…

This book is printed on paper from sustainable sources managed under the Forest Stewardship Council (FSC) scheme.

It has been printed in the UK to reduce transportation miles and their impact upon the environment.

For every new title that Troubador publishes, we plant a tree to offset CO_2, partnering with the More Trees scheme.

For more about how Troubador offsets its environmental impact, see www.troubador.co.uk/sustainability-and-community